THE BECKONING

A Story of Love

by

Nora Stangeland McNab

'Tis not too late to seek a newer world...
To strive, to seek, to find, and not to yield.
　　　　　　　　—Alfred Lord Tennyson
　　　　　　　　(1809-1892)

The saga of Andreas Knuteson Stangeland, a pathfinder with Cleng Peerson for the first boatload of Norwegian emigrants to America in 1825.

North American Heritage Press

i

International Standard Book Number: 0-942323-09-2

Cover painting by Vern Skaug
Typography by Creative Media, Inc.

Published by
North American Heritage Press
A DIVISION OF
CREATIVE MEDIA, INC.
P.O. Box 1
Minot, North Dakota 58702
701/852-5552

Printed in the United States of America

TABLE OF CONTENTS

An old photo of the Bagerbryggen in Stavanger which shows the sign for the Stangeland Bakery.

Photo courtesy of FIFO, Photo History Archives
of Rogaland, Stavanger, Norway.

PROLOGUE

HEARING MY APPROACH, a young woman rose from her garden, a basket of fresh-picked peas over her arm. I had come, I explained, from Oregon to upstate New York seeking the location of my great grandfather's farm. Old maps and deeds had directed me to this place.

She thought for a moment. "Back there," she indicated the far corner of a nearby hay field, "there are some scattered stones or bricks and what looks like old fruit trees that don't bear fruit anymore. Go take a look if you like."

As I drew near the area, vines clutched at my arms and legs, like sentinels guarding a gate, warning me to go no farther. The wild-sweet aroma of blackberries ripening in the summer sun quickened my pulse with the excitement of discovery. I looked beyond the thicket. Was that an apple tree, spindly and crooked? Another, perhaps a cherry or a peach. Seeds of seedlings. Remnants of a homesite. To the far right was a row of willows and poplars. Tall ferns grew as though along a river bank. *Bald Eagle Creek* – this had to be the place!

My quest had ended – or had it just begun?

What were the secrets beneath the sod? Cobblestones from an old cistern? Shards of broken dishes? Parts of a clay troll?

I drew from my pocket the silver button from the overcoat of my Norwegian great grandfather, Andreas Stangeland. If I rubbed the button and wished hard enough would a genie (or a nisse) appear and tell me the story of my beginnings in America? Would he tell me why, after just three generations, our family had so little knowledge of the man who was a pathfinder for the first boatload of Norwegian families to this country?

With all my heart I wanted now to recreate his story, building it around as many facts as I could find.

1

THE BECKONING

PART 1

CHAPTER 1

The
Overdue Boat

T HE MORNING DAWNED clear and golden over New York's busy harbor. October 9, 1825, brought a break in a week when leaden skies had hung close and dark over the city. Wet, cold fog had shrouded the waterfront, clinging to every man and object within its reach. Workers had gone about their necessary business silently or with curses at wet rigging rope that had to be spliced and at helpers who bungled the job. But this morning steam rose in waves from the moisture on the wooden planks. Deck hands, swinging cargo in rhythm, were anxious to launch their boats and make full use of the day.

Ignored by others except for brief glances at his odd, foreign-looking clothes, Andreas Stangeland stood alone welcoming the sun. He was a stocky, square-shouldered man of 25, hair the shade of sand and lightly curling beard to match. Shading his eyes, moving them from left to right, he again examined all vessels far out, beyond the patchwork of sails nearer by.

Two men arriving at the dock nodded to Andreas, who responded with a slight bow. After passing by, one of them shook his head and said to the other, "Those foreigners don't know when to give up."

"I wonder where he's from," remarked the other.

"Over there in Europe. Norway. I don't see the other fellow this morning. He's an older man who can speak a little English. I talked to him a few days ago. They're waiting for a boatload of their friends to arrive. Way overdue. The ocean's got 'em by now, poor devils."

After they passed by, another man approached. Cleng Peerson, slight of build, balding, clean shaven, in his forties, greeted Andreas. "Nice morning. Still nothing out there?" He spoke in Norwegian.

Above the blue eyes and heavy brows, worry lines gathered on Andreas' forehead as he answered his friend, "If they left on July 4th, their food and water would certainly be gone by now."

"Not necessarily. Not if they sailed down through the English Channel and to Maderia Island to restock. They may have spent a few days there in the warm sunshine."

"You still don't think they cancelled their plans?"

"No...no, I'm nearly positive of that." Cleng laid a gentle hand on his companion's shoulder. "But if they did, you and I will have a lot of land to farm," he chuckled.

Andreas wasn't consoled by his friend's attempt at cheerfulness. Cleng, he knew, was more concerned than he'd admit.

They walked back down the pier, watching the city of New York coming to life beyond the harbor. Wagons creaked and groaned behind horses clopping on cobblestone streets. Roosters crowed. Pigs grunted and squealed over their morning swill. Voices called to one another in a language still unfamiliar to Andreas.

Cleng stopped to talk in English with two men untangling a cargo net. Andreas returned toward the end of the pier, his tread as heavy as his heart. The swish-slap of the waves on the pilings was usually pleasant to the harbor-loving Norwegian, but today it only made him more lonesome for the inlets and fjords around Stavanger, his home and the home of his overdue friends.

His trip across with Cleng a year ago had been a young man's dream of adventure; he'd barely thought of danger. But now he called to mind all the ways the immense, wild ocean could swallow up such a small, heavily loaded sloop such at that in which his friends were sailing.

A month, a whole month, they'd watched and waited, one or both of them making frequent trips from their nearby camp to the harbor. How much longer would they keep up the watch, he wondered. Winter, even here in America, could arrive anytime. If their friends did not come, would he and Cleng stay in New York or go back to the cabin at Holley and do what clearing they could alone? Would they even remain in America? A question he hesitated to ask.

THE BECKONING

After another search of the horizon, Andreas leaned against a nearby bollard. The sun was making him sleepy. He straightened abruptly and tried to remember how he had felt when he first touched ground in America. There had been such a joy. Despite the confusion, the strangeness, the different temperament of the people and the frustrating language barrier, he had been fired with enthusiasm. He was going to be an owner of land and farm on his own, an ambition since childhood.

But his hopes had dimmed with each passing month. He now owned land but, kept to other duties, he had no time to spend there; not one tree had been cleared from it. Cleng liked to travel, keep on the move, and as his loyal companion, Andreas moved with him. It was difficult for a shy baker's assistant who'd never been much farther away from home than around the Stavanger harbor. He didn't mind the camping, like they were living now. It was the nights they'd been at the mercy of American strangers to house and feed them, that he dreaded. Social-loving Cleng enjoyed that way of life and in return for their hospitality entertained them with stories of Norway. But all Andreas could do was sit silently or occasionally say "T'ank you."

Today, in spite of the sunshine, his dream to farm seemed only that, a dream. Others had their work and were going about it cheerfully, while he had only this futile waiting and watching. The dull ache of homesickness swept over him as even the blue ocean crested with white reminded him of his mother's big blue serving plate. Absorbed with his thoughts, by habit he again lifted his eyes to scan the horizon. A far out boat, looking different from the others, attracted his attention. He stood erect, instantly alert. His heart thumped as he shaded his eyes and squinted while the object grew larger. Finally he could see a fleck of color.

"Cleng! Cleng!" His companion hurried to him. "Over there," Andreas pointed, "that boat out there by itself, isn't that our flag?"

They crowded the end of the dock, eyes straining forward. Cleng's voice quivered, "Praise God, I think it is!"

For a few moments they stood in open-mouthed silence, watching to be sure it was the sloop they had waited for so long. Bobbing and weaving among vessels nearer by, the square-rigged *Restauration* came close enough to reveal its flag of red with blue cross. Cleng began wildly swinging his arms and Andreas waved his cap. Others on the dock paused momentarily to see and be glad for them.

"I knew, God willing, Captain Helland and Lars Larson would get them over here," Cleng shouted. "Ninety-eight days in all!" He put an arm across Andreas' shoulders. "Do you realize, son, that we are greeting the first boatload of Norwegian families to America?"

Andreas nodded, his chest heaving with excitement and relief. "There goes an American patrol boat. Welcome them, do they, when they see the foreign flag?"

"Must be."

The two boats dropped sails and were tied up side by side, the gangplank was set, and four men crossed over onto the sloop. After an uncomfortably long wait, the *Restauration* began slowly following the patrol boat toward the dock. Andreas recognized faces among the passengers crowded on deck. But all were quiet and solemn, not rejoicing as they should be. What was the matter? Death? Sickness? He thought with alarm of his cousin Gudmund who was supposed to be among the passengers.

After several minutes and what seemed like confusion and controversy on board, the immigrants began slowly, hesitantly, coming ashore. Andreas waited while Cleng, leader that he was, pressed forward to hear of any difficulties.

Gudmund appeared. He was wan and thin but smiling. Andreas, shouting his name, rushed to him and the two cousins embraced. Then Gudmund dropped the news: "They're arresting the owners, Lars and Johannes and Captain Helland, because our boat was overloaded."

CHAPTER 2

Bold
Decisions

T HE 50 NORWEGIANS on the *Restauration* had looked to Lars Larson for counsel and leadership even before embarking on the journey to America. Now they needed him more than ever. But Lars was in jail.

Andreas had heard Lars' story many times from Cleng. In 1812, at the age of 20, Lars was running a blockade to deliver a load of lumber to Holland when he was captured by the English patroling the outer Scandinavian seas. He and his crew were taken captive and for the next two years were held in a prison ship off the coast of England.

During that time a Quaker book, written in Danish, came into Lars' hands. The religion of peace and inner strength so appealed to him and others aboard the ship that they sent a letter to the Quakers on the mainland to please visit them or send some of their writings. They were visited by the Friends and in time converted.

After their release in 1814 the religion was brought back to Norway and spread. Most of the immigrants on the *Restauration*, as well as Cleng and Andreas, held to Quaker beliefs.

In Norway, the Quakers were persecuted almost from the first, since they did not subscribe to the well-established Lutheran state church. In some instances a sheriff might come to a Quaker family and take children by force to a priest to be baptized. People were fined for not going to Holy Communion. Elias Tastad, a prominent Stavanger resident, had twin daughters who died and because he did not bury them in a state graveyard, he was sentenced to pay five dollars a day until he reburied the bodies according to the state church. All appeals from the Friends were ignored. Andreas remembered well this shameful event, the whispered conversations and finally that bold talk of emigrating to America.

And now, here in America it was the New York Quakers, alerted by Cleng, who welcomed the weary, disheartened Norwegians into their homes. Each family took in a family, or singles, as their house could accommodate. Although they could not understand their language, the warm-hearted Quakers fed the near-starving Norwegians, provided them with a place to bathe and wash their clothes.

The household tasks were left to the women, however, while the men returned to the grave situation at the harbor. Only Cleng and Lars spoke English so news had to come through them. All were shocked when word was spread that until a fine of $3,150 was paid, neither the men nor the boat could be released.

Daniel Rosdail, a prosperous and scholarly farmer, expressed what all were aware of: "We can't pay anywhere near that amount until the Swedish iron we brought along is sold or the sloop. And how can we sell either until the boat is released? Two people for every ton of ship's weight, the American law reads. We were overloaded by 20 people and they didn't even count the babies."

"Seems like Cleng should have found out about the immigration and navigation laws ahead of time and let us know before we started out. He's been here a year," one of the men complained.

"He realizes that now better than any of us," Daniel explained. "It just didn't occur to him that there were any such laws." One after another of the men had something to say.

"Seems like if the boat could get us over here, they'd overlook how crowded we were."

"I guess if it's the law they can't very well overlook it, at least without some authority from higher up."

"That's what Cleng is working on now, isn't it?"

"Now they say that the reason for keeping the boat is to keep us from starting a shipping business under the Norwegian flag. Well, that's nonsense. We're farmers with land waiting for us, all but the captain, and we can all vouch for him, he's an honest man."

Daniel took a long draw on his pipe which he hadn't been able to smoke, for lack of tobacco, during the last weeks on the boat. "Now I ask

9

you, who of us ever wants to get back on that sloop unless we have to?" They laughed in agreement and realized they were attracting onlookers who whispered comments, pity on their faces. Gradually the Norwegian gathering broke up and the men walked in twos along the shore to continue the discussion.

Cornelius Nelson, brother-in-law to Cleng, distinguished by a great shock of gray hair, walked with Daniel. "What will we do?" he asked. "We've got land waiting to be cleared, winter coming on, and Andreas says we have a long boat trip even to get up there."

"Only one cabin so far for all of us." Daniel stopped to relight his pipe, shielding the bowl with his hand against the ocean breeze. "We were planning on the money from the iron and sale of the boat to build those cabins and see us through the winter."

"We can't go and leave our friends sitting in jail. We'd never have made it here without them."

The good weather prevailed and on the fourth day after their arrival, following breakfast and prayers, the men again gathered on the beach. The warm sun that shone across the water and the wet sand was welcome. Andreas and Gudmund approached, smiling. "Good news, good news!" Andreas announced.

"Praise God," several of them murmured.

"Did they release the boat?"

"No, the men," Andreas said. "One of the Friends' families contacted a Francis Thompson, who is a prominent Quaker and also a founder of the Black Ball Line that runs packet ships to England. He immediately came up with the $600 bail bond. So now they're free, but they can't leave New York."

Lars and Cleng soon joined the group. The captain and Johannes Steine had been permitted to board the boat to retrieve some personal items and would join them later. It didn't take Lars long to convince the others that they should journey on to the homesites, leaving the three of them to face the charges and try to get the boat released. Cleng agreed only on the condition that he would return to work with them as soon as he could after guiding the settlers to their destination.

This arrangement disturbed Andreas even though he remained silent. Would it mean he'd be expected to lead the group after Cleng left? He couldn't speak English, nor could any of the others. He wished now more than ever that he had tried harder to learn more English words, wished that Cleng had insisted on it instead of always speaking for him.

That night before sleep came to him, as he lay rolled in his sheepskin beside Gudmund, Andreas wondered again why Cleng (who had now moved from the camp to stay with one of the families) had chosen him to be his companion for the trip to America. There were many single men in Stavanger more capable than he. Was it because of his youth and good health? The companion Cleng had taken along on his first trip to America had died, God rest his soul, before their exploration trip was completed.

It was Cleng's report of the first trip which had set the Quakers to collecting money for emigration. Cleng was to return and purchase land for them and build some kind of shelter. Did Cleng now regret his choice for a companion, Andreas wondered.

Gudmund's heavy breathing indicated he was asleep so with no one to talk to, Andreas began reliving the events which led to Cleng's choice. The first mention of emigration to America, had set Andreas to wishing and dreaming. As he sold or delivered the brown crusty loaves which his brother Ole baked, or as he kneaded and molded those loaves or scrubbed doughy tables in the back room, he thought of little else except the glories of America and owning his own farm.

After several days of meeting at the Stavanger harbor, more than chance on Andreas' part, Cleng began asking questions obviously leading to something: Was he married? No. Where did he work? At the Stangeland Bakery. His father was dead, wasn't he? Yes, six years now and his mother lived on their farm with his brother, Tollak, who was *odelsman* (oldest son with a birth right to the farm).

Finally, Cleng, 20 years his senior, looked steadily at him and asked, "Andreas, why don't you go with me when I go back to America this time? A boatload of people from Stavanger are preparing to make the crossing next spring. But I need to go back, locate land for them to settle on and make arrangements for their arrival." After a heavy pause, through which Andreas was too excited to speak, Cleng asked, "Do you have any money, son, to make the trip and perhaps invest in land of your own over there?"

Andreas considered carefully before answering, wanting to say nothing that would spoil his chances. "I...I want very much to go. As to the funds, I'd have to ask my mother and brothers."

So Cleng Peerson had gone with him to the Stangeland farm. And when Cleng talked, people listened. He had become acquainted with the Tollak Stangelands through the recently and secretly formed Stavanger Society of Friends.

Andreas stood silently by as Cleng and his mother talked. Inger Stokka Stangeland was a woman of few words, but those were spoken wisely, and with fairness. Finally, Andreas knew she was about to make a decision.

"It's a good opportunity for a young man. Knut, his father, would want him to go. About the funds, I must discuss it with my sons, but I see no reason why Andreas shouldn't have his share of the family businesses to invest in America, if that is what he chooses. Ole can find other help."

Andreas remembered well that moment of sublime joy at his mother's endorsement. Nor had he forgotten the love and pride in her smile as she turned to him. Or the private tears later when she must have realized that after he left she might never see her son again.

A tear of homesickness slid down his cheek and he rolled his head in earnest eagerness. God willing I'll prove her trust in me, he vowed.

CHAPTER 3

Booming
Cannons

A FEW DAYS AFTER the release of the three men, a huddle of women and children in straight drab dresses with bright scarves covering their hair, arms loaded with belongings, crept onto a rusting old barge. Men of the boarding party, wearing plain, homespun garments, hurriedly carried on wooden trunks, iron-banded and painted red and blue. Last aboard were Andreas and Big Nels, struggling with an iron cookstove.

"Higher, Andreas," Nels, who was a head taller, shouted with good humor, "or do you want me to carry this thing myself?"

"I got it on my shoulder now, Nels."

Everybody liked Big Nels Nelson and his wife, Betsy. The trip over had been their honeymoon. Seldom did either of them speak without kindness or pleasantry. On the desolate, cheerless days of the crossing, their jolliness seldom faltered, adding levity when it was badly needed.

The boarding of the barge at Albany followed a two-day trip in a Fulton steamboat up the Hudson River from New York. It was an extraordinary experience for the Norwegians: a comfortable boat traveling at great speed without oars or sails, belching smoke as it tore up the river and churning white water behind it. But the vibration worried some of them – would it crack apart?

The rest of the boat was filled with well-dressed merrymaking Americans, some of them waving flags or ringing bells. Women in satin bonnets were draped in silk shawls over their full skirted dresses. Gentlemen wore high black hats and stock collars above tight pants and long frock coats. The immigrants felt shy and unadorned among them. Was it the custom here in America to celebrate when boarding a steamboat?

THE BECKONING

The Quaker Society had paid the Norwegians' fare of $6 for the complete waterway trip to their destination of Holley, along the brand new Erie Canal, 26 miles west of Rochesterville. Several other New Yorkers also contributed to a fund to assist the newcomers after hearing of their unfortunate situation. The immigrants would use the money to buy provisions on the trip and to see them through the winter ahead, a cause for serious concern.

Cleng had boarded the barge ahead of his flock, checking to see that it was adequate, even though not luxurious. At least they would enjoy more freedom and privacy since they were the only passengers on the freight barge. Meals for two days on the steamship had been cold food; now they could cook and would have more room to lay out their bedrolls, even though there was little protection from the elements if the weather turned cold or rainy.

At the center of the barge was the captain's quarters, a mere cubical with a stable alongside for extra horses resting until their turn on the towline path which followed the canal.

Cleng, who had been visiting with the steersman, now turned to face the group and called, "All on, Andreas?"

Andreas looked around, then waved his gray cap, "All on, Cleng."

The gangplank creaked shut and the barge began slowly moving downstream behind the team of horses. Andreas waved a hand at Gudmund walking alongside the boys who rode and tended the horses. After his cousin had helped with the loading, he told Andreas, "I'm going to walk to the next stop. I've been on a boat so long I've got barnacles."

On board, men were sorting and stacking tools, guns, supplies and other marked boxes. Women were collecting cooking utensils to start the midday meal.

Andreas began stacking firewood near the cookstove. The stove had been brought from Norway and was ovenless, unlike the American stove he and Cleng had bought in Holley and which remained in the cabin with their other possessions.

He looked over at Lars' wife, Martha, a small, pretty blonde woman forlornly holding a tiny baby to her breast. Andreas had known her since childhood. He had gone to school with her, even though she was four years younger. She seemed too young to be alone and responsible for Lars' older deaf-mute sister, Siri, as well as the baby. Andreas had witnessed Lars and Martha's sad farewell at the dock in New York, and overheard a very solemn Lars, tell Big Nels and Betsy, "Take care of them for me, will you, until I can get there?"

As though she sensed the need, Betsy now turned from her duties, saw the solitary mother, went over to the trunk where she was sitting and placed a kindly arm around her.

"Nels and I will put our bed down right next to you and Siri. We'll all help you, Martha. And don't worry about Lars. He and the others are resourceful men; they'll come up with some solutions before long so they can come join us."

"I hope so," Martha sobbed, momentarily burying her face in the baby's cover. "How can Americans be so cruel as to arrest them for a law they didn't even know existed?"

A young girl came shyly up behind them. "When Margaret Allen is through nursing, may I hold her?"

Martha turned slightly, "Of course you may, Serene," she said to the always-willing little helper. Everyone loved the "sloop baby" as they called her, born on the crossing and named for a prominent English Quaker.

Andreas finished the wood stacking and began drawing up water from over the side of the barge and pouring it into a large cask.

Nearby, two women were dropping rounds of flatbread on the now-hot stove. Another opened a cloth sack containing potatoes, carrots and onions which had been given to them by the generous Quakers. "Come, Greta, Severine," she called to her daughters.

Daniel Rosdail took his dead pipe out of his mouth, put it in his pocket, came over to help Andreas and they began taking turns pulling up and emptying the large wooden bucket. Andreas hadn't known Daniel well back in Norway, only that he was a prosperous farmer in the Tysvaer region. He and Bertha had five children, making them the largest family to come across on the *Restauration*..

"So you had a pretty hard trip over, did you, Daniel?" Andreas asked.

Daniel shuddered, "An experience none of us would ever want to repeat."

"Awfully crowded, weren't you?"

"Below deck there was about as much room as if we were chained prisoners. You had to crawl over a trunk to get into your bunk and then it wasn't high enough to sit up in. When we were all topside, the deck was so crowded no one could move more than a step in any direction. And those terrible storms...when they came up our little sloop was tossed around like a stick of firewood there," he pointed to the neatly stacked cord. "We could do nothing but pray and try to comfort the little ones. The Heavenly Father must have thought we should be over here, because only He could have got us through it."

"Gudmund said your food and water ran awfully low."

"I'll tell you it did. Every drop and crumb had to be rationed out. When we were in sight of the harbor," Daniel chuckled, "and turned the children loose on the last of the food, you should have seen them devour it. The grown-ups were so excited about seeing land we forgot about food and drink."

The cask was full so Andreas set the empty bucket aside and leaned against the rail. Daniel again placed the pipe in his mouth.

"Your stop-over in Maderia was pretty nice, though?"

"It was like the Garden of Eden. Even though it was in our plan to stop and restock there, none of us, except maybe Lars and the captain, knew what it was like." Daniel raised his hands majestically to the sky. "Sunshine, warm soft breezes, palm and fig trees like in the Bible. And the food! Bananas, figs, grapes, pomegranates, sugar cane....the American consul in Maderia, John March, entertained us at a bountiful dinner none of us will ever forget. It boosted our spirits for those grim days ahead."

Andreas thought of the little leathery-skinned pomegranate Gudmund had brought him, knowing his cousin had never seen one before. He was especially touched after he heard of the near-starving conditions. "You didn't find any of those fruits here in America, did you, Daniel?"

"No," Daniel said with a good-natured grin, "but those apples the Quakers passed around sure tasted mighty good."

Their conversation was interrupted when Cleng rang a bell and called, "Attention everyone! There are two American words you must learn immediately." Pointing ahead he said, "Low bridge, *lav bro*, low bridge. When you hear that warning from Mr. Cassidy, the steersman," he indicated the man beside him who held a long wooden paddle with one end thrust into the water, "it is the signal for you to keep your heads down and those of your children as well."

The Norwegians practiced the words among them before Cleng spoke again. "Here is some joyful news for you. I've discovered why there are so many people and boats out. Mr. Cassidy tells me it is a very historic occasion. On October 26, while we are still on our journey, the man-made waterway, which took eight years to build and is called the Erie Canal, is being completed. The water from the Hudson River, on which we traveled from New York, is emptying into the great Lake Erie at the eastern end. On that day we will hear the booming of a cannon announcing the merging of the waters for the first time!"

There were exclamations of surprise and pleasure among the immigrants. Cleng continued, "Cannons are spaced at intervals to pass the news from one to the other all along the way to New York where a big parade and celebration will be held. The governor of this state of New York, Dewitt Clinton, is over now at a town called Buffalo, where the waters will merge. We will probably pass his boat returning before we reach..."

"Low-w bridge!" Mr. Cassidy called through a long tin horn. Immediately, obediently, the Norwegians lay face down on the dock, holding children too young to understand. Cleng and the steersman stood chuckling, ready to duck their heads, as later the rest would also.

Andreas, after completing all the chores he could think of, climbed on top of some canvas-covered freight. He had discovered on previous trips what comfort a pile of odd-shaped cargo can provide, a hollow space became a comfortable hammock. He lay face up to the blue sky overhead until the bridge cast its shadow. He turned and watched the two young boys on the towline path jump from their horses and guide them

17

underneath, showing off, he was sure, for Gudmund, who walked and talked with them.

"All's clear!" Mr. Cassidy shouted through his horn.

Relaxed as he was, Andreas began to worry. Everyone around him, except Martha, seemed too content and carefree. Certainly they deserved this break after the awesome journey, but did they really understand what was ahead of them? Dense forest to clear like nothing in Norway. Only one cabin. With the delay would they have time before winter to build even one more? Had he and Cleng chosen the location wisely?

Then Andreas thought of his own piece of property which brought a warmth to his worries. No matter how hard it would be to clear he'd make a fine farm of it. How great it would be if he could look forward to sharing it with a wife. But that didn't seem likely for a long while. The girls of marriageable age from the sloop were already engaged. Gudmund was courting Gurine Madland, a girl from a good family. Andreas was happy for him and slightly envious. He'd silently hoped to court her sister, Rakel, before discovering that Captain Helland had claimed her enroute. She had stayed in New York to marry him.

Maybe another boatload of Norwegians would be coming soon. But there was no certainty Andreas would meet them or that there would be any young women aboard. And if there were single men aboard, he wouldn't stand a chance.

He tried not to think about Katrine, his former neighbor and sweetheart. He'd courted her, but was never very sure he wanted to get married and settle down. At least not as long as that restlessness, which he hadn't quite understood, stirred within him. He had hesitated too long; she turned her attentions to another and they were married shortly thereafter. She was not one to leave her family and come with him to America anyway.

Except for Katrine, he'd always been shy with girls. Cleng sometimes had teased him as they traveled about: "You're a good looking man, Andreas. Look at those American beauties giving you the eye."

But he'd turned red and looked away from them, "They're looking at you, Cleng."

Cleng also was a good looking man, fair of features, clean shaven, and while his hair grew far back on his forehead, he kept it combed down over his ears. To Andreas' remark he replied, "Well, that's all right with me. I like pretty girls, American, Norwegian, or any other kind. But nothing to tie me down again. It took an ocean to separate me from one woman and I hope, God willing, she never finds her way across."

"You married, are you, Cleng?"

"The law says we are," he said bitterly. That was the only time Andreas ever heard him mention his wife or his marriage except to say once that the sloopers were his children, he had no other.

Banging on a kettle, Cleng's sister, Kari (wife of Cornelius), summoned the group to the midday meal. Andreas promptly rose from the canvas and got a bowl, cup and spoon from his roll of belongings. He joined the other men as Ole Olsen led the blessing. Then each man moved in turn to the kettle and was served a ladle of soup and a round of *lefse*.

The soup was made with potatoes, boiled until tender, mashed into the cooking water with other cooked vegetables added. Usually pieces of fish or meat were added also. It was a stew Andreas loved, always a reminder of home. At the cabin or over campfires, he had often made it for himself and Cleng.

When Cleng came to the kettle for his serving, he asked Kari if she had an empty bowl. She did, so he told her to fill it for the steersman who sat eating bread and cheese with his back to the passengers. He hesitantly accepted the soup, tasted it cautiously, then turned with a grin and a nod to the women at the kettle. After finishing it, he took a small package from his pocket, found another paper in his other pocket and emptied some of the contents into it. Folding it securely he sent it and the empty bowl back to the women. Kari opened the package carefully and smelled it.

"Pepper! We'll have pepper in our soup tomorrow."

Days remained sunny and warm for the travelers; nights were chilly. After prayers, the immigrants rolled themselves cozily into their sheepskin robes to sleep. Cleng was always the last down and then only after he had circled the group, answering questions, dispelling homesickness if he could, and bidding them goodnight. Gudmund joined Andreas on the cargo canvas.

THE BECKONING

When the boat docked each evening at dusk, the boys from the towline, about 12 and 14, came on board with the horses. After caring for the animals, they fell into exhausted slumber in an empty stall.

The women, after hearing that they were orphan boys, felt sorry for them and often sent food out to the towline to add to their bread and cheese. One day Bertha Rosdail used precious lard and sugar to make little round fried cakes with holes in the middle. They were shared with the boys and everyone on board. Martha was chosen to take some to the captain and his wife. Unlike the affable and jolly steersman, the captain was dour and surly, even Cleng could not get acquainted with him. Often he could be heard shouting at his young wife, words the Norwegians could not understand but they sensed their threatening intent. She always stayed within the cabin or sat on a box just outside.

"When I handed him the cakes," Martha reported back, "the captain even smiled and said, 'Thank you.' His little wife looked so lonesome...I'm going over and visit her someday when the captain is on shore. I'll try my few English words on her."

Andreas was glad to see Martha take an interest in something. To him she said, "Do they remind you of those little cakes at the Stangeland Bakery?" He nodded, knowing she understood his homesickness.

Andreas kept track of the days and on October 26, he passed around the word that today they should hear the cannons signaling. The children lined up at the rail and listened impatiently. Near noontime there was a distant boom from the west like far away thunder. "The cannons, the cannons!" they shouted.

"Hush!" commanded Daniel. Everyone stopped what they were doing and waited for the second sound. Then there was the loud volley nearer by from the east, *Ka-boom*. All stood in reverent silence, mouths agape. Finally there were loud "amens" from several of the men.

Just ahead at Rochesterville there were loud shouts, bells ringing and whistles blowing, which also put the travelers in a festive mood. When Cleng learned that their boat would be docking at the village to take on supplies, he suggested, "Let's all get off and see the town, mingle with the people. Keep track of your children, though, we don't want anyone getting lost."

To some of the shyer women, it was a frightening prospect, but Betsy soon had them putting on their bright head scarves, reversing their shawls to a cleaner side, brushing out their children's hair and fortifying each other as they clustered together, ready to get off the barge for the first time. At other embarkations, most of the men had gotten off to buy a few supplies, gather more wood, do a little nearby hunting or just to pace around on the dusty streets, watching to learn as much as possible about American ways.

In Rochesterville, the women walked in small groups, holding tightly to their children. They peered timidly into store windows and smelled the food being cooked for a surge of people in town for a holiday. The visitors, with their quaint dress and quiet ways, drew curious stares from the villagers. These "furriners" seemed so different from the fiery Irish who had worked on the building of the "canawl" as it was referred to by those who lived along it.

Cleng Peerson always found someone to visit with, in spite of his limited English vocabulary. While he seldom asked for favors, neither did he hesitate to let the Norwegians' plight be known: They were poor people who had come across the ocean, met misfortune at the harbor, and were striving to survive until they could clear the land and get crops growing. Here in Rochesterville he was given a most welcome basket of eggs, a bag of cornmeal – a kind of flour the Norwegians had never seen before – and several bushels of windfall apples. Most of the apples were peeled by the women, sliced, spread on a sail, then hung to dry, high out of reach from the hungry children.

The next afternoon Andreas saw Cornelius and Daniel standing along the rail, apparently discussing a new cabin being built near the canal. They were measuring with their hands and pointing. Andreas wondered again if they, or any of the men, realized how difficult it was to build one of those cabins. It seemed to him that Cleng should be telling them, warning them more about the difficulties ahead instead of being constantly optimistic and easy-going. Andreas didn't feel like it was his role to cast doubts and shadows, but after Cleng returned to New York...well, he didn't even like to think about it.

Further down the rail stood Oyen Thompson, alone and looking skyward above the red, gold and green panorama of leaves on the hillside rising above the canal. Oyen, a few years older than Andreas, had been a blacksmith in Stavanger. Andreas knew him well. He was a handsome man with blacksmith's shoulders, now somewhat diminished by lack of exercise and the sparse rations of the voyage. He and his wife, Carolyn, had three little blonde girls, pretty and well-behaved. Andreas approached him.

"Think it will rain, Oyen?"

"I hope not, Andreas, but there are some clouds around. Of course I don't know much about weather in America."

"I haven't got it figured out either." After a pause, as they both enjoyed the beauty of the landscape, Andreas asked, "Are you going to start a blacksmith's shop over here when we get settled?"

"Not right away. I'd like to eventually, but I'll farm with Nils for awhile, until he gets a little older. Maybe by that time I'll have enough saved up for some equipment." Nils was Oyen's 20-year-old brother and looked a lot like him. Another young man who would be looking for a wife, Andreas remembered. Nils was out on the towpath now, trotting along with Gudmund.

Eight-year-old Sara Thompson, neatly braided flaxen hair swinging across her back, came skipping up to her father. He affectionately placed a hand on her head. "Uncle Nils!" she shouted across the avenue of water between them and the towpath. Nils looked back, waved and smiled.

A loneliness swept over Andreas for the nieces and nephews and family life he'd left behind.

Several days into the journey, the captain came on deck wearing a dingy white jacket and hat instead of his usual dark, unkempt clothes. He was more friendly as he talked to the steersman and Cleng. Cleng immediately called for attention from the group.

"In a little while a packet, a small tourist boat, call the *Seneca* will pass by us." He pointed at a bright object far up ahead. "On board is Governor Clinton and other important Americans returning from the christening of the Erie Canal. Behind it is a boat called *Noah's Ark*, bearing symbols of America – an Indian, a bear, some birds and fowl and so forth. I think we should look our best and shout an American greeting to them as they pass. What do you think?"

They murmured and nodded in agreement. Then without taking out their full Norwegian *bunads*, they hurried about looking for bright shawls, bonnets, hats and coats, borrowing, swapping, laughing, exclaiming and cautioning the children. By the time the barge had pulled over and the towline slackened for the esteemed packets to pass, the Norwegians presented a colorful, smiling line along the deck, ready with their three-word American greeting. Cleng, waving an American flag in his right hand and a Norwegian flag in his left, gave the signal and they shouted in unison, "Good day, sir." Then they waved and clapped.

Obviously impressed, Governor Clinton removed his tall black hat, bowed and shouted, "Thank You!" The barge captain stood by proudly as though it had all been his doing. But the children were more interested in the boat that followed with all the animals, and were held up to the rail to see them.

On the 12th day of the canal journey, excitement grew. Mr. Cassidy announced that they would get to their destination, the little settlement of Holley, on the following day.

CHAPTER 4

Indians?

"IF YOU HAD THREE WISHES right now, Andreas, what would they be?" Gudmund Hougas asked as the two cousins lay rolled in the sheepskins beneath a makeshift shelter near the settlement of Holley.

"A hot bowl of stew, a cup of coffee and a nice warm soapstone at my feet." Andreas answered without hesitation. "I suppose you'd rather have Gurene rolled up in there with you."

"Another body to warm up? H-mmm...well maybe." They laughed through chattering teeth. "Do you suppose the rest of them are at the cabin yet?"

"They'll be caught by the dark if they aren't. It's dense up there by the lake. They call it the Black North. Big trees, lots of underbrush, really gloomy in the rain, I'll bet. Maybe we're just as well off as they are – one cabin, 20 by 24, for over 40 people, all of them soaking wet."

It had begun raining in the night before they docked at Holley, but the stoic Norwegians accepted it as a necessary inconvenience and began their chilly seven-mile walk through the woods to the cabin with only the trees for shelter. They had been able to rent one small push cart to carry a few essential possessions and the children who were unable to walk that far. Andreas and Gudmund had volunteered to stay with the remaining things until the next morning when a large wooden-wheeled wagon would be available.

"I worry about them, Gudmund – all of us – and our situation this winter. Cleng's leaving and I'm afraid they'll depend on me to know more than I do."

"Oh, what the heck, don't worry about it. Most of them are older than we are and can figure out things as we come to them. We did on the crossing. If they didn't expect to take plenty of chances, they wouldn't have started out." Andreas had to smile at his cousin's usual unconcerned attitude. Nevertheless it helped to bolster his spirits.

"How hard is it to build one of those cabins out of logs?" Gudmund asked again.

"Not as easy as it looks. First you have to find a tree small enough to handle, then the logs have to be notched and fitted together. If the trees aren't straight, you have trouble. And sometimes you don't realize it until you've cut them down. By the second day Cleng and I worked on that cabin, Cleng began to see we had to have some experienced help."

"Isn't Cleng a carpenter by trade?"

"I think all he ever built were boats and not out of logs." They laughed and Andreas, whose hands were now warm enough to take them out from under the cover, reached for two *lefse* and handed one to Gudmund. "I think Cleng would rather do what he's mostly always done, travel around trying to help others."

"Where did he find help to build the cabin?"

"He went into Rochesterville, asked around and found a carpenter whose work on the Erie Canal was finished. He explained our desperate need. The man sympathized and agreed to supervise the building for a small percentage of what he had earned on the canal. Then to help us in cutting the logs, Cleng found a couple of orphan boys who used to work on a towline. They were good workers and the carpenter was patient with them."

"That job on a towline looks like it must be a pretty good job for a boy."

"Depends on how they're treated, I guess. We sure heard some unbelievable stories from those boys who escaped from a towline job."

"What was that?"

"They'd run away before, but were always brought back and severely beaten. They worked without pay, just for a little food and a place to sleep. Then at night sometimes the captain or steersman would – would use them like women."

25

"Those poor boys!"

"It took Cleng awhile to convince them he was a good man and would watch out for them, give them enough food and a safe place to sleep."

"What happened to them when the cabin was built?"

"Cleng took them back to Rochesterville and found good homes for them to work in."

After more *lefse* and some cheese the two lay silent for awhile, almost asleep with the comfort they'd managed to create, when Gudmund asked, "Are you ever going to start a bakery here in America, Andreas?"

"No-o! I've wanted to be a farmer ever since I can remember. But I wasn't lucky enough to be born first and there wasn't enough land for all of us in Stavanger. When I looked out over that ocean, I saw that America was my opportunity."

"That's what I want to do, too. Just farm, and marry Gurene."

"Lucky cousin. Looks like I'm doomed to be a bachelor."

"I doubt it."

At daylight the next morning, which didn't come early in the still-steady rain, Gudmund stayed with the cargo while Andreas went to the farmer's stable for the team and wagon. But he had to wait because the farmer had not come out yet and he didn't know the words to go to the door and ask. At least it was warmer and drier in the stable by the horses and oxen. He petted them and talked Norwegian in their ears, wondering how long it would be before he could have animals like these on his farm.

So often he thought about those acres he owned; how he'd felt like a king as he stood there on the shore of that lake called Ontario, a bowl of blue sky overhead, and listened to the sigh and slap of the waves. As Cleng negotiated with Mr. Fellows, the Quaker land agent, Andreas couldn't believe he wasn't dreaming. That he, Andreas Knuteson Stangeland, could actually purchase 48 acres with the money in his pocket. But when was he going to be able to start work on his land or even investigate it? Cleng had kept him busy building the cabin before their friends arrived. Now he would be busy from daylight until dark helping build another one as quickly as possible.

When Gudmund and Andreas arrived, the cabin was a buzz of activity. Women were drying clothes, dressing children, rolling up beds, trying to get food cooked and everyone fed. Even without the men, who were outside, the cabin was crowded. The women had decided to make a lean-to out of extra sails brought along, for some of the men to sleep in.

As he sized up nearby trees, Cornelius overheard their plan. "Betsy's in there," he said to the bridegroom, Nels, "volunteering you to sleep outside under a canvas."

"The devil she is," Big Nels answered between swings of his broad axe against a rain-drenched tree. "If I'm out there, you'll be right beside me. Not Thomas though, he snores too loud."

"I don't snore," Thomas Madland, Gurene's father, said. "That must be my wife."

For the benefit of Andreas and Gudmund, unloading the nearby wagon, Big Nels called, "Let's let the single men sleep in the lean-to. They sleep alone anyway – or at least they're supposed to."

"Andreas," grumbled Cornelius, "Andreas, why didn't you tell us these trees are five feet thick with roots that grow to the other side of the earth? How are we going to build a cabin out of these monsters?"

"It isn't easy," Andreas called back. "We managed to find some smaller ones. I hope there are still some more not too far away."

Cleng was preparing to leave. His sister, Kari, was urging him to take along some food. Cleng protested, "All the food here is needed. By night I'll be at some wayside farmer's house and they'll be urging me to take supper with them. They always do. I must look hungry."

Andreas paused by the fire for a moment, having finished the unloading. "They want to put you up so they can listen to your stories, Cleng. I wish now I'd learned a few more English words."

"Well, you just keep working on your English, so you can talk better than I do." He clapped Andreas on the shoulder. "It's up to you now to know enough words to deal with the Americans."

Andreas flinched inwardly, wishing Cleng hadn't said that. "Go meet your American neighbor," Cleng said again. "He's a good man and could be a lot of help to you."

Andreas remembered when Cleng had walked through the brush to visit the American, about a mile away, while Andreas and the helpers were working on the cabin. At the time he'd had to squelch the feeling of being left behind; he wanted so much to see his own land again. Cleng had reported that he talked awhile to the man who he found working in his field and told him about the group that was coming. Andreas couldn't remember what he'd said his name was.

"I hate to see you start out in the rain," Kari said.

"Nonsense. Inside this old black cloak I'll be warm and snug as a hibernating bear." Cleng cinched the hood around his head with an extra muffler.

Outside, he paused with the men for a short prayer. They asked for Cleng's safe journey and that his help in New York would be effective in freeing the men still held there, along with the boat and cargo. Then with a last wave to all, Cleng climbed aboard the wagon to return it to the owner in Holley before continuing to New York.

It had already been decided on the first night at the cabin that the second cabin would be built for Cornelius and Kari, who had four children and whose land bordered Cleng's. The work did not stop except from dark to dawn and, of course, on their Quaker First Day. When any man came in to eat, rest a bit and get a dry coat, another would take his place.

A hot fire burned at one end of the cabin and steam permeated the air from a line of drying clothes pulled up to the rafters. Betsy Nelson wiped the sweat from her forehead with the corner of her apron, looked around at the women, who were cooking, making candles, tending children, and cleaning. Then, Betsy went over to Martha. They held a whispered conversation and Betsy announced, "It's too hot in here, Martha and I are going out to help the men."

There were gasps of astonishment but no one objected. Knowing Betsy, it wouldn't stop her. After all, wasn't it Betsy on the crossing who crawled up on the prow of the slooper when they neared the harbor of Funchal, and waved her plaid skirt indecently high? With no hoisted flag they were thought to be pirates and ordered to show their colors. As everyone else was frantically looking for their Norwegian flag, Betsy took charge.

So Martha and Betsy put on nearly dry coats and ventured out. The men laughed but Big Nels said to his wife, "Well, sure you can help. You can peel logs. Not much different than peeling potatoes."

"Where's your adz then? We'll skin 'em, won't we, Martha?"

By the following day, nearly all the women were taking their turns outside, sun or rain. It added levity and variety to the days and the hard physical labor helped dispel some of their worries.

Oyen and his brother Nils worked together cutting trees with the crosscut saw, hand-forged in Oyen's blacksmith shop and brought from Norway. They, like all of the other men in the process of falling a tree, took particular caution to keep children out of the area. One morning, just as a tree they were working on began to teeter, ready to fall, little Ann Marie came running toward them from the privy some distance from the house. "Papa, Papa," she shouted.

"Anne! Stay back!" Oyen yelled.

The little girl stopped, petrified, not knowing which way to run. Nils, who was closest, lunged forward and threw her away from the tree. The tree crashed. Anne Marie screamed and Nils groaned, "Oh-h, my leg!"

Oyen reached his brother in a few giant leaps and found him beneath one of the oak limbs which had caught his left leg. Hearing the commotion, the other men dropped their axes and came running over. Two of them lifted the limb off Nils while others pulled the tree away from him. By this time the news had reached the women in the cabin and they came hurrying out.

Oyen went to his screaming daughter and scooped her up. "Anne Marie, I've told you a dozen time to stay away from where we're cutting trees."

"But, but...I saw..." sobbed the child.

"I don't care what you saw. Don't come running toward a falling tree – you could have been killed!" Carolyn came then and led away her hysterical daughter.

A group was gathered around Nils, trying to decide what was best to do for him. Daniel carefully worked up the pants leg to reveal a bend in his leg between the knee and the ankle. The men looked at each other and shook their heads. Daniel looked at his wife. "You took care of Endre's leg that time back in Norway, why don't you see what you can do."

Bertha moved in beside her husband, "Somebody bring a good straight stick about the length from his knee to his heel."

Several men scurried to find one; Andreas returned first. A couple of women offered scarves to bind his leg to the stick. Carolyn, who'd sent Anne Marie into the cabin with her older sister, Sara, stooped over her brother-in-law, put her head on his chest crying, "Nils, you saved her life." He lifted a weak arm, laid his hand on her head and grimaced a smile.

With hands linked, Daniel and Oyen carried Nils, sitting up, as Andreas supported his leg. Once inside, Bertha unbound the splint and the men carefully removed his pants. Then the women took over. They needed to find a flatter board for a splint and cut canvas to bind it on.

Big Nels looked toward the pale but silent Nils, beads of sweat around his hairline. "Son-of-a-gun, you lucky devil. What a way to get out of cutting down trees – and all these women buzzin' around you." Nils raised an unsteady hand and waved it at Nels.

The men went solemnly back to work, but something stuck in Andreas' mind. He had been nearby and heard little Anne Marie when she started to say she saw something. What was it? She was known to be an easily startled and sensitive child. Often the rest were awakened in the night when she cried out from a nightmare and Carolyn had to comfort her back to sleep. But had she this time seen something of possible danger to the children – a marauding bear or a hungry wolf slinking nearby? He decided to speak to Oyen about it.

Going over to where Oyen had returned to the fallen tree, Andreas said, "I'm not as experienced as Nils on that saw, but maybe with a little practice I can man the other end of it."

Oyen looked up with a solemn face. "It doesn't take much skill, just muscle. Yes, I'd welcome your help."

Andreas stepped closer to him and spoke quietly. "Anne said she saw something. Do you think we should find out what it was?"

Oyen was thoughtful for a moment. "I forgot she said that. All I could think about is that she just escaped being...killed."

"I know."

"I doubt if she saw anything more than a rabbit or a squirrel or something. She's so crazy about animals. But when she settles down I'll ask her."

After the evening meal and an afternoon of work in which Andreas discovered the kind of strength it took to help run a crosscut, he and Oyen sat on a log with tin cups of coffee. Oyen got up, went into the cabin and brought back with him a pale and silent Anne Marie. He sat down again and pulled her to him. She looked frightened.

"Papa was cross with you today because you did what you weren't supposed to do and almost got badly hurt."

The little girl scrunched up her face into crying sobs. "I made Uncle Nils break his leg," she managed to say.

"But it will heal," Oyen soothed her. "But tell me, you said you saw something. What was it?"

She stopped crying and her eyes opened wide with the memory. "It was a man – I think."

"One of our men?"

"No, he didn't look like any man..." She paused as though unable to describe him. "He had black hair that..." she wiggled her fingers from her ears to her shoulders. "And he had an awful looking crease on his face."

"Sara was with you, wasn't she? Did she see him too?"

"No, she ran on ahead to the cabin."

Oyen frowned and looked out into the forest. Andreas asked, "What did the man do when you saw him?"

"He just jumped back behind the tree and I ran."

"All right," Oyen said, "you go back inside and help take care of Uncle Nils so he'll get well real fast."

Word was passed around among the adults about the incident, but most of them felt that what Anne had seen was from her imagination and hearing talk about Indians. But the mothers were especially careful that their children did not stray far alone.

Andreas worked long, hard days with the rest as the weather grew colder and they blessed each day without the rain or snow that was sure to come soon. Sunless days, cold biting wind, low gray clouds foretold it.

Beginning work at dawn on a Monday morning late in November, they were determined to finish by mid-week, hold their dedication service and go hunting for big game – deer, moose, bear – whatever was out there beyond the noisy stir of the settlement. They had kept the table supplied so far with small game, shot as they worked, with anybody's gun that was handy. And with fish, mostly caught by the women and older children. Cornelius had killed a wild hog early one morning. Everyone enjoyed a dinner of pork fit for a holiday, then the women rendered the lard and the children had a treat of cracklings.

On Tuesday, almost all the women and children, with numbing fingers, gathered moss and grass for chinking. Cornelius and Ole Eide were working on the door. Andreas and Oyen were trying to figure out how to make a leak-proof roof over the timbers already in place. Torstein Bjorland, who had mended sails on the crossing, was working on the windows. Sailcloth wouldn't let in much light, but could at least be rolled up on sunny days. Torstein laid down his hooked needle and the piece of canvas, and went to where Oyen and Andreas stood looking at the roof.

"Didn't we bring along enough sails to cover that roof? I think with some help I could stitch them together and make a covering that wouldn't leak a drop."

Oyen laughed. "Well...maybe. If the wind doesn't get under it and sail the house away."

"We'll anchor it good with logs," Andreas said with relief. He was thankful the cabin was almost done. And as Gudmund had predicted, the men hadn't depended on him as much as he'd expected. When Cleng was gone they just trusted their own ingenuity. The cabin wasn't well-built, but adequate.

The women were called upon to locate all the sails, and there was loud lamenting; "Not our sails, we use them for everything!" But give them up they did, taking down the lean-to, dressing room curtains, sling for overhead storage, even the piece covering a hollow stump used as a washtub. However, they were heartened when they remembered that now the population of the first cabin would be cut in half. With most of the settlers working outdoors, it was only at bedtime that the cabin seemed intolerably crowded. But soon after beds were rolled out and everyone in them, all were asleep from sheer exhaustion.

The new cabin was not so large as the first, but had a higher pitched roof, permitting a garret for extra storage and sleeping. Since it was to be Cornelius and Kari's cabin, it seemed that they should say who was to live with them. But Kari insisted that so far, it belonged to everyone and should be treated as such. So it was decided among them that each cabin should house about the same number of families with children and single men.

Andreas drew his lot with those in the original cabin, but until he had his own cabin it mattered little to him where he laid his bed roll. They hadn't decided whose cabin to start next, but he knew it wouldn't be his. The families with children must be provided for first. It would go much slower now with the bad weather setting in and the need to begin clearing for spring crops. How desperately he wanted to begin on his own ground and live in a hut of his own. To sleep and eat according to his own pattern, not God forgive him, by the will of the group. How long would they be expected to function together like this? Cleng had not been heard from. Upon leaving he said not to expect him until they saw him coming. It might be Christmas or maybe not until spring.

The cabin, with its sail roof, did indeed resemble a ship in the forest and Torstein said, "I hope and pray it sails us right through the winter."

Their dedication service was to be held on Wednesday afternoon. The meetings were patterned after that of the Society of Friends, but some of the group still held fast to Lutheran beliefs even though they had outwardly rejected them in favor of Quakerism. The Norwegians' love for bright colors, design and music prevented them from entirely espousing all-Quaker plainness. Consequently, a unique mixture of services evolved into one, like a well-done stew.

Prayers of both thankfulness and petition poured out from individual hearts. Thanks for the freedom of worship in America, for saving the lives of Anne Marie and of Nils, and for the mending that was taking place in his leg. They asked for blessings for their friends in New York who had aided them, for their families and friends back in Norway. Entreaties were poured heavenward to see them through the winter, for the progress of negotiations in New York, and "if it be thy will, Lord, free our boat and cargo so it can be sold."

The worshippers filed out and stood looking back at the cross beams above the front door, the representation in a small way of a Norwegian dwelling. Without expressing it, each suffered homesickness.

Through the chilling wind and falling dusk, women and children hurried back across the woods to the other cabin to collect belongings and carry them to the new house. Betsy good-naturedly said to Kari, "Well, you get the new house, but we get Andreas and the stove with an oven so he can bake us some loaf bread like he promised."

"If he ever gets that bread baked, you'll share a little of it with us, won't you?" Kari asked with a smile. "Except for those first few days off the boat when the New York Quakers took us in, this will be the first time since Norway that we'll cook and eat separately."

That evening the men were excited as they prepared to go hunting on the following day. Who would make up a party and which direction would they go? Andreas kept his silence until asked, then said confidently, "I've always had pretty good luck hunting alone, so that's what I'm going to try tomorrow." In his mind there was no doubt about which direction he would turn. He'd waited long enough to roam his 48 acres.

CHAPTER 5

American
Neighbors

WAKENING BEFORE DAYLIGHT, Andreas heard Thomas Madland's loud snoring, a child cough, someone sigh in her sleep and baby Margaret wimpering.

He raised one side of his sheepskin cover, reached for his pants, pulled them on over his woolen underwear and socks, sat up and put on his shirt and shoes, trying all the while not to waken Gudmund on one side nor Ole on the other. He tiptoed over and placed his rifle and axe by the door, went to the fireplace, stirred the remains of the burning log, then quietly added another.

Martha, nearest the fireplace, snuggled inside her sheepskin with the baby, raised her head. "Andreas?" she asked in a whisper.

"Yes?"

"In the cold cupboard there's some dried fish and *lefse* for you to take along. Aren't you going to wait for coffee?"

"Not this morning, thanks. I'll take some fish." He could hear the baby's contented suckling. He opened the door to look at the weather. Snow covered the ground. He went to Martha, bent over her and whispered, "It snowed last night."

The word "snow" brought up several heads, but Andreas scooped out a small handful of fish, wrapped it in flatbread and thrust it into his pocket.

The snow was not deep, only enough for good tracking. He was exhilarated with a feeling of freedom and anticipation. On his own for a whole day! By keeping the first rays of daylight to his left, he would be traveling south. The crude map Cleng had sketched showed the northern borderline of his land at the second crossing of the little creek called Bald Eagle. Thick underbrush hampered his progress and small animals and large birds scampered or fluttered out of his way.

THE BECKONING

A good-sized wild hog went snorting out of the brush in front of him. He quickly raised his gun, then hesitated. It would have been a great kill so early in the day, but he didn't want to do any gutting or packing just yet. He'd make up for it later.

He heard the creek before he got to it, but the bank was so covered with growth he almost tumbled in. It was now daylight and he could see his way downstream to where it was running in the open. He looked up and down with a powerfully possessive thrill. A little farther and it doubled back on his own property!

Against the tumult of the water, he practiced aloud the few English words he knew as he seldom had an opportunity to do with the others always around. Hello. Goodbye. Thanks. Milk. Flour. Bread. Papa. Mama. The last two words he had learned from a small boy who had taken a fancy to him at one of the homes where he and Cleng had spent a night.

He backed up a few steps, then with axe and rifle held overhead, leaped across the stream. A bright red bird flashed from one tree to the other in front of him, knocking snow from the branches, questioning his invasion with a clear sharp whistle. Andreas whistled back, thinking that at least he could do that in English.

Were the other men up and out yet, he wondered. He should have shot that pig. They weren't easy to find and the need was great. But he had looked forward to a day to himself for so long.

Here was the stream again! No Viking explorer could have been more excited than Andreas Stangeland as he looked across at his land. His own land! He knelt in the snow with raised hands and again thanked God for it. Then he silently watched a beaver emerge from its lodge and waddle upstream. "Hello, neighbor, you're lucky, you got your house built," he said to the animal.

Andreas walked east along his side of the stream, wondering how far his property went before it joined that of the American farmer. He couldn't find the stakes that were supposed to be there so he began looking for a suitable cabin site. The creek made a little nook, treeless and pleasant, but not large enough for a cabin; nevertheless it was an ideal spot with water at the door, fish too, probably. Would that corner flood in the spring? He wished his farm bordered the lake like Cleng's, but he was glad the creek was his.

36

Looking around, he recognized the log where he had sat watching a pair of squirrels busily going in and out of a hollow tree as Cleng and Mr. Fellows talked over the land purchase. If only he could leave things as they were, live like the beaver, the squirrels and the red bird in this virgin forest. But this was his farm, his living, the good earth beneath him, the sky overhead. So clear it he must. He took off his coat, picked up the axe and began swinging against a tree of medium girth, trying not to remember that he was supposed to be hunting. Only after he felled the second tree did he sit down and rest.

He'd made a slight clearing and from it he saw smoke rising above the trees not very far away. It must be from the American neighbors. He put aside any thought of visiting them today without enough English words to explain who he was. It wouldn't hurt, though, to go take a look through the trees, get an idea whether they were poor or prosperous. Maybe he would get some ideas for his own place.

Leaving his axe by one of the fallen trees, he approached the clearing as cautiously and as noiselessly as possible. Going around an especially heavy growth of bushes, he found himself directly behind what seemed to be a shed with chickens in it. He could hear cackling and flapping of wings as if someone were inside. He looked ahead to where the house sat. It was made of boards, painted white. All the other buildings were of logs. He saw no one around. If he encountered the farmer, perhaps with gestures and pointing, he could explain who he was.

He walked haltingly out into the open, stepped around the side of the building right into the path of a girl, the corner of her cloak gathered up into a catch for fresh-gathered eggs. She screamed, dropped the eggs and ran toward the house. But after several steps she plunged forward, tripping over something under the snow. She made a frightened scramble to get up until she saw Andreas quickly lay down his rifle. With red face he desperately spread his empty hands. She hesitated, then stammered, "You're not an Indian."

Andreas understood the word, Indian. "No...no. Norske." He wanted to go to her, help her up, see if she were hurt, but didn't dare approach her. He had already made her break the eggs. He looked down at them, a scramble of shells and golden yolks in the snow. He squatted down to see if any could be salvaged. How often he and the others had wished for a fried egg, and here were all these broken! He found a few still whole, cushioned by the snow, wiped them off as best he could and put them in his cap. More than anything else he wanted her to take them so he could hurry back to the privacy of the woods.

But he must in some way apologize and meet her father if possible. The meeting had to come sooner or later and Andreas didn't want them to think of him, their neighbor, as a complete fool just because he couldn't speak English.

She came fearlessly back to him, and said something which he didn't understand. Painfully he shook his head. All he could say was, "Norwegian" and point to the west, which surprisingly she must have understood, because she nodded her head and motioned for him to follow her, leaving him to carry the eggs.

At the door she hurried in, excitedly talking to those inside. He could hear a high-pitched woman's voice, a male voice, and children's chatter. But most of all, he could smell the heavenly scent of food cooking. He was reminded that he hadn't yet eaten and it must be close to noon.

A tall man with craggy features, heavy, dark, wavy hair, but clean-shaven, came to the door. A short, plump woman in a starched white cap, peeked around him.

"Come in," invited the man. When Andreas didn't move, he motioned forward with his hand. Andreas was reluctant to go in, but didn't know how to refuse politely. Besides, he still held the eggs. He set his gun by the side of the door, dusted off his knees with his free hand, stomped his feet, ran his fingers through his hair and stepped in. To the woman in the white cap, he handed the eggs, shaking his head sorrowfully. The woman looked questioningly at her daughter, who had now removed her cloak to reveal the figure of a young woman even though her dark hair was fastened back and trailing behind like a child's. He couldn't guess how old she was.

"He thinks he made me break the eggs," she explained.

The mother laughed pleasantly and, pointing to a nearby basket half full of eggs, added those in his hat to them.

The father indicated that Andreas should remove his coat and hang it by the fire. Andreas, with an embarrassed grin, revealed the fish in a pocket and pointed outdoors. The father and daughter laughed and the jacket was hung outside the door.

Settled uneasily on the bench by the fire, Andreas looked about the room. This was not the home of a poor farmer. There were books, dainty pieces of china and needlework, and a beautiful spinning wheel. Through the door to another room, he could see a large loom. But dominating the scene, tantalizing his hunger, was the turkey roasting on a spit over the fire. A white-spread table was set with pickles and other dishes he did not recognize. It reminded him of his mother's holiday table.

Did American farmers eat like this every noonday? He wanted to apologize for coming at mealtime but was helpless. What would Cleng do? He would, of course, stay and eat, entertaining them with his stories. That was fine for Cleng – he could speak English.

The father said, "Our name is Cary," pointing to himself and the others. Andreas understood from the way he emphasized the word Cary, that it was the family name. It was a name he knew well, like Cleng's sister Kari. But it seemed strange for a last name.

To show that he knew a few words, Andreas, pointing, said "Papa Cary, Mama Cary." Then he looked questioningly at the girl.

"Susan," the father said.

"Suss-uun Cary."

Mr. Cary put an arm around each small boy who had been staring at him and said, "Alexander and Leander."

Andreas was sure they were twins and the similar names confirmed it. He then introduced himself, saying his name slowly. The father made a couple of attempts to understand.

"He's saying Andreas, Papa. Andreas Stangeland," Susan said. Andreas nodded and smiled.

Mrs. Cary came with cups of coffee for the two men, followed by Susan with a plate of little cakes. Andreas uttered, "T'anks" and smiled at mother and daughter. Eating was something to do when they couldn't converse.

In the pantry, Susan spoke quietly to her mother. "If he's from that settlement of Norwegians, I'll bet he doesn't know that today is Thanksgiving. Could we ask him to stay?"

"Of course we should."

"Since cousin Angela and cousin Abner couldn't come, or Uncle Ira's either, we'll still have company," she said eagerly. "But how are we going to explain about the holiday?"

"Maybe with some pictures at the school?"

Susan's eyes sparkled with the challenge. "I'll bet I could. I'll ask Papa."

John Cary agreed to go with her to take Andreas to the school. "I want to see the benches James is making anyway. Can you explain where we're going?"

Susan paused to think how to get the idea across and Andreas watched her, thinking what a pleasant little girl she was, not only pretty, with a fluff of dark hair surrounding her small heart-shaped face but, for one so young, she seemed much more forward than a Norwegian girl of that age.

Picking up a book from the shelf, Susan patted her little brother, Alexander, on the head, looked closely at the book and said, "School."

Andreas nodded. He knew the word "school". They began putting on their coats, apparently wanting to show him where it was. So the little Norwegians could attend, he wondered.

They started down the well-traveled path, the boys running ahead. Mr. Cary pointed to a small log structure with smoke rising from its chimney. Andreas looked over at his own property, trying to think of a way to ask about the stakes, but there was no way he could explain or question.

Inside the building, a man about Andreas' age, looked up from the bench making. Andreas immediately recognized this as a schoolhouse. The young man must be the schoolmaster and Susan either helped him or was a pupil herself. Mr. Cary, after a few words to the younger man, introduced him as James Cary.

Andreas shook the extended hand warmly. He looked so much like the older Cary, he must be another son. Then Andreas tapped the slanted log on legs at the front of the room, obviously a teacher's desk, and pointed questioningly at James.

"No, I'm not the teacher." James laughed and nodded towards his sister. "She is."

Astonished, Andreas looked at her with renewed admiration. All schoolteachers in Norway were men, and never so young. He noted her embarrassment and quickly congratulated her in Norwegian, letting his slight bow and expression apologize for him.

Mr. Cary turned to the benches James had made. Susan went to a shelf beside the teacher's desk, took down a book and some drawings, then motioned Andreas over to look at a picture on the wall. It was of an American family sitting around a table with a turkey in the center and other dishes of food grouped around it. All the family had their hands folded in prayer. Well, that he could understand. Yes, he nodded, he knew Americans asked God's blessing before they ate.

She said slowly, "Thanksgiving Day" and picked up a flag and waved it. He thought of the turkey on the spit, the table spread like a holiday. A holiday for thanks to God!

He remembered now about the day in America when the harvest was finished, when families gathered together to thank God for His goodness. That was what they were trying to tell him, that he had picked the wrong day to come visit them. Trying to hide his embarrassment, but wanting to apologize, he bowed and said, "T'anks. I go. T'anks."

"Oh, no...no!" she caught his sleeve. "Papa Cary, Mama Cary, James Cary, Alexander and Leander Cary..." She pointed to herself and to him and pretended to eat.

The exaggerated invitation made them both laugh and Andreas was pleased she had communicated the whole idea to him. Then he remembered the state of his clothes. He pointed to the dirt on his knees and pretended to shoot a rifle and chop down a tree. She shrugged and went on showing him through the stack of drawings. Most of them were of a single item with the word for each beneath – an apple, potato, cow, sheep – the kind of pictures he'd learned to read by. On one he recognized the word "corn," like on the sack of cornmeal that had been given to them. He pointed to it.

41

"Yes, popcorn," she said.

"Papa's corn," he nodded.

She laughed. "No, popcorn." She closed her hands, then flung out her fingers in rapid succession. He had no idea what she was trying to tell him. She turned to her little brother, Leander, who was standing beside her. "We'll have to show him what popcorn is before he leaves, won't we? They must not grow it in Norway."

She went on to a picture of Indians being welcomed to their American feast. He noted the trussed-up deer they were bringing and thought of the wild hog he didn't shoot. Pointing to himself, he shook his head.

She quickly sorted through the papers, picked one and showed it to him. "Norske-fish." He nodded, patting his pocket. They both laughed and he felt himself relaxing around this light-hearted family.

An hour later, they were seated around the white-spread table with Mr. Cary asking the blessing. When he had finished the long prayer, Andreas raised his right hand and held it out over the table: "I Jesu navn gar vi til bords, At spise og drikke pa ditt ord, Dig Gud til aere, oss til gavn, Sa far vi mat i Jesu navn. Amen."

To Andreas, the food assembled on the table seemed to be enough to feed the whole Norwegian colony. He wished with all his heart that they could be enjoying it with him. Well, maybe next year they could have a fitting Thanks Day of their own, after the harvest was in. The bowls and platters were passed again and again, turkey, venison, potatoes, cabbage, carrots, other dishes he didn't recognize; each was welcomed. He was famished. It was the first time since leaving Norway that he had all he wanted to eat. Back at the cabin or at places he and Cleng had stopped, he politely refused when the bowl or pot was getting low. But here they urged third and fourth helpings on him. He could see that Mr. Cary and James were eating just as much and there would still be food left over.

The final dish was something they called "pumpkin pie;" it was in a round pan and cut in wedges. To his unaccustomed taste, it was too sweet and spicy, but he ate it between gulps of strong coffee, cream added. At the cabin the coffee was, of necessity, weak and seldom with milk or cream.

42

So many things he wished he could tell the Carys. That the Norwegians had completed a second cabin. That they would be greatly surprised he was enjoying a holiday dinner with an American family instead of hunting. But most of all he wanted to talk to Mr. Cary about the boundary line and about farming. And he wondered again why he hadn't seen the necessity of learning more English during the past year.

He looked across at the little-girl schoolteacher. She gave him a warm, friendly smile. He didn't feel ill at ease with her and wouldn't be embarrassed if she offered to teach him to read and speak English from her children's lesson pictures.

After dinner James picked up Andreas' gun, looked questioningly at Andreas, who nodded his head. James then took down his own rifle from the pegs above the door and handed it to Andreas. The two men pointed out similarities and differences. The stock of Andreas' gun was walnut; James' was maple. Andreas' rifle was English and bore a Birmingham proof mark. James' was a Kentucky wheellock with a brass patchbox, a curiosity to Andreas. James indicated they should go outside and he'd demonstrate how each ball, before loading, was dropped into a little "patch" to make it fit tight in the barrel.

Mr. Cary came out and the three men visited the barn where the horses, oxen and milk cows were stabled. At one side was a lean-to where a dozen sheep huddled together. They also looked into the spring house and smoke house. What a wonderful farm!

When they re-entered the house, Susan was waiting with some little yellow seeds in a cup. She motioned Andreas over to the stove where her mother had lard heating in an iron pot. Susan sprinkled in the seeds and put on the lid. With a towel, Mrs. Cary shook the hot kettle again and again. They wanted to show him something, but he wasn't sure what. The little boys were watching Andreas, their eyes full of anticipation. Then there were little explosions inside the kettle. Finally Mrs. Cary cautiously lifted the lid. To his astonishment, like magic, the pot had filled with a white fluffy mass.

It occurred to him that this was the corn he'd called "papa's corn" – it went pop, pop. Popcorn. He grinned, folded his hands and flipped his fingers rapidly like Susan had done at the schoolhouse. She nodded, smiled, gave him a small bowlful and ate some herself. It was crisp and good.

Susan than gave him a cloth bag of the seeds, perhaps as much as two pounds. She pointed to the west, toward their cabins, and said, "Norwegians."

Mrs. Cary handed him a tin pail with tight lid and said, "Maple syrup." He looked at Susan questioningly. She picked up a pitcher from the sideboard, broke off a piece of the bread left over from dinner, dipped it into the pitcher and ate it. She pinched off another piece and, after dipping it, held it out for him. It was sweet and wonderful. He nodded, remembering the taste from one of the meals he and Cleng had enjoyed with a family along the way. They had told Cleng it came from the sweet sap of trees. Andreas wondered if there were any such trees on his place.

He didn't want to leave without asking the question uppermost in his mind. Picking up the stack of word-pictures Susan had carried back with her from the schoolhouse, he pointed to her, then the cards and to himself. She seemed to understand immediately and spoke to her mother, who nodded. Susan pointed to the bench in front of the fire, and spread her hands in welcome. Then she said the days of the week as she pointed to her fingers; when she reached six she repeated "Saturday" a few times. The day before First Day, he quickly reasoned. He demonstrated his gratitude with nods and smiles.

Pointing to each in turn, he said, "Mama Cary, Papa Cary, Yames, Suss-uun...boys, t'anks, Gudbye." The two men shook hands with him, then he bent down and shook hands with the little boys, which pleased them greatly. He bowed low to the women and picked up his gun and food treasures.

It was late afternoon as he walked back across the clearing of the Cary farm onto his own heavily-wooded property, reclaimed his axe and headed back to the cabin. His mind was filled with the delightful Cary family and his unexpected visit.

But what of the hunt! Had he sinned by having such a carefree day and plenty of food while the rest were out bringing in game for the winter? Surely he had done some good for all by getting acquainted with a nearby American family. And such a devout family, too. He wouldn't be taking back any meat, but he had other surprises for them. Maybe tomorrow he'd make that loaf bread they had been asking for.

Should he tell them a young girl schoolteacher was going to help him learn English? How soon dared he go back for the first lesson? He raised his eyes heavenward and thanked God from the fullness of his heart.

CHAPTER 6

An English
Lesson

"HERE HE COMES NOW!" Oyen called out as Andreas entered the clearing where, in front of each cabin, the Norwegians were skinning and butchering their kill.

"Where's your deer?" shouted Big Nels.

Andreas tried to sound jovial, but realized any excuse would sound trifling. "I'll have to get my share of the game later. Today I got only American food." He held up the bag and the pail. "I ran into our American neighbors and they invited me in."

"I'll bet that was a lively conversation," Gudmund quipped. He was helping Cornelius skin the only bear shot on the hunt.

"Today is the American Thanksgiving Day," Andreas said as he went over to admire the size of the black bear.

Daniel asked, "You mean they have to have a special day to thank God?" Andreas was glad that Betsy and Carrie came out of the cabin just then to greet him so he wouldn't have to try to explain. Events of the day were so locked in his heart it would be difficult to share them even if he wanted to. He turned the Cary's gifts over to the women and went across to help Thomas and Oyen who were improvising a lean-to storage shed out of leftover logs to protect the meat from wild animals.

That night, before sleep overtook his thoughts, he relived each detail of the day, sensing it might have a profound effect on his life here in America. Creeping into the pleasure he felt at meeting the Cary family was a foreboding. Was he letting himself fall into something not right, not approved by God?

Just after he'd slipped off to sleep, he was awakened by the snarls and growls of wolves and coyotes. They were after the entrails from the

46

butchering, which had been dragged just beyond the clearing. Children woke crying at the sound. A little later, Daniel went to the door and shot toward the storage shed when he heard animals growling close to it.

The next day Andreas announced he was going to make the loaf bread the women had been urging him to do.

"Oh, let's have a party!" Betsy exclaimed. Other women gathered around.

"We'll fry some meat and try the sweet syrup you brought back," Carrie said.

Bertha added, "And we can make a sauce from some of our dried apples."

"I want to see how the magic corn cooks," Carolyn said. Even the usually solemn Martha smiled as she jiggled the baby over her shoulder.

So Andreas began the bread-making as the rest of the men continued with the butchering chores. Some scraped bristles from a freshly scalded pig which Endre had shot, while others finished cutting the deer into pieces that could hang from the roof of the improvised shed.

Working around Andreas, the women were rendering fat, boiling bones, making head cheese and frying meat to submerge in lard for later use. Men who came into the cabin with more parts for the women to work up, tossed good-natured taunts at Andreas as he kneaded the huge mound of dough.

"Are you hunting in the kitchen, Andreas?"

"You got flour on your beard."

"Is that easier than manning the end of a saw?"

Andreas grinned back at each comment, but silently resolved that this would be his last batch of bread he'd ever make. In Norway, baking was a profession and the mixing and kneading was done in a back room; but here in America it was a woman's job in a woman's kitchen. Men were to be hunters, builders and tillers, all the profession he'd ever want from now on.

When he rejoined the men while the bread was rising, he listened to their hunting tales and laughed with them as they teased each other.

47

Thomas said to Cornelius, "It's a good thing you teamed up with Big Nels or you'd never got back with that fat bear.

Oyen said, "Gudmund and Thomas were just lucky to get their deer right after daylight." Andreas couldn't help being a little envious.

By evening both cabins took on a festive air as women hurried back and forth to prepare the supper they would eat together. The smell of baking bread, in the only stove with an oven, permeated the whole clearing. When darkness overtook the work outside, the men came in to a feast of fried bear meat, warm bread and stewed apples.

Big Nels called to Andreas, "I guess I'll forgive you for not bringing in any meat."

Andreas answered back, "Now it's time for you to get out your squeak box. What's a party without music from you and Henrik?"

Sara Thompson broke in, "Oh, Mama, we want to see the magic seeds cooked first."

"All right," Carolyn said, "Come on, Andreas, show us how they work." She pulled the covered pot from the back of the stove to the hot spot in front.

"Put in some grease," he said and she spooned in bear fat. "Now we'll put in some seeds. I don't know how many, we'll try just a handful first. Listen," he said to the children gathered around. Even the older boys, Halvor and Ovee, just old enough to sprout fuzz on their faces, watched expectantly.

Soon they began to hear little pop-pop-pops. Carolyn lifted the lid cautiously and corn popped out of the pot. The children squealed and jumped and Carolyn quickly replaced the lid. Andreas took gloves from his pocket, held the hot pan with them and shook it like he'd seen Mrs. Cary doing. When the popping stopped, he lifted the lid.

"It's nearly full!" Ovee said and everyone else exclaimed or looked in open-mouthed wonderment.

"Isn't that something!" Betsy said. "Nels, we're going to grow some of that!"

The popped corn, after being poured into a wooden bowl, was passed for everyone to try. Some were afraid to eat it before others tasted it, then they'd take two or three bites out of each piece. Oyen, who had invented and created many things in his former blacksmith's shop, looked it over carefully. "Why, it looks like each grain just blew itself inside out. Probably from the heat in the pot."

More batches were made until each person had a generous handful, all now eating it eagerly. Andreas watched their pleasure and was glad he had withstood their barbs and helped bring some joy into the evening. They had had so little since leaving Norway.

Nels brought out his accordion and started to play while Henrik, tall and gaunt with a shock of blonde hair, tuned his fiddle. Toes began to tap, but there was no room for dancing so they settled on the floor and sang the familiar songs, swaying to the music or pumping their arms up and down and shouting with gusto during the livelier tunes. Andreas noticed Gudmund and Gurene sitting very close together in a dark corner. After awhile Henrik turned his fiddle over to Endre Dahl and went to sit in another dark corner with his intended, Martha Donalson.

One by one children fell asleep across their mothers' laps. The music ended and the group quieted into worshipful Quakers offering up their bedtime prayers.

On the following day, Saturday, since the butchering was finished, hides were stretched over boards to dry for tanning during the winter. Cornelius proudly stretched his large bear skin along the outside of the cabin. Carrie was already planning the hats she would make for her children.

As the men worked, they made plans for the coming week. A cabin for Daniel Rosdail's family of seven should come next, they decided. His land was just west of Cornelius' property and the newly built cabin. Andreas sensed the effect that Cleng's absence was having on the colony. He had encouraged them to live and work together. But since Cleng was not there and no other real leader had emerged – Andreas was most grateful they hadn't depended on him after all – they were beginning to think and act independently, deciding what they would do as families rather than as parts of a group. As for Andreas, he fervently hoped that by spring, he'd be able to move onto his own property and start building his own life.

There had been no word from Cleng or the men held in New York. Every group prayer included a petition for them.

One afternoon in early December, Andreas was splitting logs at the edge of the clearing when Martha came forlornly through the woods. She had apparently gone to the lake, as many of them did, to get away for awhile and to view a wide expanse, a place not covered with trees. He rested the axe as she approached.

"What's the matter, Martha?" he asked gently, "Just wishing for Lars?" His heart ached for her; she seemed so small and young.

"Oh, Andreas, the lake has ice on it. I'm afraid the canal is frozen over and he won't get back until spring, even if he is released." More tears came to her eyes already red from crying.

He could offer little encouragement, knowing the canal boats ceased operation as soon as the ice began to block it. "At least we can be sure he's all right. Cleng is back there, he is wise and persuasive and has many connections."

"I wish now I'd stayed in New York," she said, "and gotten a job as a serving girl or maid, if I could find anyone to hire me with a tiny baby and Siri to care for." Andreas wanted to put his arm around her for comfort, but dared not, fearing his gesture might be misunderstood. So he walked with her back to the cabin, talking about the weather. It had been getting decidedly colder every day for a week. The snow from Thanksgiving Day remained and another layer had been added before the hard freeze came. The meat was now frozen solid where it hung, and a piece at a time was brought into the cabins to thaw for cutting and cooking.

By morning the temperature had dropped even further. Andreas went into the cabin with an armload of wood, his beard frozen white from his breath. "It's cold. I'll bet Ovee and Halvor are having a hard time chopping through to the water this morning." Children sat huddled around the fire as he dropped the wood and threw another chunk into the fire.

Betsy, making candles, said, "A pan of water froze setting right over there in the corner of the cabin."

In spite of the cold, Andreas looked forward to going back to the Carys for his first English lesson, but hadn't yet found the right opportunity. On the second Saturday in December, he decided to just take off that afternoon and go, no matter what the other men said or thought. He went behind the curtain and changed into his clean suit of clothes and combed his hair and beard carefully.

"A body would think he was going courtin'," Big Nels drawled.

"I'm going to school, Nels. Didn't your mother make you clean up before you went to school?"

He found his way more easily this trip and resolved to clear a trail as soon as possible so it would be even easier to get across to his property. His face was red from the cold when Susan welcomed him in. Mrs. Cary sat in a corner spinning; Susan had been carding wool. The men and little boys were no place in sight.

Andreas showed them his tablet. "Day...good?"

Susan nodded, smiled and directed him to a bench by the fire. She was flushed, pleased that he had finally returned. In her hand was a sheaf of papers, picture-word combinations; tree, axe, man, woman, deer, bear, the numbers, and other things he recognized.

"I made these especially for you to learn English," she said. He understood her meaning and nodded his thanks.

She sat down beside him on the bench and his heart raced at her nearness. But, he must concentrate on being a good pupil and prove he was not dull. Learning English quickly should be his only goal, he reminded himself.

He pointed to the card for bear and pretended to shoot. Her brown eyes shone with interest, "You shot a bear?"

"No," he shook his head and pointed toward the colony. "Cornelius Nelson."

"Cornelius Nelson," she repeated and turned to her mother who continued spinning, the ruffle on her white cap framing a softly lined face. "Did you hear that, Mama, one of the Norwegians shot a bear?" She gave Andreas the sketch of a bear. "Let's say it now. Cornelius Nelson sh-h-ot a b-b-ear." She sounded it out.

Andreas fumbled through the words, embarrassed at the sounds that came out. "Now let's try it again," Susan said. About the fifth repeat, the sentence began to sound similar to what she was saying. "Good!" She laid her hand on his arm and he flushed at her compliment. Then he picked out the paper which had "God" printed on it, Heaven sketched above. "Gud...Norwegian."

"In Norwegian you say good for God?" Andreas nodded. Lydia Cary looked up and smiled. "We'll be able to talk to Andreas in no time at all."

Susan interpreted, pointing to her lips and then his, back and forth and nodded her head. Andreas understood and his heart was again filled with gratitude for the helpful, understanding Carys.

Mrs. Cary stopped them for tea and cookies awhile into the lesson. She tapped her forehead and Andreas knew she meant he was to rest his head.

Susan sent home with him the papers containing the new words he'd learned and he placed them carefully in his pocket. All the way back to the cabin he hardly saw or heard anything, his mind was so filled with his first English lesson.

When he arrived, full of enthusiasm, he offered to share what he had learned with the others. But, he was met with indifference or jokes. Gudmund said, "I couldn't learn funny looking words like that in ten years."

Oyen said, "I can cut trees or plant potatoes just as well in Norwegian." Only Martha was interested in learning and Andreas was especially happy to give her a new interest to help her through the winter.

But the cabin was a poor place to conduct a class. There was little time or room for them to study together and they were constantly interrupted by jokes and comments from the others. And Andreas had difficulty enough pronouncing the words himself; he worried that Martha might not learn them correctly. So she copied the words in Andreas' tablet in order to at least recognize the printed words.

After considering carefully, he asked Martha, "How would you like to go with me and hear the words from the teacher? It will mean more to you."

Martha looked startled. "Go into a strange American home without Lars?"

"I'll try to explain where he is. But the worst part is getting there. You'd have to crawl through brush and over logs."

"I could do that..." She still hesitated.

"They're very friendly."

"All right, I will."

Susan had been watching since early morning for her adult pupil to arrive from out of the forest to the west. All week her mind had been so much on this one English lesson, she could hardly concentrate on her small pupils. That morning, she had insisted that the little boys stay with their father in the barn so she and Andreas could work without distractions. They were so disappointed; she promised to call them before he left.

Mrs. Cary, kneading bread at the table, first saw the two approaching. "He has a woman with him."

Susan's heart plummeted as she hurried to the window and saw the pretty blonde girl at his side. "Do you think it's his wife? I didn't think he was married."

"Maybe it's his sister or just one of the other Norwegian women," Lydia said, amused at her daughter's obvious disappointment.

After Susan invited them in, Andreas bowed, then turned to his companion, "Martha Larson." Susan was relieved the name wasn't Stangeland. "Papa Larson...New York."

Susan smiled a welcome and wondered if "Papa" meant husband or father.

Andreas pointed to his ear and mouth, then to Martha and said, "Hear." Susan nodded but Martha's eyes were on the beautiful spinning wheel standing beside her. She cautiously reached out and touched the smooth polished wood, turning the wheel slightly.

Mrs. Cary noted the homesick gaze on the girl's face, wiped her hands and went to her. "Try it," she indicated with her hand and pointed out the wool ready to feed into it. Martha shyly looked at Andreas. "Sure, go ahead," he said. She sat down, looked it over for a moment, then set it to humming.

Andreas turned to Susan and her mother, then motioned around the room and to Martha, "Norway house." He repeated the gesture, pointed to himself and nodded.

On the way home, Martha showed more spirit than Andreas had seen in her since they arrived. "They have such a lovely home. Do you suppose Lars and I will ever have a home like that?"

"I can see it now. And when Lars builds it, you can be sure it will be done right. Much better than the two we have now."

Martha followed behind as Andreas broke trail. "Andreas, you didn't tell us your teacher was a pretty young girl."

Andreas was glad she couldn't see his face redden. "She's just a little girl."

"She's old enough to teach school. How old is she?"

"I don't know," he said stumbling over a root, "how old would you say?"

"Oh, I'd say seventeen or eighteen...and she likes you, Andreas."

"Do you think so?" he asked.

"I could see it every time she looked at you."

"Maybe you won't say anything about her being...young and pretty...back at the cabin."

"It's our secret, Andreas."

As they arrived at the clearing, they heard screams coming from the nearest cabin. "That's my baby!" Martha shouted in anguish and began running toward the cabin.

CHAPTER 7

The
Pardon

S IRI LARSON WAS Martha's sister-in-law, Lars' older sister, deaf and dumb since birth. Lars, being responsible for her, had brought her with them to America. She was seldom any trouble and did her share of work. Martha could communicate with her in a sign language all their own; the rest didn't try. They were kind to her, but in a custodial way, taking her coffee or food or babies to hold or change, which she would accept with a nod.

Aunt Siri adored baby Margaret and held or played with her often. When she wasn't busy she sat by the fireplace smoking her pipe on the special little stool kept there. If she couldn't get tobacco, which was most of the time, she went out in the woods and found weeds or moss to dry and smoke. Lighting one splinter after another from the fireplace, she spent as much time trying to fire the contents of the bowl as she did smoking. Martha insisted she smoke only by the fireplace so the acrid smelling smoke would go up the chimney.

When Martha left with Andreas, Siri was dozing, empty pipe fallen to the floor, she didn't arouse her to explain. Siri awakened and didn't miss Martha until she went to check on the baby, found her wet and looked for Martha to get a diaper. She touched Carolyn on the arm with a where-is-Martha look which the women had come to recognize. Carolyn pointed to the east. Siri immediately became wild-eyed. Carolyn then gently took her by the arms and said, "What do you want?" But Siri jerked away from her and hurried for the door.

"Don't let her out," Carolyn called to Kari, who was just coming in. "She's trying to find Martha and will get lost in the woods for sure." Kari blocked the door. Siri began pushing at her and making frantic grunts.

"Martha will be back in a little while," Kari tried to explain. But Siri never understood when Lars disappeared, why he wasn't with them or where he went. She was afraid that now Martha had also left her and the baby.

Carolyn quickly found a dry diaper and handed it to Siri, suspecting that it was what she had wanted. Siri grabbed it and ran to the baby, but instead of changing her, she snatched her out of the cradle, clutched her to her bosom and began wildly pacing the floor. The baby whimpered, then began crying, finally screaming in protest at being held so rigidly. Carolyn, Kari and Betsy all tried to calm her and take the baby away, but Siri just held on all the more tightly.

When Martha burst through the door and surveyed the scene, she was afraid the baby had been burned or had fallen. "What is the matter?" she gasped, out of breath.

"The baby's all right, but Siri apparently thought you had deserted them and she went crazy," Betsy said.

Martha breathed easier, went calmly to Siri and held out her hands. "Give her to me, Siri." The older woman relinquished the child, held her head in her hands and sobbed silently, her shoulders heaving. After comforting the baby for a few moments, Martha turned her over to Carolyn and led the submissive Siri back to her stool by the fire and handed her pipe to her.

Andreas stood silently at the door watching the scene and his heart ached for Martha. What more could he do? He went back outside, harboring an even greater desire, selfish as it was, to get into a place of his own, to make it peaceful and orderly like the Cary home.

During the cold days of December, the men kept themselves warm falling trees and chopping firewood. To clear the land, they kept a fire burning around the stumps which had to be removed or farmed around. The women stayed in the cabins mending, washing clothes, cooking, baking, doing and redoing all the domestic chores necessary to keep the settlers as cared-for as possible. There was seldom any planning in advance; if a job needed doing, somebody did it. Some worked faster than others, or were more proficient at one thing than another, but there were no slackers; the quiet good nature of the Norwegian personality prevailed. Nevertheless, each woman secretly yearned for her own home as soon as possible.

Near dusk on one of the sunnier days, Martha felt particularly confined; the walls seemed to close in on her. She had just finished stitching a dress from one of her aprons for her little daughter – a new dress for Christmas. But sewing allowed for too much thinking, she must escape for awhile. She went to Betsy, who had Nels' shirt spread over the split-log table, scrubbing homemade soap into it with a brush. "My baby is asleep. Will you keep an eye out for her? I'm going outdoors to clear my head."

"Sure. You're lucky yours is in a cradle," Betsy panted, "this little fellow takes up way too much room in here." She patted her bulging stomach. "Just be sure and explain to Siri where you're going."

Just as Martha got outside the door and breathed in fresh air, she heard the faint sound of a familiar whistle. Startled, she pulled her scarf from her ears to hear more clearly. She hurried to where Andreas was dumping more branches on the fire. "Listen," she said, "that whistle, it sounds like Lars!"

Andreas listened and also heard it. "It's one of the other men, Ole, I think. He walked to town. It couldn't be Lars – the canal is frozen over."

"It's Lars. I know it is!" She ran towards the woods just as he came into view. "Oh, dear God, You brought my husband," she cried with joy.

Lars Larson dropped a pair of skates and his small bedroll on the ground and threw out his arms to receive Martha. She leaped sobbing into them. Andreas hastened to spread the news. Everyone dropped what they were doing; women grabbed shawls to throw around themselves and all came running to greet their beloved leader and friend. He looked ruddy and fit, but very thin.

Noting the skates, Daniel asked, "How far did you skate?"

"From Albany."

"But that's 290 miles!" Oyen Thompson said. They all gasped.

"How long did it take you?" asked Nils, who had hobbled out with the aid of a stick.

"I don't know. I just skated daylight to dark every day. Then I'd stop in a little village or wherever I saw a light in a settler's cabin. People are so good and the Lord provides. I always found a place to sleep and food enough for the next day."

Before he could answer any more questions, Martha began pulling him through the crowd to the cabin to see the baby. Siri sat holding the child across her lap, smiling at her, unaware of what was going on. Then she looked up and saw her brother. Quick tears streamed from her eyes as he bent down and hugged her, then took the baby. He winked at Siri, slipped a small packet from his pocket and folded it into her hand. She looked at it and grinned – tobacco.

All the Norwegians crowded into the cabin, anxious to hear the news from New York. Lars handed the baby to Martha, then raised his arms for quiet. "I know you will all be gratified to hear that the problem of the over-loaded boat has been resolved, thanks to a politician named Henry Clay, Secretary of State. All charges have been dropped."

The men cheered and waved their hats, the women clapped; Martha, teary-eyed but beaming, stood beside her handsome, heavily bearded husband snuggling baby Margaret.

Lars continued, "Captain Helland and Rakel are getting married, probably they already are." He nodded and smiled to Rakel's mother and father, Sarah and Thomas Madland. Sarah buried her face in her apron to mourn the absence of her far-away daughter. Thomas drew her to him.

"Johannes and Martha Steine are staying in New York until he gets the boat and iron cargo sold for us. Then he wasn't sure what they would do."

"How about Cleng?" Andreas asked.

"He is still there, too," Lars nodded. "He is spending the winter with Quaker friends and will help Johannes get as good a price as possible from our property. He sent his love and said to tell you he will be back in the spring as early as possible."

Around the group, now, there were more tears than Sarah's. Tears of relief, tears of thankfulness, tears for news that broke the monotony of their grueling days in the heavy forest.

Lars took a paper from his pocket and carefully unfolded it, then paused dramatically. "This is a letter from the President of the United

States, John Adams." Murmurs of surprise and pleasure ran through the assembled group. "It is written in English and I can't translate all of it to you, but it states that because we are foreigners and unaware of the American law regulating passenger ships and vessels, we are pardoned. However, all court costs incurred must be paid by us."

"That seems fair," Daniel nodded.

"If it isn't so much it'll claim all our money."

"We'll continue to pray for God's hand in this and everything we do," Ole pronounced with preacher-like solemnity. "Let's bow our head now in thanks for Lars' safe return."

As the gathering dispersed, Andreas went thoughtfully back to his brush burning. He was ever so glad for Lars' arrival, but how would it change the colony? Under Lars' leadership, would the group solidify and work together more efficiently or would he encourage independence? He must talk to Lars privately, he decided, as soon as possible, and get his advice on several matters. One of them was his relationship with the American Cary family.

Greetings!

Whereas the Norwegian Sloop, Restauration, whereof Lars Larson and Johannes Steene and others are owners, and Lars O. Helland is Master, has become forfeited by a violation of a law of the United States, entitled, An Act regulating Passenger Ships and Vessels', and the said Owners and Master have, severally, incurred the penalty imposed by the first section of said Act; – and whereas it has been made to appear, satisfactorily, that the violation of said law as aforesaid was committed through ignorance, the said Master and Owners being Foreigners, and entirely unacquainted with the language and Laws of the United States; –

Now, therefore, I, John Quincy Adams, President of the United States, in consideration of the premises, divers other good causes we thereunto moving, have pardoned, and do hereby pardon, the offense aforesaid, and have remitted, and do hereby remit, unto the said owners and master, all and singular, the pains, penalties, and forfeitures thereby incurred so far forth as the United States have any claim, interest or concern therein; on condition nevertheless, that all costs that may have accrued in any prosecution for said breach of Law, be first paid and satisfied by the parties implicated therein.

In testimony whereof I have hereunto subscribed my name and caused the Seal of the United States to be affixed to these presents. Given at the City of Washington, this 15th day of November, A.D. 1825, and of the Independence of the United States, the fiftieth.

(Signed) J.Q. Adams

(Signed) H. Clay, Secretary of State

CHAPTER 8

Birth Of
A Star

I T WAS FRIDAY AFTERNOON, the children had gone home and Susan Cary was tidying up the schoolroom for the weekend. Christmas would be on Sunday. Why, she wondered, wasn't she as full of excitement and expectancy as in other years? Was she that far away from childhood? There would be a Christmas tree with candles, presents, and a big dinner with the cousins. But there would be no Andreas, as there had been at Thanksgiving.

He had missed his lesson on Saturday and he surely wouldn't come the day before Christmas. Last week she had made cookies to go with tea, then nervously knitted as she waited all afternoon for him.

"He's probably too busy or didn't want to hike through the snow and the brush," her mother had said.

"I think it's because he doesn't like taking lessons from a young girl."

"Oh, I don't think that is it. If he wants to learn English bad enough, he'll take it anyway he can get it."

Not wanting her mother to know how much those lessons meant to her, Susan had tried to control her quivering voice. "The only way I know to teach is the way I teach the children. I guess there are better ways to teach a grown man."

Lydia had laid down her knitting and looked carefully at her daughter. "You must not let this man mean too much to you. Remember, he is much older than you, from a different country and has his Norwegian friends."

Susan sat on a bench and rested the broom between her hands. Obviously her mother thought, too, that the pretty, yellow-haired girl he'd brought along for the lesson was about to become his wife. Thinking about it made her chest hurt, her head ache, and brought tears to her eyes. She got up and tried to sweep Andreas Stangeland out of her mind. But it didn't work. Her heart was as heavy as the rough boards beneath the broom. Could this be love? And if it was, why was it so painful? How could she love a foreigner? She couldn't marry him even if he courted her. Who would she ever marry, living clear out here in the woods? There were a few boys at church who flirted with her, but none she liked. They were nothing like the handsome, soft-spoken Andreas.

Since Christmas came on Sunday, the Quakers' First Day, it was celebrated on Christmas Eve, beginning with *ringe in Julen*, ringing of bells, at four o'clock. Every family had brought at least one small bell from Norway. Betsy spearheaded the celebration.

"Let's let the children pick the prettiest evergreen tree in the forest that has space around it for dancing," she declared.

"Shall we dress up in our *bunads* (Norwegian costumes)?" Gurene asked.

"Yes, let's do," Betsy agreed, "and you and Gudmund can lead the dancing."

"Then we can follow it with a group feast ending with *juelgrot* (rice pudding)." Kari knew, as the rest did, that any excesses would mean shortages later. Wild game and fish had so far been easy to come by, but flour, sugar and other store-bought supplies had to be frugally reserved. But this was Christmas; they would splurge. Bertha Rosdail made sugarplum treats from the remaining dried apples which were enjoyed by the children a lick at a time. Each child also received a carved animal or toy or a homemade doll from their parents.

Andreas joined in the Christmas celebration with as much joy as he could muster, but his thoughts were back with his big family in Norway. He knew he was not alone in his homesickness, although it was seldom mentioned among them. Others had close family members who were left behind also. So he read and reread his mother's letter, which had included some Norwegian money for his Christmas present, and thought of Susan.

A few days after Christmas, Lars asked Andreas to go with him for a walk along the lake. As they strode along the cold water, Andreas hoped there would be an opportunity for them to talk about some of the things that lay heavily on his mind.

Thankfully, Lars opened the conversation. "How are things with you, Andreas?" "I hear you're learning English through your neighbors, the American family." Andreas immediately wondered how much Martha had told him about Susan. "I know that learning English is important, but it isn't easy," Lars said.

"I learn the words, but later I can't say them."

"That's Martha's complaint, mine too. Maybe if the three of us try to talk in English more often it would help. I wish the others would realize how important it is."

They stopped to look out across the wide expanse of the partially-frozen lake. Finally, Andreas said, "Lars...I don't know how to ask this without sounding selfish..."

"Go ahead, Andreas, you have done so much for us, you know I'll help if I can."

"Well," Andreas said, taking a deep breath, "when Cleng gave me the honor of coming over here with him, I know it was to help our group get settled and started in this new country. But...how long are we to stay together? I mean, are we going to continue building cabins and farming as a group?"

"That's one reason I wanted to talk to you today, Andreas. I want to talk to all of the men alone to get an idea of what they're thinking and feeling. But I came to you first because you've been here longer and understand the American way a little better." Lars paused before continuing, "We came over here not only to practice religious freedom, but to expand, whether it's buying land or having a wider choice of jobs."

Andreas was already nodding with agreement.

"You and I probably know Cleng better than any of the others. You traveled with him for a year, and I've know him from the beginning of the Norwegian Quaker Society. He's a good man, and he will give of himself again and again. But he also kind of likes to stay in control. I have the feeling he would like us to continue living and working closely together, all part of a tight community...and it worries me."

"Yes, I'm worried, too."

"Well, I can't tell the rest of you what to do, but I know what I'm going to do." They stopped again and Lars faced Andreas. "Eventually I want to go into the boat-building business on my own. I stopped in Rochester, some call it Rochesterville, on my way here to check out the possibilities. With the canal finished, the town is booming, new buildings everywhere. Being a carpenter, I got the promise of a job in the spring, and I'm taking Martha, the baby and Siri there as soon as the winter is over."

Andreas already felt a heavy load lifted from his chest as Lars continued, "There may be others who want to go there, or someplace else, or stay here and farm independently. But it should be up to them, not Cleng. There will be those who perhaps can't make it without him, or prefer to follow him. That's all right, too." After a pause, he asked, "Does that answer your question, Andreas?"

"It sure does," Andreas grinned, and reached out to shake his friend's hand. "Congratulations on your job in Rochester." He had always admired Lars, several years his senior, for his leadership and devotion within the Society of Quakers and for his ability to speak openly.

After Lars' conversation with the men, they began to speak more openly to each other about their plans. Even though most of them were choosing to stay there where they had already purchased or were purchasing land, they began to think independently about their own piece of land and clearing it for spring crops.

But no one was more eagerly anticipating spring than Andreas.

On a Saturday in mid-January, Andreas was going to take time for another English lesson when Kari asked if he would go to the store in Holley for some flour and salt. He hesitated, wanting to tell her what he'd planned to do, but she would think it insignificant beside their need, when he was the only one beside Lars who could speak enough English to ask for the right item. On New Year's Day, the boys, Halvor and Ovee, had been sent to the store for *sago*, an item the women needed to thicken a holiday pudding. The boys came back with all the *sage* their money would buy. Andreas had to return with it and explain. The storekeeper then advised cornstarch. All the way home, Andreas studied the words on the box and tried to pronounce them out loud.

Ole Olsen volunteered to go to the store with Andreas, which was a small irritation because he felt Ole could have gone by himself. A devout Quaker, Ole usually led the prayers and devotions for the group, but, as Andreas had noticed previously, he was not the first to grab an axe or a saw.

As they plodded along through the crusty snow, Ole asked, "Where we going to find us some wives, Andreas?"

"Getting anxious to get married, Ole?"

"I'm hoping there will be some more young ladies coming over soon. Lars said there probably would be. I'm anxious to get established in a Friends' Society either in Rochesterville or in Farmington." He scooped up a handful of snow, made a snowball and threw it ahead of them. "They can teach me English while I help in whatever way they can use me. I'm sure they'd prefer I was married."

"Then maybe you'll find an American girl."

"No, no," Ole shook his head vigorously, "I wouldn't feel right about that. I don't think the Lord wants us to mix ourselves up, even if I have to go back to Norway to find a wife. I'll just pray and wait for God to show His hand."

"I'm going to farm, you know, so I'm not anxious to find a wife until I've got someplace to put her," Andreas said. He thought again of Susan and the missed English lesson.

As they passed a farm about midway to Holley, they approached a man carrying a full pail of milk toward his house. "Look at all that milk," Ole said. "Remember when we could come in from the cow shed with a pail full like that?"

"I sure do, Ole, and I think of it often, along with eggs from the hens. Maybe it won't be long until I can have a cow and chickens, and you'll be drinking milk in Rochester." The settlers had bought milk a few times from another farmer in the area, but his cow went dry and they had never found a safe way to carry a quantity of milk so far. They had only one small pail with a tight cover; in it they had carried enough for the just-weaned children.

Andreas had an idea, if he could get it across. They approached the farmer who looked at them skeptically. "Sell milk, Norske?"

"You want to buy some milk from me, is that it?"

Andreas nodded. "Well, I guess I can save some for you, but how will you carry it?"

Andreas did not know the word "freeze" so he went to the shed and broke off an icicle and pointed to the milk. The farmer did not understand. Then remembering his lesson for soft and hard, words Susan couldn't draw, and how she had shown him the wool yarn was soft and the bench was hard, Andreas said, "Hard milk."

"Oh, you want me to set it outside and let it freeze, like the icicle." Andreas grinned and nodded.

The farmer frowned and shrugged. "I don't know how much good a pail of frozen milk will be to you, but I'll have it ready. Come back tomorrow?"

Ole reminded Andreas that the next day was Lord's Day. "No, next day, not Sunday," Andreas told the farmer.

"Monday then, five cents and you'll have to bring my bucket back."

When they returned, Andreas reported to Martha how he had negotiated with the farmer for the frozen milk, telling her how Susan had taught him the words for hard and soft. As they talked, he was unaware that Betsy Nelson was close by and overheard their conversation.

"Who is Susan?" Betsy asked.

Andreas hesitated. Martha answered, "Oh, that's Susan Cary, Andreas' schoolteacher."

"Susan, is it? She must be young. Is she pretty, too, Andreas?"

Martha said, "Sh-h-h."

"Oh," Betsy said and came closer, "so it's like that, is it? When do I get to meet her?"

Eyeing Betsy's advanced stage of pregnancy, Martha said, "Not soon, I think, over that trail." Both women laughed and turned their attention away from the embarrassed Andreas.

Betsy and Big Nels' baby was due in February. All were excitedly awaiting the first Norwegian baby born in America, an American by birth. Everyone was hoping for a boy. Bertha Rosdail acted as midwife for Martha on the crossing and would assist Betsy also. The women made plans for the imminent birth.

As it turned out, baby Nelson couldn't have chosen a better time to come pushing it's way into stardom. It was on Sunday morning, after breakfast and before time for the Meeting to convene when Betsy, pain evident on her face, whispered to Martha, "Do the pains begin in your back?"

Martha looked up quickly and saw Betsy stooped and holding her left side. "Yes! How long have you had them?"

"Just one big pain. It was all I could do to keep from groaning."

Martha quickly gave her baby to Siri and began quietly passing the word among the women. Gurene ran to the other cabin to bring Bertha. A bed in the corner was curtained in, and all activity was speeded up to get the men and children off to the prayer service or out of the way in another cabin.

Lars passed word among the men outside that the morning service would be in Cornelius and Kari's cabin. Nels was here and there, frantic because the women wouldn't let him see Betsy, and since it was First Day, he couldn't chop wood to fight off his nervousness.

Near the end of the service, Kari stepped in behind the worshippers. Nels looked up; she motioned for him. There was a flicker of disappointment on his face as she whispered. All eyes focused on him, questioning.

"I would like thee all to join me in a prayer of thanksgiving for our new baby daughter," Nels said shakily to the waiting group. The group clapped and offered congratulations.

By late afternoon, Betsy had taken a much-needed nap and was sitting up holding her baby. The men and children came in small groups to welcome the new infant.

"She looks just like you, Nels," Daniel said, "but she hasn't got any hair."

"She can holler just about as loud, too," Oyen chided the proud father.

Andreas had gone for a solitary walk by the lake so he missed the initial visit. When he returned, Serene ran to him to say that Betsy wanted to see him.

"Do you know what we named her?" Betsy asked Andreas as he came in with 12-year-old Serene, little mother, they called her.

He tried to think of the grandmother's name, since it was a Norwegian custom to so name a first daughter. "Was your mother's name Cecelia, maybe?"

"Yes, but Nels and I decided to give her an American name. The prettiest name I could think of was Susan, like your schoolteacher. We named her Susan Ann."

Andreas flushed with surprise and pleasure. "I'm sure the Cary family will be pleased to hear that." He turned his attention to the baby, who was very fair and bald. But his mind wasn't on the little one. He was trying to think of the English word for baby, and other words he could use to tell Susan.

CHAPTER 9

Sugar
Season

ANDREAS WAS ANXIOUS to report the birth of Susan Ann to the Carys, but he didn't want to appear too eager, even to Martha or Betsy. And always there was felling, sawing, building going on, making him feel like a shirker if he took off. But he had to make a declaration of independence soon in order to get any crops of his own in, and build some sort of shelter. The latter had become of utmost importance to him.

A lack of farm tools was also a problem, as it was to the other settlers. Corn and potatoes could be planted by digging holes in the sod, but wheat and oats had to be sowed on broken ground and he had no plow or anything to pull it.

By midweek, a southerly breeze brought relief from the recent cold temperatures. Also, the third cabin was completed and a jubilant Oyen Thompson family was moving into it.

"Come on over and live with us, Andreas," Oyen invited. "I need some help on that plow I'm making."

Andreas hesitated, he did need to use that plow, but so did the others. He made a decision.

"Thanks, Oyen, it sure sounds tempting, but I'm going to move onto my own place very soon, if I have to sleep in a hollow tree." Then he turned to Cornelius and Daniel who were also near the woodpile where most conversations took place. "I have to get ready to do some planting of my own so I won't have to live off my friends all next year."

"Give us a little more time," Daniel said, "we'll get you a cabin built. You've helped build ours."

"Thanks. I appreciate that, but all the families come first. I'll work out something. In fact I think I'll go over there this afternoon and size up the situation."

Lars spoke. "It's a good day for it, Andreas. That warmer breeze makes it seem like spring is on its way."

As he was leaving, Gudmund caught his eye and winked, "Have a good English lesson."

"Thanks, Cousin," Andreas grinned. He'd finally told Gudmund a little about his teacher and Gudmund guessed the rest.

As he slogged through the wet snow mixed with mud, Andreas decided to go around by the schoolhouse to see if Susan would still be there. Each Saturday lesson he'd had to miss for one reason or another, made him miserable with the thought that he would have to wait another whole week to go back.

Near the creek, he noticed tracks, definitely not from an animal, but very unusual, large and flat with no heel print. It was like prints from homemade shoes some of the older Norwegians made and wore, he thought. He followed them for awhile until they disappeared into the underbrush which led neither to the Carys nor to the settlement. Never before had he seen evidence of any other human beings as he walked the mile to his place and the Carys.

Andreas looked around, listened and shouted "Hello" in English, but neither saw nor heard anyone. Then he remembered the "man" little Anne Marie declared she'd seen, the day a tree fell on Nils' leg. Maybe there really are some Indians around, he decided. But surely they were not to be feared. Why would they have any reason to harm a white man? Resolutely he continued towards the Carys. I've got enough other problems to work out without living in fear.

He found the schoolhouse vacant, the fireplace cold. Odd. And yet Susan had said at his last English lesson that her school ends when the sweet sap from the trees starts running, because the children were needed at home.

Walking on toward the Cary house, Andreas noted far more activity than usual. Mr. Cary and James were coming and going from the woods east of their house, buckets in hand. Large iron kettles were steaming heavily nearby, Mrs. Cary tending them. Andreas realized that with the warm days the syrup-making season had begun.

"Hello, Andreas!" James waved him over. "Ever seen a sugaring before?" He pointed to the sap dripping slowly out of the tree through the peg driven into it which also held the bucket. James replaced the nearly full pail with an empty. "Sugar maple," James said, placing his hand on the tree.

Andreas looked closely, noting the gray bark and ridged trunk so that he might identify sugar maple trees on his property.

He walked with James to the steaming kettles, where the full bucket was emptied into a waiting kettle. He greeted Mrs. Cary and nudged the little boys, who always seemed happy to see him, but Susan was nowhere in sight.

James started back with the empty pails and Andreas reached for them. "I carry." With a welcome nod, James gave them to him and picked up two more empties.

When Andreas returned with the full pails, Mr. Cary was at the kettle. "Thank you, neighbor," he said. "Susan has supper almost ready; you must stay and eat."

Andreas carried sap and James watched the kettle while the elder Carys went in to eat. When Andreas was called in, together with James and the small boys, he brushed off his clothes and nervously ran a hand through his hair. He greeted Susan shyly, but she seemed quiet and restrained.

The meal was simple in comparison with the Thanksgiving feast: bowls of stew and thick slices of bread set on a bare table. Susan did not sit down, but went back and forth from stove to table, serving everyone and giving extra help to the little boys. Andreas wondered if Susan's silence was because of him or because she alone was responsible for the supper. He tried not to look at her, concentrating instead on his food and the others at the table.

The little boys finished their meal and went back outdoors. Susan sat down with her chin resting on her hands, and shyly smiled across at Andreas. "You have been busy?"

"Yes."

"And how is Martha?"

"Martha very happy. Huss-band come from New York."

Andreas saw a flush spread up over Susan's face. Flustered, not sure what it meant, he began naming things on the table to show he hadn't forgotten. "Potatoes. Cabbage. Bowl. Knife. Meat."

"Sausage. Sausage meat," she added.

"Sausage," he repeated. "Maple syrup, pitcher, bench, table, chair, fire."

"Good! Now say a sentence."

He thought for a moment, his eyes twinkling with amusement. "New Norske baby...name Su-suun."

Her eyes opened wide with surprise and pleasure. "Really? James, did you hear that? The Norwegians named a baby after me."

James, grinning, replied, "He didn't say they named it for you, just that the name is Susan."

Andreas understood the teasing. "Mama Betsy...think Susan pretty name...when I told schoolteacher's name."

"There, James, see!"

"Want American name. First Norske baby born in America."

"And she has my name!" Susan's face glowed. A sudden rush of feeling for this girl swept over Andreas. He felt strangely weak, strongly aware of her presence.

James pushed his chair back. "I've got to get back outside."

Andreas stumbled to his feet. "Me too."

Susan stopped him. "Wait, I want to find something to send to the new baby." She thought for a moment, then disappeared into her bedroom. When she came out, she carried a tiny chain with a pendant on it. She dropped it in Andreas' hand and when he looked more closely, he could see it was a large bird rising in flight. "An eagle," she said. "The eagle stands for America. I want to give it to baby Susan. "Andreas was deeply touched and felt so inadequate to express his thanks. "Betsy...love...," he hesitated, then tried "big?"

72

Susan laughed lightly, "Much, I think you mean. You're doing all right, Andreas. Keep it up." She touched the sleeve of his coat.

How very much he wanted to touch her! But he settled for a warm smile as he looked into her brown eyes, "T'ank you...much."

Susan followed him out to the kettles to tell her mother about the new baby. When Mr. Cary returned with full pails, he said to Susan, "We could sure use some help. Ask Andreas if he'd want to come and work for us during the whole sugaring season."

She thought for a moment, then turned to Andreas, "Papa...wants you to help make syrup tomorrow...next day...next day...for money."

Andreas understood immediately. "Yes, yes work...no money...pay schoolteacher...learn English."

"No, I'll pay you," Mr. Cary laughed. "Learning English doesn't cost that much."

"Then maybe use plow...ox...my farm?"

"Sure, we can do that. Trade work for any of my farm tools." Mr. Cary swept his arm in an arc around the farmyard. After thinking for a moment, he added, "Maybe another Norske could help, too, for pay, two Norwegians." He held up two fingers. "One to work with James at night, keep the kettles boiling. The other to help all day." Susan went over the request more slowly, waiting for Andreas to understand each word.

"Yes...yes," he nodded happily. "Maybe baby Susan's papa, Big Nels." He flexed his muscles and looked at Susan.

"Strong?"

"Strong...yes. Big." He held his hand several inches above his head.

"Good," said Mr. Cary. "Why don't you go home and get some sleep, then come back at dark. The other fellow can come at daylight and work with me." Susan then interpreted what Andreas didn't already understand.

"If Big Nels doesn't speak English, Susan will be around to help us out." Mr Cary smiled at his daughter.

Andreas understood that statement and tried not to show his disappointment, that, instead of him, it would be Big Nels working days when Susan was around.

Before Andreas left, Mr. Cary explained, "I think some of the trees we are tapping are on your property. Rather than trying to separate the sap, would you be satisfied to take some of the finished syrup?"

"I'm happy to hear I have some sweet sap trees. Yes, I like a little. I use only a little. I soon live by myself."

Andreas hurried back to tell Big Nels the good news, thankful he had a reason for choosing him, since any of the men would more than welcome an opportunity to work for money. He fingered the pendant in his pocket; how surprised and pleased Betsy would be!

That evening the men around the woodpile grew excited as Andreas explained what he could understand of the sugar-making process. To think that they had a surprise new crop right under their noses without plowing, planting or cutting down trees! If just one farmer was hiring two Norwegians, surely others would need help. But how could they go out and ask for the jobs?

"Well," said Lars, "I'm leaving for Rochester soon, but tomorrow I'll go toward Kendall to see if I can find where men might be needed."

"We'd be mighty thankful to you, Lars," Daniel said, then turned to Andreas, "Could a couple of us go with you, Andreas, to visit the Carys and find out as much as we can about the sugar-making process? Maybe we can tap our own trees."

Within the next few days, Lars had found jobs for all the men and older boys. Most of them worked 12-hour shifts for 50 cents and at least two meals.

Word spread that the Norwegians were good, tireless workers and completely honest. But, because they could not understand English, they also got the reputation of being not very bright. Not all farmers were patient or had the time to be. Instead of showing what was to be done, they just shouted a little louder, thinking that would make them understand. Some of the Norwegians came back to the cabins so humiliated it was all they could do to make themselves return the next day. They turned to Andreas and Lars to learn a few essential words – bucket, tree, kettle, numbers one to ten.

Hard maple trees within the perimeter of the cabins were bored and tapped for the women and younger children to tend and make syrup.

74

Without more equipment, such as pails and large kettles for boiling, it was all they could tackle the first year. It was a busy but happy time for the women. They were learning a new process, would have more sugar to use, strange tasting as it was, and there was far less cooking to do with the men eating out.

Andreas had little opportunity to talk to Susan during the unusually long sugar season since he worked nights. But he learned as much as he could about the whole sugaring process. He knew that the season began when the nights were still very cold, and lasted until the buds on the trees began to break open.

He learned from Mrs. Cary when to add a few drops of cream to keep the steaming, bubbling sap from boiling over, also about skimming off the impurities as they came to the top. She showed him how the syrup "aproned" when it was ready to be removed from the fire. As she lifted a dipperful of the amber syrup, it sheeted back into the kettle. "Like a woman's apron," she smiled.

James, emptying a pail full of sap in the empty kettle to start a fresh batch, said, "It takes about thirty or forty gallons of this sap to make just one gallon of finished syrup." Andreas was astonished. No wonder it was so much work and so time consuming.

Susan worked hard, long daylight hours in the kitchen, baking, cooking, washing dishes, carrying bowls and pans of food from the house out to the kettles, and helping to jug the syrup. But her heart was light, she now knew that Andreas was not engaged to Martha. She tried to get up early enough in the morning to get a glimpse of him through her bedroom window before he left in the mornings. Maybe he would never court her, but she could dream.

She so wanted to know what her mother and father thought about an American and a foreigner together, like sweethearts.

Often, the men had hoe cakes for breakfast, baked in the fire and served with some of the warm syrup. One morning near the end of the season, when the sap had slowed and Big Nels would be no longer needed, Mr Cary persuaded Andreas to stay for a breakfast of the cornmeal cakes. Susan joined them. While baking the cakes she said, "Andreas, do you know what your name is in English?"

75

"Is-s it not the same in English?"

"A little different. It's Andrew."

He tried it a couple of times, then turned to Big Nels. "What do you think? You want to start calling me Andrew?"

"Oh, yes, I do think we should start calling you, And-ro-o-o!" The new name reached his friends at the cabins, and in jest they often used it. There was no longer any secrecy about his schoolteacher having her hat out for him.

Andreas wondered what his family would think if he changed his name. How very much he wanted to send some of this unique sugar syrup to his family to taste with brother Ole's good bread. Perhaps soon he could send a small pail of it with someone going back to Norway; maybe even deliver it himself if things went well.

CHAPTER 10

Prodigal
Son

S UGARING SEASON ENDED. Bald Eagle Creek was running full and Lake Ontario was high with runoff from many creeks. Birds were coming back to the greening trees for the nesting season, and it was then that Cleng also returned.

The settlers expected him and began a watch to see who should spy him first. The men, and some of the women, were again spending long days chopping trees, burning stumps, planning and beginning more cabins and outbuildings. It was a busy, noisy island in the forest and no one heard Cleng's clarion whistle the day he actually arrived. Moving into the clearing, his walking stick in one hand, a small bundle in the other, his black cloak open to the sun, he shouted, "Kill the fatted calf, the prodigal son had returned!"

"Cleng! Cleng! Cleng's here!" the cries resounded. Then everyone was upon him at once, inundating him with hugs and handshakes. Children clung to him. It was as though he had brought a little of Norway back with him.

"So you missed me, did you?" Cleng reveled in the adoration. "But you all look as though you wintered pretty well. Anne and Sara, how you've grown! Betsy Nelson, let me see that baby. A girl?" Betsy nodded. "Three new cabins you got built, I see."

The women immediately began to plan a get-together supper with music afterward if Cleng wasn't too tired. "No, of course not. I've been getting my rest each night. I'd love to have a party. Just between us, I'm a little glad to get away from those strict and quiet New York Quakers."

The supper included hot loaf bread, which Bertha had now learned to make, and some of the new maple syrup. Then they were eager to hear all the news from Cleng: the developments in New York about their friends who remained there and his journey back.

"I'm afraid I don't have very good news about the sale of the boat and cargo," he began. "The boat couldn't be moved until the fine was paid, so we had to take what we could get for the iron where it sat. Nor did the boat sell for near what we'd hoped. Just $400." There were audible gasps around the room as they turned pityingly toward Lars; he was a major owner of the *Restauration*. They seemed to be ignoring the fact that it was profit from the iron ore, in which each family had a share, which they were intending to use to pay on their mortgaged land.

"I've already talked to Lars," Cleng continued, "and he agreed to the plan that Johannes and I worked out for the division of the money. And since no one is pushing you yet to pay on your mortgages, we should use the money from the iron, small amount that it is, to buy farm implements and tools for all of you to use so you can have good crops this fall."

Andreas sat cross-legged on the floor at the front corner of the gathering. He looked around at the faces of his friends to get their reactions to Cleng's decision. None of the money belonged to Andreas from either the boat or the iron ore, but if it had, he was sure he would want some say as to how it was spent, even though farm tools seemed like a very sensible decision. Thankfully, there seemed to be no disapproval among the men. Andreas felt fortunate; his land was paid for and farm tools had been offered for his use. Beside a place to live, he only needed money for seed and for taxes.

Cleng went on to tell more about his winter spent in New York and the many encounters on his way back. He included stories to interest the children often enough to keep them interested. "You should have seen the flocks of wild geese and ducks I saw flying back for the summer," he told them. "And I saw several beavers working together to dam up the water on a creek."

"Why do beavers build dams, Cleng?" a youngster asked.

"Well, Inger, it helps catch their food and store it for hard times like we must do here in the forest. We all work together to build houses and plant crops so that we'll have a place to live and food to eat. We must always be 'busy as beavers,' like they say here in America."

Cleng answered more questions, then finally turned to Big Nels and Henrik, "Now, I'm about ready to hear some music. How about the rest of you?" He was answered by cheers and clapping.

After a rousing interval of fiddle and accordion music with lusty singing, the Norwegians settled into their evening prayers. From-the-heart impromptu prayers were spoken by most of the men and in spite of the financial disappointment, love flowed through the group like a blessing.

The next morning Andreas got up at daylight as usual. Cleng, who was sleeping beside him, whispered, "Wait for me, I want to walk over to your place with you."

Andreas was hoping for such an offer so that Cleng could help him establish his exact property line. Mr. Cary had helped him locate the stakes between their adjoining farms, but Andreas had not yet located any markers to the west. On the day of the purchase, Andreas had been caught up in the magnitude of realization that at five dollars an acre he could become the sole owner of the 48-acre piece with the money in his pocket. He had paid little attention to details.

As they made their way along the path, carved out and tramped down during sugar season, Cleng said, "I had an opportunity to talk with Lars last night at the woodpile. He tells me you're beginning to speak English pretty well."

"I can understand it better than I speak it, but I know most of the important words. It's connecting them that gives me trouble."

"Yes, I know," Cleng chuckled. "I still get mixed up sometimes. It's good to be back and rest my wits with Norwegians for awhile."

"I'm very fortunate to have the American neighbors. They've been very helpful in my learning English." (Andreas was not ready to tell Cleng the whole story.) "Mr. Cary agreed to let me use his farm equipments in exchange for the help I gave him during the sugar season, as they call it."

"Well, now, that's a big boost for you. And it will be closer by than our collective equipment. Besides that's going to be kept pretty busy," Cleng laughed. Andreas thought he should say something about the constant reference to living and making decisions as a group, but, since he'd already made a little wedge in gaining his independence, he didn't want to interfere in what was going on at the settlement. There was Lars or Cornelius or Daniel to speak up, and they could do it far better than he.

After they leaped over Bald Eagle Creek, Cleng's black cloak swirling behind him, Andreas said, "One of my first priorities is to split a log and build a bridge across this creek."

Now on his property, Andreas pointed out some of the many maple trees he owned. "I'm sure glad now I didn't have more time to start clearing my land. I might have cut a lot of them down." He patted a nearby gray-barked tree lovingly and looked up to its leafing branches. "The sugar trees seem like a godsend to us, coming at a time before other crops need attention."

"I agree," said Cleng, "but it also might give a false sense of security. All the men got jobs this year, because, as I understand, it was a good year and the farmers could sell the syrup. But another year the weather may not be so favorable or the market so good and the farmers couldn't afford to hire help."

Sharp of mind and memory, it did not take Cleng long to locate the hidden stakes. "Now where will you build your cabin?"

"Where would you suggest? I keep wanting to get started, but between helping Carys and falling trees at the settlement, I have made no definite plans yet. I'm determined now though, to get something to live in over here if it's no more than a cave or a hollow tree."

Cleng looked around thoughtfully, "You know, you might have something there. It reminds me of a conversation I had with a fellow passenger on one of the boats coming back. He was headed farther west into the prairie land where there are hardly any trees. It's hard to realize, here in the forest, that there is any such place in America, but he assured me there is. I'm anxious to travel in that direction and take a look sometime. Anyway, he was telling me that he intended to build a sod shanty for himself."

"Sod, like grass?" Andreas asked with surprise. "How could he do that?"

"The way he described it, it made sense. He was going to cut out squares of sod, stack them up, one block on top of the other, angling them enough to come to a dome at the top."

"U-m-m. Sort of like a house made of ice, but using sod instead."

"Yes. He said there are a lot of pioneers, as they call the people out there on those prairies, building them for first dwellings. They're warm in winter and cool in summer."

They had reached the cleared nook by the creek which Andreas favored since that first visit on Thanksgiving day. It was bordered by a huge oak tree.

"I've thought of building right here by the creek, but it isn't really big enough for a cabin. Maybe I could build a sod shanty there right against that tree. It would give me a place to live until I can get something better."

"The rest of us will help you build a cabin, before you get a wife anyway," Cleng laughed.

"Ole Olsen is more worried about finding a wife than I am. He wonders whether there will be other immigrants from Norway before long."

"Oh, yes, I'm sure there will be. There are letters going back there all the time about the advantages over here. I wouldn't be surprised if another boatload of Norwegians arrived this summer. Maybe even more than one."

THE BECKONING

PART 2

CHAPTER 11

A
LOSS

HE LARSON FAMILY, the Simon Lihmes and Ole Olsen all moved to Rochester early in the spring of 1826.

Cleng Peerson might have tried to delay the beginning of the breakup of the first Norwegian colony in America if it had been anyone but Lars Larson who led the trek westward. But Lars was as staunch in his convictions and determination as his demeanor implied, so Cleng, along with the rest, bade them farewell and "write often." Simon would seek work as a merchant, which was his profession in Norway, and Ole would find himself a place with the Friends Society in Rochester, and wait for a Norwegian wife.

The last family cabin was being constructed. It was for Torstein Bjorland, a shoemaker by trade, who wanted eventually to return to that business.

Farmers, who had bargained for land expecting to pay the first installment after sale of the iron ore, were worried. They were honest men used to paying their obligations on time. But they also agreed with Cleng's reasoning that they must buy farm equipment in order to raise crops and make enough to pay their debts in the fall.

So Cleng scouted the area for bargains and found a cast iron plow and two oxen along with other badly needed items, including two 35 gallon kettles needed for maple syrup season, for butchering, for making soap and for boiling white clothes to remove the grime of winter. To the women's delight, he also found a churn, a couple of spinning wheels, not as good as those left behind in Norway, but useable, also a small loom.

With the money the men had earned during the maple syrup season, each family purchased a cow, a most coveted animal for the milk, cream and butter-loving Norwegians. Some of the cows had already been bred to the bull which ran with Mr. Cary's cows. When time came for one cow to dry up, the other families would share their milk.

The farmers could only wonder how many valuable maple trees had been cut down during the winter of clearing and building cabins before their introduction to maple syrup.

Oyen Thompson observed a farmer pulling stumps with a rigged-up set of wheels, reminding him of an apparatus he'd worked on in his blacksmith shop in Stavanger. So with help from Nils, he got materials to make wheels in graduating sizes to add power to the work of one ox. The device proved a great success and it speeded up stump-pulling for all the Norwegians.

A few orphan lambs had been given to the settlers by nearby farmers who had hired the Norwegians during sugar season and knew of their hardship and their desire to collect livestock. The women and children took them over to wean as they had in Norway. By thrusting a hand into a pan of milk, they would convince the lamb to suckle a finger, then finally begin drinking from the pan. A few adult ewes were purchased so that their flocks would increase more rapidly. The few clothes they brought from Norway would not last much longer with the hard use they were receiving; they would need wool to make more.

Andreas began working on his sod hut soon after Lars and the others departed. It was not an easy task to cut out sections of sod from the tough growing virgin turf, but, at least he was doing two jobs in one: building his house and digging furrows to plant corn and potatoes. Mr. Cary suggested that Andreas plant more potatoes than he'd need for himself, just as he was doing, because it was a commodity that kept well and might be a saleable item to ship east on the canal.

As the dwelling progressed, Cleng often came over to offer suggestions and encouragement, but as Andreas often noted with chagrin, he never brought along a shovel or any implement to help dig. Andreas surmised there would always be people whose best work was accomplished inside their heads. Nevertheless, he couldn't help but feel that a little physical work with it couldn't hurt.

As the shanty rose and took shape, snuggling up against the big oak tree, Andreas became more and more excited and anxious to move in. It was hardly more than six by eight feet in size, but roomy enough for a bed and a few items.

Squirrels in nearby trees, at first curious and scolding, now accepted him and his work while they went on with their lives, leaping from limb to limb or making scallops across the ground, waving their question-mark tails. Andreas loved his land and every tree and creature on it, wishing again and again that he didn't have to demolish so much of it in order to farm.

When his hut began to close in at the top, whimsically he lifted a few chunks of sod containing wild flowers, violets and daisies. The roof blossomed with spring and was almost invisible to anyone passing by.

Joy of freedom and accomplishment settled over Andreas from the first night he spent in it. At the same time, it was quiet, very quiet at night without the human sounds he was used to. He tried to keep his thoughts from turning to Susan, but here they were overwhelming him. Even if she ever were to become his wife, he could never ask her to sleep beside him in a little earthen hut like this.

By fall, other living arrangements would have to be made, but for now he happily cooked over a campfire and bathed and washed clothes in Bald Eagle Creek. After the hut was built, he worked nearly every hour of daylight clearing and planting. On First Day, he went back to the cabins for Meeting and always there was an invitation to someone's house for dinner.

The English lessons with Susan had ceased when Lydia Cary suggested it might do Andreas more good to come one evening each week for supper to join in conversation with all of them. They settled on Wednesdays for the visits and Andreas marked the days until midweek. If his Norwegian friends knew, they would consider it courting night, but he dared not think of it as such. He still did not know Susan's age, or how to find out. And he wondered if her parents would approve of a foreigner courting their daughter.

One Wednesday, a warm day in the middle of June, he quit work a little earlier than usual. He took down his clean shirt and trousers from where he had hung them after yesterday's washing. Then he went to the nearby brush covered area of the creek to take his bath, shuddering from the first cold plunge.

Later he carefully combed his hair and beard, holding a small mirror in his hand, his thoughts constantly on Susan.

His cousin, Gudmund, was be be wed the following week. It was the second romance begun on the sloop to culminate in marriage. Rakel and Captain Helland in New York had been the first. The third would be Henrik and Martha Donalson, later on in the summer when Henrik had finished his cabin.

Andreas wished he could muster the courage to ask Susan to accompany him to Gudmund and Gurine's wedding. The Norwegians, who hadn't met her, were anxious for him to bring her over. He wasn't sure how much of his hesitation in asking her was fear and how much was from a reluctance to take her into a strange culture, especially one with such severely plain living conditions. If only he could take her to his mother's nice house. His heart ached.

The Carys knew about his sod hut. Both Mr. Cary and James had visited it and were impressed with the summer shelter; it was unlike any they had ever seen. He always kept his campsite neat and clean, just in case Susan came to see it.

As he walked through the woods to the Carys, his spirits were as light as the spring around him. There was a velvety feel to the air, the scent of forest, moss and green growing things.

Susan was drawing water from the well as he approached. He watched her bend over, look in the well, then strain to wind up the bucket. He noticed with a thrill how her body had acquired different form during the winter. Her breasts, only slightly rounded before, were now full and womanly. Her waist was thinner and her hips...well, maybe that was what corseting did to a woman. He did not know when a girl was supposed to start wearing a corset.

"Hello," he called. "Wait, I help you."

"Oh, hello Andrew." She appeared flustered, but the American name rolled off her tongue like she'd been practicing it. He lifted the bucket and followed her into the house. Yes, the proud and straight way she walked, as though trying to over-come a certain awkwardness, must be due to a corset.

THE BECKONING

The supper consisted of thick slices of smoked ham, hot biscuits, dandelion greens and fresh spring radishes from their garden. To top it off, was a custard pie Susan had made. It was delicious and he complimented her on it.

They talked of many things. James asked, "Have any bears got into your cave yet, Andreas?"

"No bear," he grinned. "Much mosquito bugs. Wild flowers bloom on top of my house."

"Oh, Mama," Susan said with little girl delight, "can we walk over after supper?" Then looking at Andreas, she added, "May we?" He nodded a welcome.

"Perhaps," her mother said. "We haven't been out to see the wild flowers yet this spring." Lydia Cary was a quiet woman, but Andreas could tell she was the backbone of the family without noticeably influencing them. Her face was rounder than Susan's and made fuller by the white ruffled cap she always wore. She was not as tall or big boned as Andreas' mother, but he greatly admired her. The proud way both Mr. and Mrs. Cary often looked at their daughter demonstrated their feelings, perhaps even to the point of sometimes indulging her. But being an only daughter, that was understandable, Andreas thought.

He told them as best he could about the upcoming wedding. That the women were busily getting ready for it. But it would not be as grand as a typical Norwegian wedding festival. Susan asked about baby Susan.

"She have a round face, many smiles..." Not knowing the word for dimples, he pushed his fingers in his own cheeks. Susan nodded. "She is-s a big girl, make her papa proud."

When they rose from the table, Susan pleaded, "Let's go see Andrew's house before we wash the dishes, Mama." So the elder Cary's, the little boys and Susan all walked with Andreas across the trail to his hut. Susan was ecstatic. "Isn't it beautiful! Built right into a tree, and flowers on the roof!" Andreas picked a small nosegay of violets for Mrs. Cary, another for Susan.

"May I look inside?" Susan asked. Andreas nodded. She peeked in through the rolled back canvas he used to cover the opening. It was bound to a stake and could either be rolled open or tied to another stake on the other side when he wanted it closed.

"Is-s not a door will keep animals out," Andreas explained, "but I don't keep much food to invite them in." He pointed to a limb overhead where a pouch was attached to a rope to either raise or lower it. "I keep t'ings up there. I also have a dugout place by the creek, keep milk and butter cool inside a covered wooden bucket."

"What fun you must be having," Susan said gleefully.

"You're a neat housekeeper, Andreas," Mrs. Cary said.

"Do you care if fishworms go through the roof of your house?" Mr. Cary asked.

"One dropped on my face at night, I care." They all laughed.

Andreas started back with them, Susan walking primly beside him. Every once in awhile she pointed to or picked up something, expecting him to name it, a squirrel, a beech tree, a twig, which he called a branch. She corrected. A pine cone, moss, a piece of bark.

Near the border of their properties, Susan said, "Look, strawberries!" Searching carefully through the grass, they saw several, then many more. The twins were sent home to bring a pan and Andreas and Susan helped them pick all they could find. The boys hurried on ahead with the mound of sweet, red berries while Andreas and Susan strolled more slowly towards the house.

"What a lovely evening," Susan sighed as she sank onto a stump near the house. "If it weren't for the mosquitoes." She waved away another swarm.

Andreas sat in the grass beside her and began mashing a few red berries he had carried along with him. Susan watched curiously. "What are you doing, Andrew, making strawberry jam on a maple leaf?"

He looked up at her and grinned. "I make ink."

"Ink?"

"You teach me English. Now I teach you Norwegian."

"The whole language with ink from three strawberries?"

"Only numbers to ten. Give me your hand, pleas-se."

She held it out palm up and he felt the thrill of holding her hand for the first time. With a twig he wrote a number on each finger. When he got to five, she held out the other hand. That the markings were completely illegible mattered not to either of them. They sat laughing as she helplessly held out two red stained hands.

In Norwegian, he said the numbers slowly, picking up each finger. She tried to repeat. "Now...how many year you?" he asked.

She colored slightly. "Guess."

"Eighteen?" She shook her head. "Nineteen?"

"Other direction." She pointed down.

"Seventeen?" She shook her head. He hid his disappointment. "Sixteen?"

She nodded. "Next month." She was *fifteen* years old.

"How many years...you?" she asked playfully. But for Andreas, the game had lost its zest. His hopes had fled.

"Old man," he said pulling together two of her fingers.

"Two," she said; then he held one of his fingers beside five of hers. "Twenty-six. I thought you were about James' age. He's twenty-five."

Andreas left shortly, with many thanks to Mrs. Cary for the fine supper, but without inviting Susan to go with him to Gudmund's wedding. He walked home to the privacy of his earth house with a heavy heart, to think and try to reshape his dreams. Now he'd have plenty of time to build a cabin. He was certain Susan cared for him, but now he was afraid it was just an infatuation. American boys would be courting her soon. She could never love him, like he did her, enough to last a lifetime. Bumble-speaking Norwegian that he was, what did he have to offer but 48 acres of land? Perhaps he should begin thinking again about other immigrants headed for America, single Norwegian girls coming over. The thought brought tears to his eyes and an ache to his chest. He didn't want just a wife. He wanted Susan.

The nuptials on Thursday went well. The feasting was as bountiful as the settlers dared make it. The men had helped Gudmund finish his cabin and the happy couple left to spend their first night in it, carrying with them a basket of food.

Andreas stopped for a moment's visit with Thomas Madland. "You're losing your daughters fast, Thomas. Two in one year." He referred to Gurine's older sister, Rakel, who had wed Captain Helland in New York.

"Wish I had another one the right age for you, Andreas."

"Maybe I'll just wait for Serene," he winked at Thomas' 12-year-old daughter standing nearby. She giggled shyly. It was an insignificant conversation which might have been forgotten. But Andreas would always remember, because it was the last time he ever spoke to Thomas. He died the following week. His new son-in-law, Gudmund, saw the oxen hitched to a plow standing a long time idle in the hot noonday sun. He went over and found Thomas face down in the furrow. There were no signs of an accident. Apparently his heart had just given up. At 46, he had died in a new land, far removed from his blacksmith shop in Stavanger and his older married children there. Left alone, were his wife, Sarah, and the daughter, Serene.

His friends, with heavy hearts, had to deal with the funeral, create a graveyard, and bury one of their number. Lars and Martha and the other people in Rochester had walked the 23 miles to the wedding and could not be notified in time to come back to the funeral. Nor would the daughter in New York know about his death until days later. The children in Norway would not hear for weeks.

After the short service and the sad burial of the rough-hewn box with its revered contents, Gudmund went to his sorrowing mother-in-law and took her hand. "Our cabin is yours, too, Mother Madland. Come home with us. There is room for you and Serene with Gurine and me."

Andreas, standing nearby, was touched and proud of his cousin.

The Sloopers had enjoyed a birth and a wedding. Now they had suffered the first death.

CHAPTER 12

A Picnic
And A Birthday

"MAMA," SUSAN SAID above the sound of the churn she was turning, "do you like Andrew?"

Lydia Cary looked quickly at her daughter, then turned back to the jam she was making. "Yes, I like him. Why do you ask?"

"Well, I...I just think sometimes he'd like to court me. And I don't know if it would be proper...him being Norwegian."

"He hasn't said or done anything yet, has he?"

"Oh, no...no. It's just the way he smiles at me, sometimes."

Lydia lifted a spoon of strawberry jam and let it sheet back into the kettle, noting that it was done, then lifted it off the stove. "Does he know how old you are?"

"Yes, he asked me the other night while trying to teach me numbers in Norwegian." Susan sighed. "So now I don't suppose he's interested in me any longer."

"But you wish he would be?"

"Yes, I like him a lot. Is that sinful?"

"No, of course not. God wants us to love everyone. And so long as you conduct yourself in a proper manner, you and Andreas can be friends."

Susan wildly cranked the churn to match her drumming heart. "Then because he's a Norwegian doesn't make any difference if maybe sometime, a long time yet, he might want to marry me?"

Lydia laughed lightly, "Since your father is half Irish, I'd have to say no, it doesn't matter. But marriage for you, dear, is a long time off, so don't think about it yet."

"Mama, I'll be sixteen soon. Didn't you marry Papa when you were seventeen?"

On Saturday evening, the first of July, Daniel Rosdail came to visit Andreas and to see his sod hut. Andreas had just finished his supper and was returning the milk, which the Carys supplied, to the cache in the creek. After hearty greetings, Andreas showed him around. They walked out into the fields where his wheat was coming along nicely, as well as his corn, potatoes and a small patch of garden vegetables. When they returned to the camp, Andreas pointed to a nearby log. "Sit down, Daniel, I've got some coffee left heating over the fire." He went into the hut to find another cup, then settled down beside Daniel on the log.

"Nice place you got fixed up here for yourself, real nice."

"Yes, for the summer it's fine. Don't know yet what I'll do once winter comes."

"You're always welcome at our cabin, you know that."

"Thanks, Daniel. Right now winter seems a long time off." He waved away mosquitoes in the sultry heat of the evening.

"Lots of folks sick around these parts," Daniel reported. "Cleng found many ailing in his visits around. What they call ague and malarial fever. Can't seem to figure out what's causing it; certainly can't be blamed on cold wet weather now. The women keep vinegar boiling in all the cabins, thinking that will help. An American woman at the store told Cleng about it."

They talked on for awhile, then Daniel remembered, "By the way, Andreas, I'm to tell you, we're planning a little celebration next Tuesday, July 4. It will be a year from the day we left Norway for America. Cleng says it is also the American Independence Day. So we're going to take the afternoon off and go over by the lake for a picnic. It's so soon after Thomas' funeral, people probably won't feel very lively. But it will be nice to get together for a quiet visit away from the cabins, and for the kids to kick up their heels."

"Count me in, I'll be there," said Andreas, immediately wondering if he would have nerve enough to ask Susan to go along. "Are the folks from Rochester coming over for the picnic?"

"I wouldn't be surprised. Cleng hiked over to tell them about Thomas' death and the picnic. He came back yesterday and said they wanted to come pay their respects to Sarah and the girls and visit his grave."

After an easy silence, Daniel continued, "Cleng is always on the go. No more than home from one place until he starts out somewhere else. 'On the steeds of apostles,' he says. Takes his hickory walking stick and away he goes."

"I know. You should try to keep up with him for a whole year."

"I'm sure you know about that." Daniel laughed.

"I have lots of admiration for him, though. He's always thinking of other people, how he can help."

"Yes, but sometimes I wish he wouldn't try quite so hard, especially when he makes us out to be such poor people. We came from prosperous Norwegian farms and jobs; we want to make it on our own, without charity, even though it will take time to build up again." He sighed. "If we hadn't lost all that money in Norway before starting out."

"I heard about that, but never knew what happened."

"Nobody else knows exactly what happened, except the man who lost the money. We were too trusting. That fellow said he could invest our money and double it. It was just a gamble. He lost almost all of it. I think that is one reason Cleng is working so hard for us now; he feels it was his fault. But I don't think so. All of us should have looked into it a little more." He shook his head. "It was a bleak time; our plans for emigration just about ended right there. But, with most of our things sold, we'd have had to start over anyway, might as well be in a new country where we wouldn't be constantly harassed for being Quakers."

Andreas liked Daniel and appreciated his visit. As for the July Fourth picnic, if he were going to invite Susan, there was something he must do first.

Monday, he worked in the field farthest to the east and kept watch, hoping to see Mr. Cary leave the house alone. Finally, after the noonday meal, his neighbor started out with the team of oxen toward the field next to Andreas'. John Cary waved and Andreas settled his hoe by a nearby tree and went to meet him.

They visited for a few minutes under a cottonwood tree at the edge of the field while the oxen chased flies, waving their heavy tails and shaking their massive heads. "I want to ask you something, Mr. Cary," Andreas said hesitantly with a slight tremor in his voice. The older man nodded encouragingly. "I care for your Susan. I wish...if you could let me court her...some."

Mr. Cary took off his straw hat, waved away mosquitoes, and laughed a little with fatherly pride. "It looks to me like the courtship has already begun. You know how old she is, don't you, Andreas?"

"I know she's young...maybe don't know what is good for her. Maybe Norwegian not right for her. I do not want to...to hurt her life...in any way."

Mr. Cary reached out a hand. "You're a fine young man, Andreas. Go ahead and spend time with her once a week or so. It's the only way to find out if you're good for each other. If not, one of you will discover it before the summer's over. As to her being young, she's always been ahead of her years. She walked when she was hardly nine months old. She talked everything by the time she was two. In school, always ahead of the teacher. When he moved on, they hired her at barely 15. Probably the youngest teacher in the state of New York. But she taught those kids just fine."

"I learn because she's patient."

"One thing, though, Andreas, if things go good between you two, wait for marriage until she's at least seventeen. By that time, she ought to know her own mind."

"I will wait," Andreas said earnestly.

Andreas didn't know if any of the conversation would be reported to Susan, but not knowing would make him self-conscious when he saw her. Now that he'd asked to court her, he didn't know what he should do differently. In Norway, courting Katrine had come naturally, they just grew up together. He realized, now that he thought about it, his love for Katrine had vanished completely. She was a pleasant memory. Nor did he feel jealousy for Pedar, the man she married.

THE BECKONING

Taking some flowers to Susan certainly wouldn't be out of place. He remembered seeing a different kind of daisy growing along the southern edge of his clearing.

Susan was shelling peas on the front porch when he arrived carrying a small bouquet of flowers. As she took them, her face broke into a smile. "Do you know the name of these?"

"Orange daisy? They look like white daisy."

"They are kind of a daisy." Her mother heard them and came to the porch. Susan showed her the flowers.

"Where did you find the black-eyed Susans, Andreas? I haven't seen any yet this year."

"Is-s that really the name?"

Mother and daughter laughed.

"You have a baby named after you, now a flower."

"It's the other way around this time," said Mrs. Cary. "When her father first saw her he said, 'She looks as bright and pretty as a black-eyed Susan.' So that's what we named her."

After the flowers were placed in a vase of water and there was a little more small talk, Andreas took a deep breath and began. "Norwegians have a picnic at lake tomorrow. Celebrate day they left Norway on boat."

"They left on July 4, our Independence Day?"

He nodded, then turned to Mrs. Cary, "I want ask Susan to go. Don't know American...rules. Do girls need...need...woman to go along?"

"Chaperone is the word I think you mean," Mrs. Cary said kindly.

Susan said, "Oh, Mama, I want to go instead of to the celebration in Kendall."

"We'll wait and ask your father."

A few minutes later Susan saw her father coming from the field and hurried to meet him. Andreas watched. She pleaded; he frowned. Finally his face spread with a grin. She hugged him; he waved to Andreas, "Now mind," he said loud enough for both to hear, "home well before dark."

The picnic was planned for two o'clock. Andreas walked over for Susan at one. He carried with him his one cooking pot, in which he had placed a small bowl of the wild strawberries he'd picked that morning, plus a plate, spoon and knife for each of them.

Susan was lovely in her light gray summer dress and matching bonnet with pink ribbons around the crown and tied under the chin. They walked slowly along the paths, Andreas hurrying ahead if there was anything he could move out of the way. He had made a split log bridge over Bald Eagle Creek which she crossed easily, but Andreas stayed very close behind her. She seemed quiet; he was sure she was nervous about going into such a large group of strangers.

"You have met Martha," he said. "I think she will be there today with her husband, Lars."

"Will baby Susan be there?"

"I'm sure."

"I'm kind of scared, Andrew."

"I'll take care of you," Andreas said, his heart melting as he put an arm behind her and touched her lightly on the shoulder. "Cleng will be there, too. You have met him."

To his relief, Lars and Martha were the first people he saw on the beach. They sat in the sand talking to Cleng, year-old Margaret playing beside them. Martha, who could now speak fair English, immediately took Susan in hand, making her feel welcome. Cleng was also stimulated into using his best English with the young and dainty Susan. When Susan was introduced to the other Norwegians by Martha or Andreas, they would politely nod or say, "Hello," a word most of them knew. They could say little more to her, so they went back to talking among themselves.

When she met Betsy, Susan was most anxious to hold little Susan. Andreas interpreted for her and the mother smilingly handed her over. Little Susan was immediately fascinated by the pink ribbons on Susan's bonnet, so she removed her hat and waved the ribbons for the baby. The women all took the opportunity to cast secret glances at Susan's lovely white skin and heavy coil of dark brown hair. From her pocket, Betsy withdrew the eagle pendant on a chain, which Susan had sent to the baby and said, "T'ank you!" Then she patted the baby.

THE BECKONING

Susan ate slowly and sparingly of the smorgasbord of food spread on the makeshift table. Andrew knew it was mostly strange to her, and ate much less himself than he would have liked.

Later, when Cleng was talking with Susan, Andreas had an opportunity to tell Martha he had found out that she wasn't yet 16. Martha laughed. "I didn't guess very close, did I? But that's all right, many girls marry at sixteen. And she'll always have you to take care of her, Andreas."

The afternoon went by pleasantly with little groups of people visiting together, shifting, being joined by others. Cleng made the rounds, as usual. The children joyfully waded or swam in the lake, constantly admonished by parents to "stay in close."

Andreas watched the sun and the time. Finally he suggested to Susan they they should start home. He didn't want to be one minute late.

On the trail again, Susan breathed an audible sigh of relief. "Now I know how you felt when you first met our family and couldn't understand any English," she said, "I really do want to learn some Norwegian, Andrew, so I can talk with them a little."

"You will learn. I teach you one word at a time."

After a pause, he asked hesitantly, "Do you suppose some of the Norwegian children could come to your school when classes open?"

"Oh, Andrew, I'd love to have them. Do you think the parents will want them to come?"

"Now that they have meet you, I'm sure."

"Do you think they like me, Andrew?"

"They like you fine and think you pretty...beautiful. Like I think you are beautiful."

"Oh, Andrew," she said demurely.

He helped her over a log, then continued to hold her hand. "I'm so glad you came today. Sorry you miss other celebration."

"I wanted to come with you, really, I...I hope I didn't act too...childish in front of your friends. Sometimes people expect me to act older than I am, because I teach school, I guess. I don't always succeed."

98

He wanted to take her in his arms, protect her against any such unreasonable expectations, but he dared only to hold her hand a little tighter. "You always be just right. When with me you be big girl if you feel like it, be little girl if you want. I...like both Susans."

She looked up at him. "Thank you, Andrew. You say such nice things."

"You teach me right words." They laughed and happily held hands until they were in sight of the house.

July 16 was Susan's 16th birthday. Mrs. Cary had invited Andreas for dinner right after Sunday services. His gift to Susan was lying in wait. Soon after the English lessons began, Andreas had written a letter to his mother asking that she buy a brooch or something in Norway which was appropriate for his young schoolteacher. After several months, the package came, along with a new homespun suit of clothes for his own birthday of September 1. When he found out about Susan's birthday, he decided to save the brooch to give her at that time. At least once a day he got it out, looked it over carefully and lovingly. It was small, made of gold filigree and surrounded by shiny spangles. He knew it was expensive, and was pleased to have something of value to give Susan for all she had done for him.

At the birthday dinner were two foods new to Andreas, sweet corn and tomatoes, neither of which he'd ever seen in Norway. The Carys had introduced him to popcorn; now he was going to try roasting ears, as they called them. Seeing the corn on the table, brought merriment to Susan and Andreas. She giggled, he grinned. She had to explain to the others that when he was learning the word "ear", she had drawn a human ear on a cornstalk.

"I never forget that word," Andreas said.

Andreas wondered how a whole ear of corn was supposed to be eaten until he saw others butter it, salt it, then pick it up and start nibbling. He did the same and liked the taste. The thick slices of red tomatoes would take a little getting used to, he decided.

At the end of the meal, a lovely cake with 16 hand-decorated candles was brought out. "Oh, Mama, it's beautiful," said Susan, her eyes shining in the candlelight. "It's too pretty. I don't want to blow them out." But finally she puckered up and blew out all 16 with one breath.

Everyone clapped and James said, "Oh-oh, you know what that means, Susan. You'll be married within the year." She blushed and avoided looking at Andreas whose forehead also turned ruddy beneath the tan.

When there was a pause, Andreas laid the small wrapped package in front of her. (It was her only gift at the table since the dress she wore had been her parents' present to her. Muslin, she called it.)

Susan looked at the package, then at him questioningly. "My mother send it from Norway for my schoolteacher."

"All the way from Norway!" she said turning the package over and over reverently, then finally unwrapping it slowly and cautiously. The little brooch lay in her hand. She held it up and let the light shine on the spangles. "Mama, look! Isn't it beautiful?" She handed it to her mother to admire.

Her father said, "You'll look like a princess wearing that."

Susan looked lovingly at Andreas, then stood up, went behind him and kissed him on the cheek. "Tell your mother I send that to her." Andreas was too happy to be embarrassed.

CHAPTER 13

Strained
Friendship

URING JULY'S SOARING temperatures, the Norwegian men worked harder than ever, not only harvesting their own crops, but working for other farmers. The Americans who hired them for heavy work during the sugar season, asked them to come back and flail wheat. This time they were paid in kind; one bushel of wheat for every 11 threshed. After saving out enough for next year's seed, they took their portion to Bascom's Mill, five miles away, where it was ground into flour. Most of the men carried the sacks on their shoulders, two at a time.

One night, Big Nels said to Betsy, who was knitting while nursing baby Susan, "You know, I think I'll take a couple of sacks of wheat to Rochester. Lars said when they were here for Thomas' funeral that it was selling for so much more there."

"Wouldn't it cost as much to take it on the boat as the extra you'd make?"

"Boat? No-o. I'd pack it on my shoulders. A hundred and twenty pounds on each shoulder will balance out fine."

"Oh, Nels, it's over 20 miles."

"Well, I know that. I didn't say I wasn't going to rest before I got there."

"Then I'm going with you," said Betsy, "I'll put Susan on my shoulders part of the time or tie her to my back. We can stay over with Lars and Martha and have a good visit. Let's do it!"

Determined to get money together for a frame house, Andreas saved and earned everywhere he could. When he had his own threshing done, he helped Mr. Cary and James. After he'd saved out seed wheat (little flour was needed for his own use), the remainder was hauled by ox cart with Mr. Cary's wheat to the mill. It was a busy month with little rest for anyone.

But the August heat brought sickness and sorrow to the little Norwegian settlement.

Hearing that so many of his friends were down with the fever, Andreas took time one evening in mid-August to visit the cabins. The strong smell of boiling vinegar permeated the hot, humid, windless air surrounding the homes. He knew the droves of mosquitoes added to the settlers' misery.

While there he prayed with some of the men for cooler weather and relief.

"I'm afraid it's God's will to cause a pestilence among us," Cornelius said as they remained by the centrally located woodpile. "For what, I can't understand; unless we're mixing up too much with the Americans..." Seeing Andreas' quick frown and remembering Susan he added, "I mean working for them, doing their threshing and all."

"Maybe it's the difference in climate," Andreas said, trying not to sound offended. "Norwegians aren't used to such hot weather and hard work mixed together."

"Oyen's down now, you know," Daniel said.

"Is that right! I must go over and see him." Andreas was genuinely distressed. "It's hard to believe this mysterious fever can bring down a man as strong as he is."

Andreas went across to the Thompson cabin and found the pale, thin, bedraggled Caroline moving from one patient to the other. Anne and Sara, although weak, were well enough to sit outside on a blanket, but little Berta Karene, just a year and a half, was gravely ill. Carolyn was using all the herbs and folklore she knew, while the rest were praying for her hourly.

Andreas went to Oyen's bedside, laid a hand on his arm and prayed with him. "I'll beat this thing," Oyen murmured weakly.

"Sure you will."

"Nils is doing two men's work...and helping Carolyn, too."

"Your brother's a fine young man; I'll stop by and have a word of prayer with him, too."

On August 26, little Berta Karene Thompson breathed her last. When Andreas received word of the death, he went over to help dig a grave and build the tiny coffin. So many of the rest were sick, he knew they needed his help. A few days later, Halvor Revheim came over early one morning with the sad news that Oyen had died during the night. Andreas was stunned with disbelief. Beside Gudmund, Oyen seemed closer to him than any other man in the group.

After Halvor left, Andreas wept, then mournfully again went to help and to pay his respects to poor, dear Carolyn. Betsy led him to where she lay prostrate on the bed, mute and ashen, eyes staring emptily at the rafters above her. He took one of her cold and clammy hands, in spite of the hot day. He uttered a few words of sympathy, to which she did not respond.

Betsy followed him back outside. "She's even too weak to care for the two little girls she has left. Poor little things," she sobbed, "just eight and nine and so frightened and sad."

Andreas patted Betsy on the shoulder, shook his head and with tears in his eyes, picked up his shovel and walked slowly toward the plot where the grave was being dug. The trail to the little Norwegian graveyard was well-trod and sprinkled with many tears.

September and cooler weather finally arrived, eliminating some of the problems. Most of the settlers were restored to health. Gardens had produced well and root cellars were dug to store whatever would keep.

Not only were sweet corn and tomatoes new to the Norwegians, but also squash and pumpkins. Those who planted a few seeds were greatly rewarded with the huge yellow vegetables which they marveled over, but did not know how to cook. On his visits around the area, Cleng brought home some ideas. One was for pie, which seemed strange and too complicated to be considered. Another suggestion was to use them in a cream soup, which they didn't care for either. The method they preferred was to cut up the pumpkin or squash into chunks, let it bake next to the fire or in an oven, and then eat it with salt and butter right off the shell.

THE BECKONING

They found that even the seeds could be cleaned, toasted and eaten. The children begged for them.

The harvest was good for a first year on new ground, but the settlers realized very little cash profit and were again disappointed and embarrassed that they could pay no more than the interest on their mortgages. Even Nels and Betsy's trip to Rochester netted little more than a pleasant visit to the fast growing town and an overnight with Lars and Martha.

Even though Andreas had no mortgage, approaching cold weather presented him with another kind of problem. Where would he spend the winter? From lack of both time and money, his house was not so much as started. He knew his friends were willing and waiting to give him help to put up a cabin, but secretly he wanted more. He wanted a well-built little house made with lumber and he determined to keep working toward that end. He tried to think of some way to heat his sod shanty, but it was so small, any kind of stove would suffocate him even if he cut out a window.

After living independently all summer, he hated to think of going back to the cabins. Cleng's would be most logical; all the other families had moved out, and Cleng was gone much of the time. But often visitors passing through or folks from Rochester slept there when they came to stay overnight. Andreas was afraid he would have to spend too much time playing host, as Cleng did, instead of working on his farm and building a house.

Like an act of Providence, Andreas' problem was solved for him before he had to make a decision. An American came to him one afternoon just as he finished plowing in preparation for planting his winter wheat.

"Good day," the solemn visitor said, "I'm Abner Whitcomb, trustee for Eagle Creek Township. We need a caretaker for the Holley school and I've been told you might consider taking the job. James Cary has been doing it for his sister, but now has a job in Kendall for the winter."

Andreas didn't understand all of the words the man had used, but got the sense of what he said. He knew James had been offered a job in Kendall, but he didn't know that his work at the school was anything more than just helping Susan.

"It doesn't pay much, just a dollar a week," Mr. Whitcomb explained. "In most schools, the teacher does these things, but the little Cary girl, who does such a fine job of teaching, can't be expected to chop wood, shovel paths, carry water and all."

Of course he wanted the job! But Cleng's cabin would be too far away for him to watch over the schoolhouse properly. He pondered over an idea so long that he was afraid Mr. Whitcomb would think he didn't want the job. Finally, he decided to ask.

"Maybe I could sleep there at night, keep animals and thieves away?"

Mr. Whitcomb misunderstood. "Oh, no, you don't have to live there, just come early to build a fire."

"I mean if I want to sleep there on my sheepskin bed, roll it up in the day and hide it, would that be all right?"

"I don't see why not, if you want to. The place would be a lot safer with someone in it."

"See...my winter home too far away when snow comes, might not get there in time to get the school nice and warm."

"You work that out anyway you want to, as long as the work gets done. John Cary said he'd vouch for that."

"Mr. Cary's nice to tell you that. Thank you."

Andreas spent the rest of the afternoon with a mixture of feelings. Having a job like that with pay and a place to sleep, seeing Susan everyday, working with her, helping with the Norwegian children. Why, it seemed like paradise. Nevertheless, an uneasy feeling lurked in the back of his mind. Would it endanger Susan's reputation if he were to sleep in her schoolhouse overnight? He must again go talk to her father.

He found Mr. Cary in the stable doing chores. He told about the visit from Mr. Whitcomb and about his own idea for sleeping there.

"That's one reason I suggested you for the job. I knew you'd have to get in out of the cold before long. The little school building is snug, and Lydia and I knew you'd keep things picked up."

"Thanks," Andreas said, flushed with pleasure. "Do you think it would be...proper?"

"If we're agreeable, I don't know why the other parents wouldn't be. We know them all, but the Norwegians. If you or Cleng can explain the situation to them, Lydia or I will talk to the folks around here."

"I will talk to my friends right away tomorrow."

"Well, come on in to supper," said Mr. Cary. "I saw the women stirring up some cornbread and beans. We'll have a go at them and talk it over."

Andreas' winter was set up for him in a way he couldn't possibly have predicted. Surely, the Lord was favoring him, expecting big things. And he was sure it had something to do with teaching the Norwegian children.

The next afternoon he walked over the trail to the cabins to visit the parents with children of school age. After the frost, the forest was putting on its autumn dress of red-gold, scarlet and crimson. Andreas walked joyfully, leaping over logs, breathing in the autumn freshness, the mosquitoless air in a state of ecstasy, imagining Susan by his side, as he did almost everywhere he went.

First he went to Carolyn Thompson. She was gradually getting over the deaths, grimly going about her tasks, talking to people again, caring for her two girls. Oyen's younger brother, Nils, was continuing with the work on the farm and living with Cleng.

Carolyn was brushing Sara's hair as she and the two girls sat in the sunshine; the long, blonde tresses shone with each stroke. Andreas joined them, visited for awhile from a nearby stump, then told them about the school. "I'll be helping Miss Cary with both the caretaker duties and any language difficulties, as well as sleeping there nights to protect the school."

"I've been wondering where you were going to stay this winter," Carolyn said. "That will be handy for you and give you an extra job, too."

"Andreas," Anne said shyly, "will the pretty lady you brought to the picnic be our teacher?"

Andreas beamed. "She sure will be, Anne." Both girls ran to tell their Uncle Nils, who was working in a nearby field.

106

As Andreas started to leave, Carolyn rose and walked with him. "I'm so thankful to you, Andreas, for helping get the girls in school. Oyen always believed in education for them and I'm going to see that they get it."

He turned at the parting and took her hand. "You're a brave woman, sister Carolyn. Few of us can really understand what you've been through with two deaths so close together."

After this encounter, Andreas was a little too shaken to go directly to the next cabin where there were children, so he went for a short visit with Cleng. He, too, was sitting in the autumn sunshine, a book in his hands.

He greeted Andreas, then held up the book. "This Scottish writer, Sir Walter Scott, has a beautiful way with words. The Kendrick family loaned me a book of his poems. They have a son attending Colgate College; he brought it home. Listen to this:

'Ah, County Guy, the hour is nigh,

The sun has left the lea.

The orange flower perfumes the bower,

The breeze is on the sea.'

Isn't that beautiful?"

Andreas nodded absently. "I've just come from Carolyn's. She seems to be recovering and beginning to take an interest in things again."

"Yes, bless her heart, with God's help from our many prayers, she's coming along just fine."

"I told her that the children were welcome to go to the little American school which Miss Cary teaches. The girls are willing to go there and Carolyn wants them to." Although he didn't know why he should, he was hesitating to tell Cleng about his moving into the school for the winter. "By the way, I've got a job at the school this winter...caretaker. I'll stay there nights and build a fire to get the school warm before the children come in. I'll only stay there days if Miss Cary needs me to help with language difficulties."

"H-m-m," Cleng said. "Well, that will give you a warm place to sleep, but you know you are more than welcome to stay in my cabin. Right now there is just Nils and me."

"Mr. Cary suggested I stay there. I can keep wood chopped and protect the building." Andreas wanted to change the subject. "Who all do you think I should contact about attending the school? I don't know where I should draw the line on age."

"I say invite them all. Ovee and Halvor and Olaf need to learn to speak English and they can see the little ones safely to and from school. Talk to them; I'll talk to them, too."

After the visits, Andreas went home, content that he had spent a purposeful afternoon.

He was in no way prepared for the shock of Cleng's visit to his cabin the following day. Surprised to see him so soon after yesterday's visit, Andreas supposed he was on his way to visit the Carys or perhaps even the schoolhouse. But Cleng settled down on the visiting log, and for him seemed a little hesitant to speak. "You look like you came up with an idea, Cleng," Andreas said pleasantly. "What great plans have you got in mind this time?"

"Well, Andreas, you may not take to my idea right off. But I've always known you to do what is right for the sake of our little group, for the betterment of all of us and those that come later."

Andreas' mind sent up a warning signal. What suggestion was Cleng going to make? He had a dark foreboding, certain it had something to do with Susan.

Cleng cleared his throat and continued, "Carolyn Thompson is a wonderful woman with property and two nice girls. You need a home, Andreas, some place besides a schoolhouse. That's no place to live. Also, Nils wants to go back to that home; he misses Carolyn and the girls."

Andreas, astonished, stiffened and spoke to Cleng more icily than he'd ever dared. "Are you suggesting that I *marry* Carolyn Thompson?"

"Well, yes, Andreas, I see that as the thing for you to do. Think of the advantages, for you and for her. Oh, I know you have been infatuated with the Cary girl. She's a beauty, and I could get all steamed up over her myself, even at my age..." He turned to wink at Andreas, but Andreas sat stonily silent, rage fomenting within. He had to grip his hands together to keep from hitting Cleng. He wanted to knock him right off the log.

Cleng went on calmly, "Carolyn is still a handsome woman. Comes from good stock. She's not more than eight or nine years older than you. She can give you children yet; you'd have a good solid marriage."

Andreas was hearing only part of what Cleng was saying, but when he again referred to Susan, it registered. "Otherwise it's not going to look very good for an unmarried man like you to be working so closely with the young lady schoolteacher. Marriage to Carolyn would remove any doubts about your intentions. Getting the children in an American school, learning English, that's the important thing right now for the future of our little group."

Andreas controlled himself enough to stand and to speak. "Cleng, surely you realize this suggestion comes as a shock to me. Could you leave me now to think it through alone?"

Cleng stood. "Why, certainly, Andreas, I hope I haven't been too straightforward with my suggestion, but you know me. That's the way great things are accomplished. Ideas!" Cleng held out his hand. Andreas hesitated, then extended a limp hand. At that moment, he hated the grip of the other man's fingers.

With clenched fists and a tight throat, Andreas watched Cleng as he walked briskly back into the forest and disappeared from sight. Then he went into his hut, threw himself on the sheepskin bed and began praying: "God...surely Thou dost not ask this of me. I've seldom known Cleng to be wrong. Am I thinking of Susan with only selfish desires? How could a man love a woman any more than I love her? And Carolyn...she's like an older sister. I'd do anything in the world for her. But to marry her, physically give her my body..."

Tears flooded his eyes as he tried to find some peace from his wretchedness, but no peace came. Instead he cried out, "Susan, oh Susan...I can't live without you!"

He tried to formulate some logical solutions. Give up the job at the school? Then who would help the Norwegian children? Cleng wouldn't stick around all winter. Maybe one of the women? None of them spoke enough English. He had to talk to someone about it, get another view on Cleng's interpretation of what was right and what was wrong. Should he talk to Mr. Cary? No, certainly not him. Daniel? Cornelius? Betsy? Lars! Lars and Martha. He'd leave for Rochester early in the morning.

That decision made, he suddenly had a great longing to see Susan. In the past hour, it seemed as though she had been disembodied. He wanted to see her ready smile, her bright brown eyes, her round lovely figure. She had planned to work in the schoolhouse for a few days before the children came; perhaps she would be there this afternoon. He'd go there first. He'd think of some excuse.

He approached the little log building where he had anticipated making his home for the winter, a dull ache in his chest because now it might never be. His heart leaped when he heard her singing, "Blest be the tie that binds, our hearts in Christian love. The fellowship of kindred minds is like to that above."

Could she be thinking of him as he was thinking of her? He tapped on the door and the singing stopped. She lifted the latch and peeked out. He noted how her face lighted up when she saw him. "Andrew! Come in. I've been sweeping and scrubbing all afternoon to get ready for all the children, American and Norwegian together. Are you as excited about it as I am?" She was barefoot, had on a dress that looked like she'd outgrown it, a little girl's frock, shapeless and plain. Her hair was covered with a cloth and tied at the back like a peasant, wisps of curls escaping. Somehow it enhanced her, made her more beautiful than ever. Her cheeks were flushed with happiness and exertion. Best of all, was her enthusiasm and obvious delight in his being there.

Just looking at her, he forgot to speak. Her smile turned to a frown. "Is something wrong, Andrew? You look so pale. Are you sick?"

"I'll be all right. I just have some worries on my mind...I want to talk over with Lars. I came to tell you I'll be gone to Rochester two, three days."

"Is it the Norwegians?" she asked with alarm. "You didn't get some bad news from your family, did you?"

"No...not either that." He shouldn't have mentioned it when he couldn't tell her. "I know more when I get back."

He stood looking at her for another long moment, then stepped closer, picked up one of her hands and laid his cheek upon it. "Before I go, Susan, I want to tell you...I want to tell you...I love you." He clutched her hand in both of his, looked deeply into her eyes and watched them fill with tears. Then slowly, he let go of her hand, turned quickly and walked out the door. After he'd gone a short distance, he heard her calling his name. He looked back. She threw him a kiss.

CHAPTER 14

A Long
Journey

A T DAWN THE NEXT DAY, after a nearly sleepless night, Andreas began his 20-mile walk to Rochester. The morning was heavily overcast, like his mood. The pain in his chest was a swirl of rage, guilt, frustration...and love for Susan.

Even if they married, would she soon tire of him? Marriage, working hard, bearing children would rob her of youth and beauty so soon. Is this what he wanted to do to her for his own selfish desires? Was God really against nationalities mixing? Would their children be shunned? Was Susan's reputation threatened if he worked with her at the schoolhouse and slept there? Oh, God, give me answers, he prayed!

So absorbed was he in his conflicting thoughts and worries, Andreas was only vaguely aware that something seemed to be keeping pace with him just out of sight in the forest beside the canal path on which he walked. He began paying attention and heard the light crunch of leaves with the rustle of branches overhead. While not really afraid, he realized he had no weapon. Was something really stalking him? He remembered the several times during the summer when he'd heard a slight disturbance as though a large animal or person were nearby. But nothing ever showed up nor was nothing in his camp disturbed that could be attributed to a large marauder. Of course there was the night half of his milk from the pail in the creek cooler seemed to disappear. But the lid was still on so he decided the foam on the fresh milk had made it appear fuller than it was.

After another mile along the canal, the presence of something unknown seemed to disappear and Andreas dismissed it from his mind.

When the sun was high in the sky, he stopped to eat the bread and cheese he had brought. He watched a small boat go by. Where was the little packet boat of well-dressed passengers going, he wondered, as he waved a greeting to the tow boys. Were they just sight seeing? Traveling from New York to Rochester, or beyond? What was out there, beyond the haze of the green forest? If he had to break up with Susan, maybe he'd just head in that direction. Travel like Cleng, never knowing where he'd sleep. Let the Lord provide. He'd have to do something to get Susan out of his mind; without her, his life wasn't worth much anyway.

He rose with a heavy sigh, drank from the nearby stream, then journeyed on, reading any signs along the way, greeting the few travelers he met, some on foot, some in buggy or cart.

It was a long walk, not as far as he'd walked at other times, but the burden of unresolved problems made it seem farther. He was glad to see traffic picking up and smoke billowing. Rochester was just ahead.

Andreas followed directions to the Larson house. Lars answered his knock and after the surprised greeting, he took on a worried frown.

"No bad news this time," Andreas hastened to tell them. "For some reason the sickness seems to have left with the colder weather. It's more of a personal problem I've come with."

"Well, I hope we can help," Lars said, "But first, let's have some supper. We're just about ready to sit and ask the Lord's blessing before we eat."

Andreas nodded to Siri as she came from her chimney corner to join them. He smiled at baby Margaret and tickled her on the cheek as she sat at the table tied to the back of a high stool. He talked little and ate sparingly. But he found that even a little food and relaxation within the warmth of this loving family prepared him for what he must discuss with Lars, and to accept whatever advice this wise friend had to give.

Supper ended with a welcome bowl of Norwegian rice pudding. Then Lars said, "Come on into the other room by the fire, Andreas, and tell me what's on your mind. I can see it's pretty heavy."

Andreas settled into a chair and took a deep breath. He told his story from the afternoon he was offered the job at the school. It seemed like a month ago.

"Why, that's great, Andreas. If Mr. Cary approves and sent the fellow to you, I see no problem there."

"I didn't either. It seemed like a good opportunity to get our Norwegian children speaking good English by next spring. But, Lars, Cleng came over to my place yesterday and made a suggestion I can't accept, although I feel that I should, as he said, for the sake of the group." Andreas gulped and went on.

"He said I shouldn't be working over there as a single man; that if I were married it would give me the respectability to help educate the children. That Carolyn Thompson would make me a good wife, provide a good home, and permit Nils to go back to the house again, which he wants to do."

Lars frowned. "Cleng suggested that you marry Carolyn to accommodate everyone else?" Andreas nodded.

Lars shook his head. "What will Cleng come up with next? That's old world thinking. Martha, come here," Lars called to his wife, who was getting the baby ready for bed. She handed Margaret to Siri and came, wiping her hands on her apron.

"Cleng has told Andreas that he is supposed to marry Carolyn. What do you think of that?"

"Carolyn Thompson?" She looked at Andreas. "How does Andreas, and how does Carolyn feel about that?"

"I don't think Carolyn has been consulted. Such a thought never occurred to me," Andreas said shakily. "She...she's like a sister."

"Of course she is. And how about Susan? Is it over between you two?" Martha asked.

"Oh, no...no!" Andreas exclaimed.

"Then what right has he got to try marrying you off to someone else, ten years older than you, and a husband just a month in his grave?" She laughed shortly. "Why doesn't he court her himself? We hear that the wife he had in Norway has died."

As Martha talked, Lars, staunch Quaker that he was, realized where the conversation was headed. He circled his beard with thumb and forefinger in characteristic manner. "Let's not be too hard on Cleng," he said kindly. "I don't think he knows about marrying for love. About the

114

kind of marriage Martha and I are privileged to enjoy." Martha moved over and put her hand on his shoulder.

Andreas, not yet convinced, said, "I have to wonder...if Susan is too young, and being a different nationality, might soon regret marrying me."

"If there was any problem with you being Norwegian," declared Martha, "I'm sure her family would not be encouraging your relationship. As to age, I was a little older than Susan when I married Lars, but there were sixteen years between us and I've never regretted marrying him, for more than a few minutes at a time anyway!"

"Give Susan plenty of time, don't rush her, that's all." Lars reached up to pat Martha's hand.

"I promised Mr. Cary we wouldn't marry before she's seventeen."

Martha went back to put the baby to bed. Lars threw more wood on the fire. Andreas leaned back with an incredible feeling of relief.

"We're expecting another little one early in February," Lars confided.

"Congratulations, I hope you have many more daughters and sons. As for me, Lars, to have a friend like you is wealth beyond measure. I'll forgive Cleng, knowing he, too, can make mistakes like the rest of us."

"Well, maybe Cleng will find the right woman someday and then he'll understand love in a new light."

Martha rejoined them and they continued the visit.

"In the spring," Lars said, "I'm starting a boat-building business of my own. Want to join me, Andreas?"

"No, but many thanks, Lars. I'm a farmer like I always wanted to be. Life here in the city would be easier and if I had to give up Susan...I'd have to come here, go back to Norway or something. But now I'll go on with my plans as before, and build a house on my property so that we can live right there next to her parents."

"I suspected that would be your decision as well as most of the rest of the Norwegian men from the sloop. But there will be others coming."

"Tell him about the house we're going to build," Martha said, excitement evident on her face.

Lars beamed. "Yes. After I get the boat business underway, I'm going to build a very large frame house on ground I've already purchased. We will use it as a sort of host house for new Norwegian immigrants coming over. It will give them a place to stay until they can get a job and lodging."

"It's been an ambition of ours to do this," Martha confided, "knowing how hard it was for us. Without the New York Quakers, we really would have been lost."

"That sounds like a mighty generous and Christian thing to do," Andreas said. "I'll certainly pray for your venture."

As the evening grew late, Andreas nodded off. Martha gently woke him and showed him to his room. It contained a bed with feather tick, pillow with a white lace-edged case on it, wash stand and bowl with pitcher, rag rugs on the floor, curtains at the window.

It was the first bed he had been in since one he shared with Cleng on a night during their travels. Susan and all the Carys slept in beds like this every night, just as he had until he left Norway. He tried to remain awake to enjoy the rich comfort. But it was only a short time before he was in deep, welcome slumber. He dreamed that he and Susan, as man and wife, were visiting his mother's house in Norway.

The next morning when Andreas got up, Lars had already gone to work, Siri had porridge made for him and was frying eggs. Martha was milking the cow.

Before he left, he thanked Martha again for their help and encouragement and Siri handed him a generous lunch for the trip home.

Andreas no longer felt bitterness toward Cleng. He was going to turn the other cheek. That evening upon arriving home, he went right away to Cleng's cabin. Cleng was alone.

"I want to apologize for my attitude the other night," Andreas said. "But Carolyn seems too much like a sister to me to ever consider marrying her. Also, since neither Mr. and Mrs. Cary nor Mr. Whitcomb objected to my sleeping at the schoolhouse, I've decided to go ahead with the job."

Cleng smiled. "I didn't think you were taking too kindly to the suggestion. But things will work out for Carolyn. Nils and the girls keep her from getting too lonesome. They invited him over there for supper tonight so I'm eating fish alone. Join me, there's more than enough." He pulled up a bench for Andreas, then brought food from the stove.

Cleng usually had a story to tell and tonight it was a retelling of his encounter with an Indian on his first trip to America. An Indian greatly admired his Norwegian-made coat and wanted to trade for it. First, he offered his wife, then finally the deed to a large piece of property on the shore of a lake called Michigan in the town of Chicago.

"I considered this trade," Cleng said, "thinking it might be a good place for our immigrants. But in asking around about it, a man warned me that it was just an undrained swamp, all mud, he said. I often wonder if I should have taken him up on the deal."

"For the wife?" Andreas laughed.

"No, no, it took me less time to decide about that than it did you about taking on a wife. But with work, the land might have been drainable and made us good homes for the price of my coat. Of course, I might have got pretty cold before I could afford another one."

"Do you suppose he really had a deed to it?"

"Oh yes, I saw it. Looked legal. I don't know how he came by it."

The evening after his return from Rochester, Andreas was expected for supper at the Carys. He only had a brief opportunity to speak to Susan alone, on the porch before supper.

"Lars and Martha send you their greetings."

"Did you get your problem worked out?" she asked with concern. "You look happier."

"Lars and Martha are wise. They give me good...thoughts..."

"Advice?"

He nodded. "I'm not worried now." He smiled warmly, ignoring her questioning look. He couldn't tell her now, if ever. So thankful for his new lease on courtship, he was determined to abide by the most stringent rules. There must be no further words of love between them at the schoolhouse.

THE BECKONING

School began and Andreas was proud of the little group of Norwegian children who got there early, well-scrubbed and neatly combed. Two big boys, Ovee Rosdail and Halvor Reveim, had been willing to come and try it. They sat silently at the back of the room on benches too low for them, looking very much out of place.

After the first week of school, Susan went home on Friday afternoon, tired and tearful. "Mama, I just don't know what to do for those big Norwegian boys. It's all I can do to keep up with helping the little ones. The big boys have to just sit back there and listen. And their...their eyes just follow me everywhere. In Norway, they probably got as much schooling as I have. All they need is just to learn English. And I don't have time to spend with them."

The mother put an arm around her daughter. "You're hardly more than a child yourself and trying to deal with such big problems." She thought for a moment. "Why don't you have a special day for them, maybe just an afternoon or two each week without the little children there. Then you could teach them like you did Andrew. Maybe he could help you on those days. Let's talk to Andrew and Mr. Whitcomb about it."

Everyone concerned thought it was a good idea. Since the Norwegians were within the township, they had to be educated along with the rest of the children. The boys over 12 were to come on Fridays and either Andreas or Cleng would be there, along with any other Norwegians who would like to listen in, learning what English they could.

At her mother's suggestion, Susan spent the first school day for older Norwegians telling them their American names. Pedar was Peter. Tomad was Thomas. Gudmund was Goodman. Henrik was Henry, and so on. She went over familiar objects with them to make a few sentences. "I walk to school. This is a pencil. This is my right hand. This is my nose." And so on. They chanted the words together, over and over. Before the afternoon ended they were laughing, having a good time and speaking a little English.

After school, Andreas helped her tidy up the room and brought in more wood for morning. Susan was exuberant. "They will learn quickly now, I think."

"I need to hurry and read, keep ahead of them," Andreas said eagerly.

"I'll bring some books from home which are easy to read."

"It's dark longer now. I'll read them each night before I get too sleepy."

But there was another matter on his mind that evening. Halvor had confided in him that his family and a couple of the others, whom he did not identify, were seriously thinking of moving on west because they'd heard that land could be bought for practically nothing and it was much easier to farm.

The old urge for adventure again stirred in Andreas. He wouldn't give up his farm and he wouldn't leave Susan. But going along just to see what it was like, that wouldn't hurt, would it?

Did other men feel that same deep urge, Andreas wondered. He had felt it in Norway down at the harbor when Cleng talked about America. So well he remembered, he could almost smell the sea water. It was as if a power beyond himself were tugging at him, enticing, "Come further, see what lies out here." He had come and here was his own land and a woman he loved passionately. Here were his friends he trusted and knew.

And yet....

Andreas shivered and attended the fire into which he had been gazing. Did it never end, this thirst for adventure, for moving on? The powerful pull had eased when he reached America; it was more of an insistent whisper now, a beckoning.

CHAPTER 15

Eventful
Holidays

THE DAY BEFORE THANKSGIVING, a team of oxen and wagon with two men on board approached the Norwegian settlement. Since it was a most unusual occurrence, all who heard came out to look. Cleng went to meet the visitors.

"Well, Joseph Fellows, welcome!" Cleng greeted the friendly American Quaker who had been so much help to the settlers. He was the agent who had sold them their land under the most lenient of terms.

"We bring thee a load of provisions," said Mr. Fellows. "Our granaries are full this autumn and we want to show our appreciation to our Heavenly Father by sharing." He waved his hand behind him toward the sacks of flour, cornmeal, potatoes, apples and cabbages. "Where would thee like us to unload it?"

It was hastily decided that the Cornelius Nelson cabin was the most conveniently located and also had an attic for storage. After helping unload, each Norwegian man in turn went to the Quakers to shake hands and say, "T'anks! God bless!"

The settlers rejoiced that now they could enjoy a more bountiful Thanksgiving than they expected. But the thrifty Norwegians were thinking more of the winter ahead before fields and gardens would produce again, and portioned out the provender sparingly.

In mid-December, Cornelius Nelson went to Farmington to bargain for a team of oxen and wagon which they had heard were for sale. His friends waited anxiously for his return, listening hopefully for the sound of wheels. What they heard was, "Fire! Fire! HELP!"

There was a dash for the Nelson cabin. The whole end of the house with the sail roof was ablaze. There was no hope of saving it or anything within. Confusion was everywhere.

120

Big Nels shouted to Kari, "Is everyone out?"

Hysterically Kari answered, "I don't know where Karine is!"

Nels strode fearlessly to the cabin, and thrust his powerful shoulder against the corner of the building. Flames spiraled out, forcing him back.

"Here she is, here she is!" someone shouted and held up a terrified and screaming little girl.

The next moment they heard oxen pounding down the path, followed by the squeaking wagon. Kari, followed by two of the children, ran sobbing toward him.

"Kari, Kari, are the children all out?"

"They're all safe, Cornelius," Big Nels called to him.

"Oh, thank God, thank God," he cried, springing from the wagon and falling to his knees with upraised hands.

How the fire started was a mystery. Kari said she was preparing supper, stirring the soup kettle which was hanging on the trivet over the fire, when there was a big boom up in the attic where the produce the Quakers had given them was stored.

"There was a big cloud of black smoke," Kari sobbingly reported, "then...then flames leaped around the whole cabin. All I could think of was getting all the children out."

The women shepherded Kari and the children away to another cabin, but the men remained by the smoldering produce that lay on top of the blackened heap.

"Do you suppose some gunpowder could have been accidentally packed in with the flour or cornmeal?" Daniel suggested. "Or even on purpose by some cruel person?"

"But what would be the spark that set it off?" Gudmund asked.

"It seems like we're doing something to displease the Lord," Cornelius said in a broken voice. "Surely it can't be my new team and wagon."

"If the Lord had a part in this," said Cleng, speaking firmly like a father, "it was in seeing that Kari and the children got out safely. Now we must see that they are comforted and provided for until they can get on their feet again and rebuild." He turned to Cornelius. "Of course there's room for you in my cabin."

Kari took more than a little comforting. She continued crying, wringing her hands and moaning. Cornelius finally put an arm around her and led her away from the group of women and they walked toward the lake.

"It won't be long before we get another cabin up, probably yet this winter, maybe even better than that one," Cornelius murmured.

"But everything is destroyed!" sobbed Kari. One end of the long braid she always wore around her head had come loose, her face was smudged, her dress torn. "The few things we brought from Norway are all gone, my mother's shawl, the children's clothes for school that I just finished making...oh, I just want to leave this horrible forest where life is so hard." She clutched her husband's arm pleadingly.

"Well, that's a decision we must not make overnight," he soothed, "but we'll think about it this winter and get as much information as we can about that land further west."

Andreas was in Holley at the time of the fire. He saw flames in that direction on his way home, but thought it was brush burning. He didn't learn of it until the next morning when the school children excitedly told him about it. He went right over, saddened by the misfortune of his friends, but glad it hadn't been necessary for him to move back and further crowd Cleng's cabin.

He appreciated the cozy little school building where he could spend the long winter evenings in front of the fireplace whittling or reading books Susan brought for him. Her presence was everywhere and always with him no matter what he did. Sometimes he looked for things she had left behind, a handkerchief or words printed on a card for teaching the children. But in the presence of the children they were formal, calling each other Miss Cary or Mr. Stangeland. It was only at the Cary home with the family that they dared carry on their courtship.

Andreas and James became good friends. James stayed with a family in Kendall during the week while he worked, but Saturday nights he often visited with Andreas at the school until late at night. Andreas saved questions from his exploration of books and maps to ask his neighbor. Sometimes James knew the answers and sometimes he didn't, but it made for interesting discussions.

One night James confided to Andreas, "I haven't told anyone else this yet, but I'm thinking about striking out westward next spring. I hear that land can be purchased from the government for $1.25 an acre."

Andreas was surprised and a bit envious. "Is that in the part of America warm all winter?"

"No, that's south. The Michigan Territory is what I'm interested in, about straight west of here." He held out his arm in that direction. "I could get there almost all the way by boat. Want to go along?"

"Oh, I would like that. I would like to see every part of this big country. But I think for now I stay close by your sister, Susan." Andreas laughed, his color rising.

"Yeah. Well, I don't feel that strongly about anybody yet. Susan sure seems taken with you. Looks like you're her first and last sweetheart. Since she's known you, I've never seen her interested in anyone else."

Andreas was filled with love and pride. "We can't be brothers too soon to suit me."

Why couldn't he be two people, he thought with chagrin. One of him to stay and marry Susan, build a fine prosperous farm and raise children, while the other part of him was off exploring, being one of the American pioneers?

As Christmas time approached, Susan planned to invite the parents to the school for an evening so the children could put on a little program. The mothers could help furnish holiday sweets and popcorn for the conclusion. Inger Nelson and Sara Thompson carried word to the Norwegian parents who agreed to make *fatteningman* and other *kake* for the event.

The twins, Alex and Leander, would be shepherds and carry rolled up sheep skins for lambs. Andreas was at the Carys when they planned the pageant. He noticed how much the boys had grown just since he'd known them. At school they were bright and talkative, but had no special privileges. They had to address their sister as Miss Cary, which to everyone's amusement often carried over at home.

With the emphasis at school on Christmas, Andreas began to wonder what he could get Susan for a Christmas present that was special. Maybe he should make another trip to Rochester where he had a chance of finding something out of the ordinary. It hadn't snowed yet; it was chilly, but not unbearably cold, nice hiking weather. He decided to go over and see if Gudmund would go with him for company. But as he walked, he remembered that his cousin had said he didn't like to leave the women alone overnight.

Who else should he ask, he wondered. Nils! Nils Thompson. The trip would do him good; he'd been working hard trying to take Oyen's place on the farm. He found him working alone, cutting up a tree.

"How about walking over to Rochester with me tomorrow, Nils?" Andreas said to him. "I'm going over to visit Lars and Martha before Christmas."

Nils didn't hesitate. "I'd like that, I haven't seen them since...since we buried Oyen. I guess I can take off a couple of days' work if you can."

"I'm going to get Ovee and Halvor to do the chores around the school. They want a chance to camp out in my hut overnight anyway, if it doesn't snow."

They started their walk at daylight the next morning. Having someone to visit with shortened the trip; Andreas was surprised how fast the day went and soon they were being welcomed into the warm and cheerful Larson household. Lars and Martha were, as usual, eager for all the news. They hadn't known about the fire or the ox team and wagon. Before bedtime, the three men walked the dark streets to Ole Olsen's place where Ole persuaded Nils to spend the night with him for more visiting.

Next morning after they had said their goodbyes and were headed out of town, they passed by Morgan's store, where they slowed and looked in the window with its display of Christmas gifts. "Let's go in and have a look around, Nils. Won't cost anything to look."

In the store a salesman in a plaid suit was smiling broadly and saying, "How do," to everyone who passed by. He stood with his hand on a stack of small boards with polished edges. After several people had stopped to look curiously at the boards, the salesman began his spiel.

"Step right up, folks, and let me show you the latest invention right out of New York City. It will sweep the country by storm, revolutionize industry and education, as well as the stock market." He held up one of the boards. "This is a remarkable little board called a slate. S-l-a-t-e. Slate. Watch now." The salesman held up a small stick, "I'm going to write my name on this little slate board." He wrote B-E-N in large letters with the white stick. Andreas and Nils watched from the back of the group.

"Can everyone see that? Can you men at the back see it?" Andreas nodded. "Now I'm going to take this piece of felt and rub off my name, just as simple as that!" Everyone looked at each other with surprise as the white lines disappeared.

Ben bent down to a girl in the front, "What is your name, little girl?" he asked.

"Anna."

"Anna? That's a nice name. We'll write it on the slate." He held it up again. "Now, isn't that remarkable, folks? Write, rub off, write, rub off as many times as you want.

There were smiles and murmurs throughout the audience. Ben next wrote sums on the slate. "Just think how fast our children will learn when each child in school has one of these. Some day schoolrooms will have large sections of this material on the walls to write on and draw maps for the children to see all at once."

"How long will they last?" someone from the audience timidly asked.

"The slate will last indefinitely," Ben said. "The little white marker, it's called chalk, does wear down after a long time and must be replaced, depending, of course, on how much you use it."

Then there was the inevitable question, "How much do they cost?"

"Just one dollar! That's all, folks, just one dollar and you've got the finest, most useful Christmas present anyone could give. Carry it anywhere, write anything you want and rub it off. A revolutionary invention."

As soon as the price was announced most people walked away. Andreas reached in his pocket and fingered the dollar bill he had earned for work at the school. He hoped the writing board wasn't just a gimcrack that wouldn't really work after he bought it, but it did seem like it would be useful for a teacher. With little further hesitation, he took out the dollar bill, straightened it and stepped forward. He waited for two other people to make their purchases. Then Ben turned and winked at Andreas. "You're making a wise choice, sir. Better take two of them." Andreas shook his head and held up one finger.

Nils had turned and was looking at some white linen handkerchiefs on the counter behind them. He chose one and handed it, with his money, to the clerk.

When they got back outside, Andreas asked, "You got a girl, too, Nils?"

Nils hesitated and cleared his throat before answering. "No...I just thought I'd get if for Carolyn. She's working hard making things for the girls and...and I just thought she deserved something, too. I know Oyen would have bought or made her something."

"That's nice of you, Nils; I imagine you miss being over there with the girls and Carolyn."

"Yes...it was home," Nils answered with a tremble in his voice. They walked on in silence for several minutes.

Nils spoke again, "Andreas, if I ask you something, would you not make fun or laugh at me?"

"Of course, I wouldn't laugh unless you meant it to be funny."

"Well...then..." He stopped for another long pause.

"Go on. What?"

"What do you think, and what do you think the others would think...if after a decent length of time...I...I courted Carolyn?"

Andreas felt himself becoming angry. Now Cleng was working on Nils, even younger than himself. He controlled his voice to answer. "What I would think depends on whose idea it is. When you look forward to marrying someone, I think it should come from the heart, not because someone else suggests it."

"Oh, no," Nils said defensively, "Carolyn hasn't said or done anything out of place. I...I guess it was only me that's sinned all these years, coveting my brother's wife."

"Cleng didn't suggest it?"

"Cleng? No-o. He probably has no idea how I feel, me being fourteen years younger than Carolyn."

Inaudibly, Andreas sighed with relief. God and his wondrous ways! "I think I'd try to find out how Carolyn feels about it first thing. I'm sure Cleng and all the others would give their full blessing if she could come to feel more for you than just a brother. Your Christmas present for her seems like a good beginning. Give it to her with love in your eyes, and see how she reacts."

"Thanks, Andreas. I'm glad I asked." Nils was jubilant.

The stop at the store had delayed them and they would have to hurry, with little time out to rest or eat the lunch Martha and Siri had sent along. It was not a pleasant experience picking one's way through the dark forest after night. Andreas was glad he'd asked Nils to go along, – doubly glad.

On December 22, the schoolhouse was filled with people. Along one wall, a long sideboard was spread with inviting sweets. At the front of the room, Ovee and Halvor held up a blanket to curtain off the scene behind it until all was ready. Children sat, prim and nervous, on benches at the side of the scene, Susan in their midst.

On cue from the teacher, the boys opened the curtain to reveal a small Joseph and Mary and a well-swathed doll on a mound of hay. The Cary shepherds in long robes stood tall and serious on either side with their long staffs and imitation lambs.

One by one each child came forward, knelt before the doll Christ child, then rose and told the audience what he or she was giving.

"I will obey my mother and father."

"I will always think pure thoughts."

"I will remember my prayers each night and morning."

"I will learn one Bible verse each week."

Now it was time for the Norwegian children. First came Carolyn's older daughter. Sara shyly bowed to the Christ child, then to the audience. "My name Sara Thompson. I give...I give... quick learn English to...to..."

"To praise," prompted Susan in a whisper.

"...to praise God," Sara finished triumphantly.

There were pleased murmurings from both the American and Norwegian parents. The pretty little girl with long golden hair and wearing a brand new dress captured the hearts of all, as did her sister Anne Marie, who spoke next. Teary-eyed Carolyn sat close to the front between Cleng and Nils.

As the pageant ended, Ovee walked back with his corner of the blanket to close the curtain. The boys stood together in their colorful Norwegian vests over full-sleeved shirts, looking proud and confident. Each of them gave a short Bible verse, first in Norwegian, then in English.

Preacher Haines, who had a boy in the school finished the program with a prayer; then it was time for refreshments.

The children crowded toward the table of sweets where Mrs. Cary passed them out. Beside the *fatteningman* cookies, which the Norwegian women had made, there were sugar cookies, molasses cookies, taffy and a popcorn ball for everyone. The Norwegians had not yet seen popcorn in a ball and, after a few nibbles, took them home to savor later.

After everything was eaten to the last cookie, there was more visiting among the parents. The children ran around the school yard. Soon families began leaving for home. Some had come in sleighs over the frozen, lightly snow covered ground, but most had walked, as did the Carys. Two sleepy boys walked between their parents as Andreas and Susan lingered behind in the pale half-moon light.

"Your program was nice," Andreas said. "Everything went well and they think you do a good job teaching."

"Yes, it went pretty well, didn't it? But I'm so tired, Andrew. I'm glad it's over."

He released her hand to put his arm around her, and pulled her to him, wanting desperately to share her burden. They walked slowly and silently to the house, where the rest of the family had already entered. His arms circled her; she laid her head on his shoulder. He nestled her close, felt her tremble, heard her sigh and wanted to lift her lips to his. But the time had not yet come. He gave her one last warm hug and said, "Good night, dear Susan." He slowly released her, turned and walked quickly back toward the schoolhouse.

CHAPTER 16

Two
Proposals

NILS THOMPSON LIKED TO WHITTLE and the long January evenings gave him plenty of opportunity. For Christmas he had whittled little animals for Anne Marie and Sara and was rewarded by their delight in them. Now he was finishing a bowl for Carolyn's birthday. He sat in the corner near the light of the blazing fire, working with loving care to smooth the rough edges. He listened, but seldom entered into the conversation of Cleng, Kari and Cornelius. Tomorrow he would take the bowl to Carolyn.

When he gave her the handkerchief at Christmas, she had been grateful, but nothing more that he could discover. He hoped, with this present, to be bold enough to find out if he had a chance with her. He must use the right words that wouldn't offend her. If she couldn't care for him in the same way he cared for her, if he were to be cut off from her and the girls...well, anything would be better than that.

When the girls left for school, snow crunching beneath their feet, Nils was chopping wood. They waved their bright new Christmas mittens at him; he waved back. Shortly after, he slipped into Cleng's cabin and got the bowl. He looked it over in the daylight, removed a few last imperfections, then headed toward Carolyn's house.

As he approached her door, he could hear the hum of the spinning wheel. He knew it was her week to use it, because he had carried it over. The latch string was out so he lifted it and entered. Moving a few feet into the room, he waited for her to look up. Finally, she raised her head, and, with a start and a puzzled frown, exclaimed, "Oyen!"

Nils said nothing, just stood waiting, faintly smiling.

"Oh, Nils, I'm so sorry." She rose and came red-faced toward him. "I do and say such crazy things these days, sometimes I wonder if I'm...losing my mind." Suddenly she picked up the corner of her apron and began crying into it.

Immediately, Nils put the bowl on the table, wrapped his arms around her, held her to his chest, and buried his face in the mound of her blonde hair. She clung to him. "No one has done more for me...or understands me better than you, Nils," she sobbed.

"That's because I love you, Carolyn. Not just as a brother, but as Oyen must have loved you. I love the girls as my own. Could we marry and become a family again?"

She backed away and looked at him with a frown. "Nils, are you saying you want to marry me, at my age?" Her tear streaked face reflected astonishment.

"I didn't mean to blurt it out so suddenly, but it's true, Carolyn, I love you," Nils said earnestly, "I want to support and protect you and the girls. Age doesn't matter to me; does it matter so much to you?"

Carolyn hesitated, then looked at him as if she were seeing him for the first time. "No.....no, I suppose not."

He smiled. "You can even call me Oyen sometimes and I won't mind. I loved him, too, you know."

She stood looking at him for several more moments. Then to his delight, the lines around her blue eyes and her mouth softened. Her lips parted in a slow smile. "No, Nils, I don't think it will take long for me to care for you in, in the way you want me to."

His hands trembling, he picked up the bowl and held it out to her. "Happy birthday, my beloved."

She examined it inside and out without really seeing it. She caressed it as she would a child.

"You have always been so good to me, dear, dear Nils." She touched his arm. Feelings she had been trying to suppress were suddenly being rekindled. Impulsively she set the bowl on the table, moved to him and drew his face down to hers.

It was the first time Nils had kissed a woman. But in that long moment all his questions were answered.

Andreas saw Nils coming leaping over logs, whistling, and slapping his mittened hands together. When he came closer, Andreas could see a big smile spreading across his ruddy face. His breath made puffs of steam on the frigid air.

"You look like a man with good news!"

"She loves me, Andreas! Can you believe that she loves me!"

"Yes, I can believe that, you big, handsome ox!" Andreas grabbed him by the shoulders and shook him affectionately. "It looks like you'll have a bride before I do!"

"Well, you see, Andreas, I don't have to wait for my girl to grow up." They both laughed. "But we're going to wait until after sugar season. I want to earn enough money to take her on a canal boat ride to Rochester. Also, that will give everyone time to get used to the idea of Carolyn and me together."

Andreas was glad for Nils and Carolyn, but it made the time before he could propose to Susan seem a long time off. She wouldn't be 17 until July; how long before that was a respectable time to ask her? He knew so little of American customs, only that a girl should not be kissed before she was engaged.

In the meantime, he worked hard on his English. It hurt him deeply when he sometimes saw a slight frown on Susan's face at his mispronounced words. She'd correct him, then ask him to say the word with her.

The slate Andreas had given Susan for Christmas was a sensation. Parents came to the school and asked to see it. And for the children it was an honor when they earned the right to take the slate and write on it.

A mile away in the Norwegian colony, it was a difficult winter. The summer had brought sickness and death, the autumn, a fire and now the cold months saw their food supply diminishing rapidly. Most of them were ready to move on to someplace more hopeful. Some even talked of returning to Norway if it weren't for the humiliation of it. Cleng encouraged them to hang on, tried to bring them hope and prayed with them, but he was being urged by nearly every family to go West and seek a better place for them to farm. Talking Cleng into taking another trip was never difficult, so when he saw that moving the settlement was his only possibility of keeping them together, he agreed to start out as soon as the canal opened up.

The welfare of his friends was of major concern to Andreas. He wanted to do as much as he could to help them, knowing his lot was better than theirs. His farm, like Cleng's, was paid for and his close association with the Carys permitted him extra privileges.

A couple of times, he had left flour and potatoes with Cleng to pass out where they were most needed. But he must save every bit of money he could in order to build his cabin. He realized now it could not be the frame house he'd hoped for.

Sharing with the settlers was a subject of concern when Andreas visited Lars a week after the birth of their little girl, Inger, on February 18. They were as proud of their new daughter as they had been the first one. "We've lots of time to have sons," said Lars.

On the subject of the settlers' dire needs, Lars said, "Yes, Andreas, it's true we do have more than the others, but we can only give so much without neglecting our own responsibilities. Martha and I have set our sights on building a hospitality house. It will be done before long. If any of them get destitute, they're welcome to come here with us for awhile. We will have plenty of room and work for them to do to earn their keep. I've already told Cleng that. As for you, you're going that extra mile to educate the children and help them learn English. That's your share. Don't deny yourself a life of your own, marriage and family. Our friends will survive; they're from pretty hardy stock."

Andreas again took his good friend's advice, thinking it through as he returned from Rochester with new slate markers and a brand new lead pencil as well as another writing tablet. As he walked, he planned in detail how he would get everything ready to build his cabin so he could propose to Susan. He wanted to pick the right time and place. When would the moon be full, he wondered. The next day he slyly checked Cleng's copy of Poor Richard's Almanac.

Discussions of religion and places of worship hadn't come up much in his visits at the Carys. He knew they attended the little community church nearby. And they knew he spent his Sabbath with the Norwegians in

Quaker-like service at one of the cabins. Now it was time for him and Susan to make a decision together. Since Susan could not understand the Norwegian service, there seemed no choice but for him to go to her church. It troubled him greatly to think of leaving the Quaker religion which was so dear to him. But it wasn't as though he were leaving God. He knew the Carys were just as devout; only the outward form of worship was different.

Winter began to wane and the sugar sap started flowing. The settlers tapped their own trees, then left the women and children in charge while they went to work for others. Cleng was mapping out his journey and getting as much information as he could. Things were looking a little brighter over there, Andreas decided after a visit.

The schoolhouse was closed for the season, but Mr. Whitcomb paid Andreas an extra week's salary to do some repairs and to dig new pits for the privies. He also encouraged Andreas to live there as long as he liked, seeing that the place was better kept with him in it. But Andreas was anxious to move back to his little hut as soon as weather permitted because he was working long days and into the night with his own first sugar season in cooperation with the Carys.

The pile of logs he'd worked hard to accumulate during the winter was ready for at least a small cabin. Other rooms could come later.

Andreas and Susan saw little of each other during the sugar season except for a hasty wave or a few moments of conversation around the boiling kettles. Leander and Alexander were considered old enough this year to bring half-full pails of sap to the kettles. They worked hard and in competition, until monotony set in; then they had to be urged on.

One evening toward the last of the season, Susan and Andreas had a little time to themselves. They sat on upended chunks of wood near the fires and steam that warmed them.

"Susan," he began, "I think I'd like to attend your church sometime. I've never gone to a church house here in America, only to our Friends' service."

"Oh, Andrew," she said with surprise and pleasure, "I'd love to have you come. Would you like to come this Sunday?"

"Could I come to the evening service? That way I could attend the Meeting at Cleng's cabin as usual."

So it was planned that Andrew would walk with Susan to the seven o'clock evening service at the little Holley community church.

He dressed carefully in the deerskin tunic the Carys had given him at Christmas time. It was a beautiful shirt which Susan made with her mother's help. James had shot the deer and Mr. Cary and the little boys had tanned the hide, so it was really from all of them, Susan said. It had eyelets at the neck, laced through with leather strings, fringe around the bottom and at the end of the sleeves. He wished so much that his family could see it, but he had to be content with writing them a letter. By now, they must be getting the idea that this American teacher was very involved in his life.

The sermon seemed long, loud and demanding compared to the quiet informal Quaker services where anyone so moved offered up a prayer or dedication. Between those Quaker prayers were times of silence when the feeling of togetherness reached from soul to soul. In contrast, he learned from Preacher Haines that he could end in a fiery hell if he didn't mend his ways. But the presence of the girl at his side kept him from taking the words too literally. Occasionally she peered around her gray bonnet to discreetly smile at him. Out of a small window, he saw the moon rising above the trees and impatiently wished for the final prayer.

At the door upon leaving, the preacher, perspiring from an overheated stove as well as a fiery sermon, shook Andreas' hand and urged him to return. Then the two lovers were on their way home. Other couples and families were in front and behind them, turning at their own lanes or overtaking them. Andreas and Susan strolled along slowly, holding hands. Finally they were alone, no one behind them, no one in front of them.

Susan sighed deeply. "Oh, Andrew, isn't it a beautiful night? The freshness of spring in the air and the moonlight...I feel as though I never want to get home." His answer was a tighter grip on her hand. He could not yet trust his voice to speak.

A little further on, where the moon shone through the trees full on them, he stopped and pulled her to him. Overwhelmed by her loveliness and the fever within him, he said in a broken voice, "I had so lot of

135

words...beautiful words...think up to say to you...to ask you to marry me, but now all I think to say...is-s Susan...Susan, I love you, I want you be my wife...and live with me for ever and ever."

"Oh, Andrew," she whispered, tears glistening in the moonlight, "I've waited so long to hear those words."

He untied her bonnet, pushed it back and brought her to him, aware of her firm body next to his wildly beating heart. The fur muff dangled as her arms wound tightly round his neck. Her lips on his filled him with an ecstasy he'd never known before except in dreaming. Finally, they walked on, each with an arm still tight around the other. "Andrew...I forgot to say, yes."

"I like the way you show me better. I promise your father we wouldn't marry until you are seventeen. But I wish it was sooner."

Susan pulled away from him and stopped, then asked with amusement, "Now, when did you two decide that for me?"

He chuckled, "Long time ago. Before Fourth of July picnic last year."

"He never told me...nor did you!"

"I had to wait for right time." They walked along in loving embrace until Susan broke the silence again.

"Andrew...I want to get married in June, before it gets so hot."

"Oh, Susan, I want to marry you tomorrow if that be possible."

"Do you mind if I talk to Papa?"

"Of course not. But you better wait for the wedding until I get our cabin built. We have no place to live."

"Don't worry. I've got a feather bed and four pillows to finish. And the geese aren't even ready to pluck." They laughed happily and stopped to kiss again. They were engaged. Surely now nothing could keep them from marrying.

CHAPTER 17

Chastisement
From God?

ILS AND CAROLYN WERE MARRIED in Rochester on May 2. Ole Olsen had gone back to Norway to seek himself a wife and had made arrangements with Nils for the newlyweds to live in his house during his absence; while there, Nils would work for Lars in the boat business. They would decide later whether to keep their family in Rochester or eventually move back to the farm. Anne Marie and Sara were excited about going to the city to live and especially with their much-loved Uncle Nils.

Cleng hadn't been heard from since his departure to the West in April. The men put crops in, knowing their land would be worth more if they should want to sell and move West before harvest. If they had to stay, it would be needed.

Susan had little trouble convincing her father that she and Andrew wanted to marry in June rather than wait for the hot and humid month of July. The two men discussed the decision late one morning as they stood in the shade of a big beech tree along the rough road separating their properties, while the oxen drank from Bald Eagle Creek.

"I told Susan that it was up to her and her mother now, and you, of course, when the wedding should be," Mr. Cary said. "Looks to me like you two will hit it off all right."

"Thank you, Mr. Cary. I pray I always be worthy of that precious little girl. She is so wise and good."

"She is that, all right. How is your house coming?"

"I'm building small," Andreas said. "Nice and tight. What you call...cozy? Build more later."

"As the children come along," Mr. Cary smilingly added.

137

"Babies, yes. Hope for many babies." Andreas looked away, coloring. "Need more room then, sure."

They saw Susan in her calico sunbonnet come out of the house, pick up a hoe and start toward the garden. Seeing them, she leaned the hoe against a tree and came over, walking rapidly as if she were trying to keep from skipping or running. She came up between them breathing hard and smelling as fresh as the May morning and newly-made soap. Her father put his hand on her shoulder, caressing it lightly. Andreas could only look with love into her laughing brown eyes.

"Are you two standing out here making plans for the wedding? Mama and I have some ideas, too, you know."

"Not the wedding; we leave that to you. We talk about the house."

"When do I get to see it?"

"When it's done I let you see it." Andreas promised as Mr. Cary prepared to return to the field.

Andreas had little trouble finding help to build his house. Almost every evening one of the Norwegian men or older boys came to visit and help. Most often it was Ovee and Halvor; they seemed to hold a special affection for Andreas. Due to Susan's teaching and their desire to learn, the boys now spoke English reasonably well. The small Norwegian children, as well as Alexander and Leander, gathered and carried cobblestones for a large cistern in the cellar beneath the cabin. To them it was like play, laying the stones in the mortar for Andreas.

James, when he came home from his job in Kendall, also spent most of his free time helping. But he was getting anxious to leave for the West. He waited only because his sister begged him not to leave until after the wedding.

Susan's Uncle Ira gave Andreas invaluable help. He spent winters in New York City, but had a house on the tract of land owned jointly by him and his younger brother, Susan's father. Ira had already turned his farm over to his son-in-law, freeing him to work, wherever he wanted. He loved building things with wood, and he had taken a special liking to this quiet, hard-working Scandinavian and enjoyed working with him. Ira had the knowledge for detail work which Andreas lacked; fine cutting, fitting, joining, the kind of exactness which had given the settlers so much trouble in building their cabins.

Ira was impressed with features Andreas was planning to build into his house, and said the Norwegians must be very innovative people, wise with space. Andreas was building a bench with a back that moved from one side to the other. Facing one way it was a seat at the table. The back, pushed to the other side, made a warming bench by the fire. Andreas had trouble making the hinges work smoothly, but with Ira's expertise, the problem was quickly solved. A table Andreas planned was also hinged so that it could be hooked up flat to the wall, out of the way when not in use.

It was a busy time and Susan and Andreas saw little of each other except at the meals to which he was frequently invited. But one Saturday in mid-May, he decided to take the night off so that he and Susan could discuss their plans. The wedding date had been set for Friday, June 8.

"Isn't it exciting?" Susan said as they sat on a bench by the purple lilac bush outside the Cary house. "We'll have the first Norwegian-American wedding! We'll have to use some Norwegian customs along with American. What do they do at weddings in Norway?"

"I don't know very much about weddings. I only gone two or three. I like any kind of wedding, when it's with you." He pulled her closer; she laid her head on his shoulder.

"Three weeks seems like a long time to wait, doesn't it?"

"A long time."

They sat close for several moments, then Susan spoke timidly, "Andrew...?"

"What is it, my sweet?"

"The first night after our wedding...?"

"Are you afraid?" he asked gently.

"No," she said quickly. "I mean...could we spend it in your little sod hut?"

He laughed. "Instead of the nice house I build for you?"

"Oh, I'm looking forward to our little house, but I've wanted to sleep inside the hut since I first saw it. It's kind of like a little playhouse."

"I think that is little girl Susan talking now. But that's all right. I like to play house with little Susan. I will see what I can make of it. Maybe make a wedding...what you say?"

"Bower? Wedding bower?"

"Does that mean like flower?"

"Sort of, I guess. I'm not sure what it means. I've just read it in a poem."

After a few thought-filled moments, Andrew spoke again. "Might be best place for us. Some Norske boys and maybe your brothers might come and bang pans, ring bells, make noise by the cabin to bother us. We'll be in the hut all the time not hearing them."

"That would be fun and a joke on them," Susan exclaimed. "Do you think all of the Norwegians will come?"

"I think so, if you want them to."

"Of course I want them to."

"They dress different...don't speak much English."

"I love it when they wear their colorful clothes. As to the way they talk..." she raised her head, looked at him and began circling his beard from ear to ear with her forefinger, "I loved you before you could speak English."

He pressed her to him. "Oh, Su-suun, I loved you from the first day when I see you were not just a little girl gathering up the eggs." Their impatience for each other was as powerful as the heady, sweet scent of lilacs behind them.

By staying busy, the weeks flew by for Andreas. He rose at dawn to work in the fields, cultivating his few cleared acres planted to wheat, corn and potatoes. His crops were coming along well and he wanted them to be weed-free by the day of the wedding when surely the men, both Norwegian and American, would be observing them.

The cabin now had a roof, door and windows. He moved his sleeping pallet inside and dreamed of the time soon when Susan would be beside him in the bed he was building. It was in a corner, the foot end enclosed from floor to ceiling, a deep boxlike bed which would hold Susan's feather tick. Since it was high off the floor with storage space beneath, he would build detachable steps for use as a stepstool during the day.

Andreas spent all of one rainy day carving scrolls on the canopy over the bed and across the fireplace mantel. Ira appeared and said he was going to build a low, wide corner cupboard for Susan to store her dishes, with room on top for washing up. He had already made a shelf beside the fireplace for making bread to be baked in the dutch oven built into one end of the fireplace.

Two days before the wedding, Andrew swept out shavings, tidied up the cabin and went to invite Susan for her first look.

"Oh, Andrew, I'm dying to see it! Can we go right away? Shall we take the feather tick and see if it fits? When can I take my dishes? Mama, do you want to go with us?"

"No, dear," Lydia Cary said, glancing at a grinning Andrew, then laughing at her grown-up little girl's excitement. "It is right that you two inspect your new home alone. Perhaps tomorrow you can take me over. Why don't you take the hand cart, put the feather tick and pillows on it with the dishes on top?"

So they loaded up the cart. When Andrew went to get the feather tick from Susan's room, he saw a long white garment on her bed, a froth of lace beside it as though it were being sewn on. At first he thought it was her wedding dress, then realized it was probably a nightgown. He tried not to look at it.

Susan hurried along the path ahead of him as he pushed the cart carefully to avoid as many ruts as possible. "Wait for me!" he called.

"I'm trying, but my feet won't stop running." At the sight of the cabin she stopped and gazed in rapture. He caught up to her and she said softly, "It's just beautiful. Our own little house."

He set the cart down carefully and put his arm around her. "It not all done, but we've got the rest of our lives to work on it."

"Let's go inside," she said pulling him by the hand. He lifted the latch and she stepped in, and looked around with open mouthed amazement. "Why, it's like a little...fairy house."

"I thought you'd like it. It's Norske house, blessed by the good *nisse*."

"You and your trolls!" She hugged him. "Let's bring in the feather tick and see if it fits."

It did.

He showed her how the convertible bench worked, and how the table could be hooked up out of the way. She was thrilled with everything. Together they unpacked the new white dishes and Susan lovingly placed them in the cupboard Uncle Ira had made.

"Papa and Uncle Ira are getting us something special for a wedding present, but I don't know what it is. Do you?"

"No, I heard nothing. They've done so much already. I wish they would not do more."

"Me, too, but I know they will. It's something big, that has to be gone after. I heard them talking and they stopped when I came up to them. I'm kind of hoping it's a stove."

The dishes in place, they left reluctantly. "Is it all right if I bring Mama over to see it?" Susan asked as Andreas latched the door behind them.

"It is your house now. You come and go when you want."

"We'll bring covers and make up the bed," she said eagerly. "I'm anxious to see how my quilt looks."

"You still want to sleep first night in my hut?" he asked.

"Oh, yes, Andrew. I've wanted to for so long."

Thunder rumbled in the distance and Susan and Andrew looked out at heavy gray clouds forming overhead. Susan frowned anxiously. "What if it rains on the wedding? We've planned everything for outdoors."

"Then I guess we'll have to get married in a pretty tight squeeze in the house or barn." Noting the bleak look on Susan's face, he added. "I think the rain will come and be all over by wedding time."

He stopped the empty cart, picked her up, held her close for a moment, then set her on it. She held on, laughing as she jolted and bounced the rest of the way home, where her mother met them at the porch. "I have to keep her feet from running away from me," Andreas said grinning.

For the rest of the humid afternoon, as he worked on the sod hut, thunder continued to rumble and lightning scratched the sky. But there were only a few sprinkles of rain, though the sky did not clear.

Suddenly, a volley of pebbles fell on him. He looked up to see who was throwing them, and saw that they were coming out of the sky. Completely frightened, he stood paralyzed as the stones stung his face, his back and arms. Finally, he crawled inside the hut. They came faster and faster, beating on the roof of the nearby cabin and making a fearful racket in the trees. They were stacking up outside on the ground. What was God trying to tell him? That he and Susan were not supposed to marry? He remembered Ole Olsen's warning before he left for Norway to find a wife: God doesn't want us to mix like that.

Reaching out through the opening, he picked up a handful of the clear, white stones. They felt cold like ice and melted in his hand. How could there be an ice storm in the summer time?

Then the phenomenon stopped as fast as it had begun. The icy pebbles lay all around, an inch or two deep. He hurried to the Cary farm. But before he reached the clearing, the pebbles disappeared, making him even more frightened. On just his land, they were meant for him! He went back and scooped up a large handful, then ran to Mr. Cary's barn where Andreas found him feeding the stock.

"What's the matter, Andrew, you're pale as a ghost?"

"I think maybe I see ghost or maybe wrath of God. These little stones come falling out of sky like rain. Just on my place," Andreas added tremulously.

"That's hail, Andrew. Don't they have that in Norway?"

"You say...hell?"

"No, no, hailstones. Frozen rain. Is that a word Susan didn't teach you?"

"Ice storm in the summer time?"

"You'll have to have Susan look it up in one of her books. I don't know why, but it often hits just a small area. I didn't hear any over here. Was it hard enough to hurt your corn and wheat?"

That possibility had not occurred to him. His spirits plummeted. "I don't know. I was too afraid to look one way or the other. I'll go see now."

"I'll go with you. I can see how a hail storm would scare the bejebers out of you if you didn't know what was going on." They approached the cornfield and since it was nearly dark they couldn't see the foot-high corn until they were up to it.

Andreas groaned. The beautiful weed-free corn was in shreds. Mr. Cary put his hand on his young neighbor's shoulder. "Some of it might come back."

"The wheat and potatoes," Andreas said lamely, "would it take them, too?"

"Well, let's go see. It's hard to say. Your cornfield could have been on the very edge of it." But they found the wheat flattened as well.

"Wait a minute," John Cary said, hurrying along the edge of the field. "I think it's only this side that got hit. Look over here, you've got wheat left. And the potato patch is only about half gone."

But it was small consolation. Mr. Cary invited him over to the house for some coffee and companionship to cheer him up, but Andreas politely refused, saying he had so many things yet to do. "Well, don't worry too much," John Cary said. "Don't let it spoil your wedding. Ira and I have come through tough luck, time and again, hail and dry summers, wet summers, late cold spring weather. We've had it all, but we're still a kickin' pretty lively."

"Thanks," Andreas managed. He stood for awhile watching his father-in-law-to-be walking back through the woods; then he trudged toward his cabin.

It was too dark to do any further outside work and Andreas didn't have the heart for it anyway. He went inside and threw himself on the pallet.

His corn ruined and part of his wheat and potatoes! How could he support Susan and make a nice home for them with crops like that? But that wasn't all that was troubling him. For the past few days, before he dropped off to sleep or when he was eating alone, he had had this vacant, lonely feeling.

Homesickness?

A tear slipped out of his eye, and he knew that was it. Only one more day before the wedding. He was marrying a girl who was as sweet and dear and loving as any man could hope for. But his mother and none of his family could be there. They would probably never meet her. He missed them all so terribly.

He tried to be thankful that his cousin, Gudmund, would be with him. When Susan was trying to decide who should stand up with them, it was Mrs. Cary's suggestion that they ask Gudmund and Gurine. Even though they spoke little English, there wouldn't be much need of it. They were a good-looking couple and their Norwegian costumes would add a colorful accent.

Andreas didn't know how many other settlers were coming, if any. He hadn't even heard if Lars and Martha could make it. He tried to find out by asking around who was coming, but all he got were evasive answers: "Not sure yet" or "Oh...maybe."

"Do you think I should take time off just to see you get hitched?" Big Nels had asked jovially.

Maybe they weren't giving the real reason, Andreas thought miserably. Maybe they weren't coming because Susan was not one of them.

He had apologized to Mrs. Cary because he didn't know how many of his friends were coming for the feast. But she assured him, "Don't worry about it. There will be plenty for all who come."

Then there were his clothes. He didn't know if his outfit would look right at an American wedding. He had borrowed from Gudmund, who had extra clothes left from his father-in-law. Since the Carys suggested Norwegian dress for Gurine and Gudmund, Gurine and her mother helped him put together an outfit, that was part American, part Norwegian.

Would his idea for the hut work? Would Susan like it? Then his mind returned to the ruined crops. The wedding ring had taken most of his money. Now what?

Finally, he rose to his knees. "Lord, if you're trying to tell me something, you'll have to make it a little plainer. This thick Norwegian head does not understand hail storms that ruin crops and wipe out hard, honest work. Surely it can't be wrong for two people, whose love is as sure as ours, to marry. Even if we were born in different countries. I try to do thy bidding, Lord, but when I'm as lost and lonesome as I am tonight, you'll have to give me a little boost."

He lay back in the pitch darkness and gradually felt a warmth filling the emptiness inside his chest. Yes, of course his mother and brothers were thinking about him and his bride and were praying for them. Maybe someday he could take Susan to see them. And the loss of his crops? Well, he'd just have to figure out something after the wedding. Mr. Cary's words come back to him, "We're still kicking pretty lively."

Suddenly he realized he was hungry. He got up, ate some clabbered milk with a sprinkle of sugar and a piece of bread, returned to his bed and went to sleep almost at once.

A short distance away, Susan lay in her bed after prayers. Tears dripped on her pillow as she whispered as though Andrew could hear her: I wanted to go to you, my sweetheart, but Papa wouldn't let me. He said you wanted to be alone. How frightened you must have been about the hail. And your crops ruined. But don't worry, we'll both work hard and make up for it.

Finally, she quieted. She began wondering what tomorrow night would be like. A quiver of delight went through her, followed by wonderment and a little fear. Did it hurt? How could it help but hurt a little? But she'd be brave. Andrew was so good and kind and she did want to please him. He had enough trouble right now.

She sighed and went on thinking. I'll be a woman after tomorrow. No more skipping and running around like a little girl. How soon will we have a baby of our own? Oh, I hope it doesn't take too long. And I wonder what it will look like.

CHAPTER 18

The
Wedding

T HE NERVOUS BRIDEGROOM took one last look inside the hut, checked his pocket for the ring, latched the cabin door, then joined Gudmund and they started down the path. The wedding ceremony was planned for two o'clock. Gurine and her mother would be along later.

Andreas was so uneasy about the ordeal ahead that he hardly noticed the sweet forest smells and sounds around him, blossoming wild flowers and a symphony of bird songs. A beautiful June day with the lushness of early summer everywhere.

"Does my hair and beard look all right?"

"You look just fine," Gudmund answered. "Maybe even that American word, handsome."

"How many of the others are coming?"

"I'm not sure. But don't worry, a couple of Stokka cousins can handle it. Now relax. It'll all be over in a few hours, then just think what's waiting for you. It's worth it," Gudmund grinned.

The Cary relatives and neighbors seemed to be there already. Through Pastor Haines, a general invitation had been extended to the congregation of the Holley church, so most of the guests were strangers to Andreas. Clusters of men stood about the yard. Dressed up children sat giggling on benches. Susan was nowhere in sight, but then he didn't expect her to be. Andreas nodded and spoke to people as he and Gudmund passed them.

Nearing the house, they heard Susan call in a loud whisper, "Andrew...over here." He saw her face outlined by her bedroom window and moved cautiously in that direction.

"Oh, Andrew...you look so handsome!"

Gudmund nudged him. "Didn't I tell you?"

"I didn't know you had all those clothes!"

"I don't." He pointed at Gudmund.

"They're very nice. I'm scared, Andrew. Are you?"

He nodded. "Can you come out so we be scared together?"

"Mama said I must stay in here and just watch for awhile. Will you stay close by?"

"I'll be right here until someone tell me to move."

Being close to Susan and fortified with her compliments, Andreas felt a little more at ease. He watched, waited and prayed to see some Norwegians coming. Surely Ovee and Halvor and the older school children would come, if their parents would let them. Instead of thinking about it, he tried to concentrate on the people around them. Who were the men visiting with Mr. Cary? Did he recognize any of them from the church service? Where was James?

The women were going in and out carrying dishes, silverware, cups, pickles, eggs, and covered dishes. They must be expecting a lot more people. He would be so embarrassed if none of the Norwegians showed up. Mrs. Cary saw them and paused long enough to say, "My, you look nice, Andrew. Susan does too. She probably told you I'm making her stay in until almost time for the ceremony."

Over the talking, laughing and hustling about, Andreas thought he heard music and bells coming from the woods, familiar music, or was it just wishful thinking? Other people turned to look, and he saw Mrs. Cary smiling at Gudmund. Aware of the Norwegians' love of jokes and tricks, he guessed the secret. It was all he could do to keep the tears back as the grandly decorated wagon came into view. It was loaded with women and children dressed in full Norwegian dress, their costumes accented by pieces of jewelry saved for very special occasions.

Henrik and Big Nels stood in the middle of the wagon playing the Norwegian tunes Andreas had grown up with. The other men marched along side, singing, laughing, and waving. Cornelius' big wagon, even the harness and oxen, were decorated with every kind of bright ribbon.

Andreas took in the dear familiar faces – Lars and Martha, even sister Siri and the babies; Nils and Carolyn and the girls; Betsy and little Susan, specially dressed for the occasion; and all the school children.

Susan called from her spot at the window, "You knew about this didn't you, Mama? That's why Ovee and Halvor were here talking to you, wasn't it? Why didn't you tell me? Oh, Mama, can't I come out now?" Lydia Cary laughed and nodded.

The wagon stopped at the edge of the yard and so did the music and bell-ringing. Led by Uncle Ira, everyone clapped and cheered.

While attention was on the wagon, Susan appeared at the doorway. She wore a white dress with brown and yellow ribbons laced through eyelets at the neck and hem. The Norwegian brooch, Andreas' gift to her, sparkled at her throat. A yellow ribbon was twined through her thick brown hair, which she wore in a chignon low on her neck. A cinched waist emphasized her full breasts and round hips.

Andreas was nearly overcome with pride. This lovely American girl was about to become his wife, and in the presence of his friends. "My beautiful, beautiful brown-eyed Susan," he murmured as they walked hand in hand toward the wagon.

Men were helping women down, many of whom were carrying covered dishes and wooden Norwegian *tines* of food. Big Nels was first to offer his hand. "Congratulations, my friend."

Andreas shook his hand warmly and said, "I was afraid you wouldn't make it."

"We just wanted to surprise you." As Nels laughed, Andreas noticed that the colorful vest had more slack than when he'd worn it in Norway. "You never saw a Norske pass up an opportunity to go to a wedding, did you? Especially a friend who's done as much for us as you have."

Andreas could say no more; he had to move on. "That's a fancy *kubberulle* you got there Cornelius; it would outshine all the boats at a Midsummer's Eve Festival." Cornelius pulled one of the ribbons from the oxen's harness and wound it around Andreas' neck, then jovially shook his hand.

Susan hugged all her little school children and her namesake, Susan. She felt honored by the presence of the Norwegian colony – Andrew's close friends. But at the same time, she felt strange that she soon might be expected to become a part of these people so colorfully dressed in foreign costumes. She was too full of joy to even think of it now.

The Norwegians grew quiet as they moved toward the house. The oxen, left behind with the deserted wagon, shook their massive heads, protesting all the decorations hung on them. Mr. Cary suggested unhitching them so they could be taken to the barn. James, who was nearby, went to help Cornelius.

Pulling Andreas by the hand, Susan hurried to where Mr. and Mrs. Cary were talking with the preacher. "Could we have the ceremony on the pretty wagon, Mama?" Lydia looked questioningly at Pastor Haines.

"Certainly, if you want," the preacher said.

"But it's in the wrong place down there, Susan," her mother reasoned.

"Oh, dear, and they've already taken away the oxen," lamented Susan.

"Let's move it anyway," Mr. Cary said. "There's plenty of men here."

"Sure," Andreas said, and began passing the word among the Norwegians.

The men, Norwegian and American together, surrounded the heavy vehicle. Under the direction of Cornelius and amidst laughter, exaggerated grunting and misdirected moves, the wagon rolled into place beside the lilac bush.

The preacher swung himself up on it and waved his hands for quiet. "It seems our plans have been changed a little. The bride wants the ceremony up here. If you will gather around, we'll get the necessary people assembled to solemnize this marriage. Then the merrymaking can continue."

After a final straightening and smoothing by her mother, Susan was lifted up on the wagon. Her father handed her a bouquet of black-eyed Susans. Gurine was lifted up and the men leaped aboard. Andreas whispered to Susan, "I think your mama and papa should be up here, too."

So chairs were brought and the parents, after protests, were persuaded to join them.

The crowd grew quiet, but the birds, attracted by the Norwegians' music, twittered and sang from the edge of the forest. And somewhere in a nearby pasture, a mother ewe bleated to her young lamb that all was well. Susan glanced at her mother. They had hoped and prayed for a day so near-perfect. She knew there were tears hiding behind the calm expression. The solemnity of the occasion did not escape Susan. Here was a major event in her life, one she could never regret nor turn away from.

The ceremony began. Rev. Haines, his voice more gentle than in his shouted sermon, read scripture, instructed, admonished, asked for promises, each to the other and both to God. Andreas tried to take every word to heart, realizing he was privileged beyond measure. A final prayer, then Andreas slipped the gold ring on her finger as she looked up at him with the promises of a lifetime. He kissed her tenderly. The preacher pronounced them "Mr. and Mrs. Andrew Stangeland."

The fiddle and accordion music resumed and the wedded couple climbed down, to be engulfed with congratulations, hugs and the babble of English and Norwegian voices. Some of the women hurried to get food to the table while others chased flies and children away from it.

Andreas and Susan led the procession to the wedding dinner and the feasting began. People ate at tables, on stumps, on the grass, wherever there was a place to settle and balance a heaping plate. After all had eaten, Aunt Helen, wife of Ira, began passing a plate of fancy little cakes she had brought from New York. Andreas tasted of the cloud-soft cakes and was reminded of the trays of sweets at his brother's bakery. He forced back a pang of homesickness and smiled at Susan who was exclaiming over the decorated confections.

Empty platters and dishes were removed from the long table and presents were brought and placed upon it. Most of the gifts were unwrapped, treasured pieces brought from the giver's home, and intended to honor the couple and help them set up housekeeping.

Susan and Andreas admired each gift in turn, a teapot painted with pansies, an embroidered "HOME SWEET HOME" hanging, hooked wedding spoons, a hymn book, baskets, lovely glass pieces, a vase, a cheese box and a butter mold.

151

"Thank you all so very, very much," Susan said. Andreas bowed deeply.

Daniel and Gudmund went quietly to get something covered with sailcloth. Andreas had noticed the men taking it off the wagon earlier. As they set the object down in front of Andreas, he looked questioningly at his grinning friends. Then Gudmund pulled off the cover. It was the stove with an oven, freshly blackened and polished.

"First thing bought in America," Andreas explained shakily.

"We're coming over to your house for some loaf bread," Betsy called out. Andreas smiled broadly and nodded, "Susan bakes better bread than I do, and we'll invite you all over for some of it."

At that moment they heard the slap-slap of harness to horseflesh. People turned toward the barn. Ira Cary sat grandly in a two-seater, shiny black buggy, a new black-snake crop lightly touching the back of a dappled gray horse led by John Cary. They stopped just short of the crowd. Leander and Alexander were sent to bring Susan and Andrew. Ira crawled out and handed the crop to Susan as John handed the bridle reins to Andrew. "Oh, Papa, Papa...Uncle Ira...is this ours?" Susan cried.

"All yours." Uncle Ira bowed with a flourish.

"No racing now, son," John said affectionately to a silent Andreas, too overwhelmed to speak.

Finally, he was able to stutter, "Too over...too much...thank you. No...no racing...Papa," he grinned.

The celebrating continued with more music, rides in the new buggy, visiting, laughing, chasing, flirting. The Norwegians were shy, the Americans bolder, but all were enjoying themselves.

Betsy beckoned her husband and Henrik to a corner of the yard and started a Norwegian polka. She took Ovee for a partner and told Halvor to bring Susan and show her the steps. Susan loved it, caught on quickly and was soon dancing with everyone.

More Norwegians joined them, women with white head dresses and *bunads* of colorful waists and skirts. Men and boys in bright vests buttoned over full-sleeved embroidered shirts, wore breeches held tightly at the knee with gold braid above their long socks. Betsy urged more Americans into the circle. Soon nearly every young person was dancing to the sprightly Scandinavian music.

Andreas stood talking to Lars and Martha as they watched Susan stepping to the music, ribbons flying. Martha said, "A lot of water has gone under the bridge since that day you first brought me here. Now I have Lars back and my nice house. And you're married to Susan."

"I keep thinking this must be a dream," Andreas shook his head. "I can't believe we're actually married. From the very first it didn't seem possible."

"You've made history, Andreas," said Lars. "The first Norwegian-American marriage. If you hurry, you might get to have the first half-American baby."

"Lars!" Martha scolded. Andreas, embarrassed, looked away.

Lars hastened to change the subject. "Did anyone tell you yet that Kari and Cornelius got a letter from Cleng yesterday?"

"No," Andreas was surprised. "What did he have to say; did he find anything?"

"He seems to have found a perfect place for the group to move to. It's south of the town of Chicago, he says." Andreas remembered Cleng's story about the village that was mostly swamp. Lars continued, "It's all fertile soil on a treeless prairie next to a river, he writes."

"That sounds like good news. When will he be home?"

"He wanted to do a little more exploring and won't be home until later in the summer. He thinks they shouldn't plan on moving until next spring."

Andreas almost wished Lars hadn't shared the news. It momentarily turned his own thoughts westward when he wanted this day to center entirely on Susan.

"Look who's dancing with Susan now," Martha laughed.

Andreas could hardly see his wife with Big Nels' beefy arms draped around her. She hardly came past his middle. "You better go rescue her." Martha gave him a little shove.

"Dance with her in front of all these people?" Andreas protested.

"Sure, you're a good dancer. I almost wish I could join them." She glanced at Lars and quickly added, "But we're strict Quakers now, these worldly pleasures are behind us."

Andreas worked his way into the group and laid his hand on Big Nels' shoulder. "Aw, Andreas, we just got started and she dances like a feather."

"You better go start a hat dance," Andreas laughed, as he positioned himself in front of Susan, and gave her a quick squeeze before they broke into the dance. Nels was already dancing with Betsy.

People stopped dancing to watch the newlyweds, then applauded. Andreas felt clumsy beside his perfectly tuned partner, but his several years' advantage doing those same steps favored him.

When one tune ended and before another started, Susan asked breathlessly, "What is a hat dance; is it some kind of joke?"

"No," Andreas laughed, "but it's very difficult. Big Nels and Gudmund are the only men in this group can do it, that I know of, unless Ovee or Halvor has learned. It takes weeks of practice and then you have to keep it up."

"My goodness, what do they have to do?" Susan asked again.

"A girl stands on a chair or ladder and holds a hat on a stick about eight feet off the ground or floor. The man is supposed to dance and then jump high enough to knock it off."

"That high! Can you do it?"

"No, I used to try, but I gave up long time ago."

The late summer dusk was creeping over the forest as the next dance started. Susan bobbed over to Andrew and whispered, "Andrew, let's slip away while the party is still going on so they won't miss us."

"Sound good to me," Andreas said eagerly. They deftly danced to a nearby stump where she sat down laughing and fanning herself. When attention was turned away from them, she whispered in his ear, "I'll meet you behind the house in about fifteen minutes. I want to pick up my things and tell Mama we're going."

"I tell James to care for horse and buggy. We can take the long way around so no one will see us."

Susan changed into a darker frock and rejoined her husband. She carried a towel-covered basket and a satchel which Andreas suspected contained the nightgown he'd accidentally seen. "Mama sent along some fried chicken, cakes and lemonade for us later." She handed the basket to him.

They made a hasty exit to the woods, turning back once to see Lydia and John Cary watching from the back door, in the deepening twilight. Susan threw them a kiss and Andreas bowed and waved.

"Do we get to stay in the hut tonight?"

"If you still want." He hoped it was as he had left it and that it would meet with her approval. At the clearing, Andreas put the basket down, took the satchel from her and set it on the ground also. "Welcome home, Mrs. Andrew Stangeland." He took her in his arms, kissed her and they clung together, daring now to enjoy the intimacy. He spoke hesitantly, "Susuun, my sweet...if I do anything tonight...or any night...to hurt you...or you don't like...will you sure to tell me don't?"

She colored slightly, looked down, then up at him with a shy smile. "I promise."

They hesitated at the entrance of the hut and he nodded for her to look inside. She stooped to look. Even in the fading daylight, she could see the violets and daisies planted, some of them upside down, all over the interior of the hut. The fresh smell of earth and wildflowers permeated even the clean sheepskins that covered the floor.

She backed out and trembled as she looked at him with wonder and amazement. "Oh, Andrew, it's just beautiful! No bride ever had a nicer wedding bed. Our...our little flower-bower. May I go in alone for a few minutes?"

"Take all the time you want, sweetheart. I'll be right here until you call me."

She disappeared inside with the satchel. He sat down on the log outside. Turning toward the cornfield, he grimaced, then tried to erase all troublesome thoughts from his mind. He looked at the nearly-finished cabin so lovingly built. Would he and Susan, and their children, live there for the rest of their lives together?

Shortly he heard her call softly, timidly, "Andrew...you may come in now."

He hesitated one long moment, took a deep breath, arose and peered inside, expecting to see her in the lacy nightgown. His breath caught in his throat. She lay before him slightly curled and smiling, her bare white skin glowing in the semi-darkness, her long dark hair falling around her. The nightgown lay at her side. Without further hesitation he hurriedly removed his clothes, shoved them through the door and to one side, then crept in and tied the canvas across the opening.

He lay down, slid an arm beneath her shoulders, savoring the feel of her bare, slightly moist skin. His hand cupped around her full breast, the touch he'd yearned for for so long. She inched closer to him, murmuring, "We'll always be together now, my love."

PART 3

CHAPTER 19

Dinner At the
Cobblestone Inn

"OH, ANDREW," SUSAN SIGHED as the two sat over supper one evening a couple of weeks after their marriage.

He looked up quickly. He loved the way she spoke his name. It suddenly struck him that as he had grown closer to Susan and her family, his new American name had come to be as comfortable to him as had the Norwegian version he had used all his life. In fact, twice now he had introduced himself to strangers saying, "My name is Andrew Stangeland" and not found it strange at all.

"Is-s something wrong, my sweet?"

"Oh, no!" She shook her head. "I was just thinking how much I'd miss the children this fall, and going to the school."

"Maybe Mr. Whitcomb would let you teach again, if you really want to."

"No, I wouldn't even ask. A married woman? Do married women teach school in Norway?"

"No women teachers. All men I know of."

Susan shrugged. "I guess we're supposed to stay home and have babies."

"Do you think maybe...already?"

"I...can't tell yet." Susan blushed and turned to the stove for the warm gingerbread she had brought from her mother's kitchen. "Are you going to be caretaker again?"

"No, I'll stay here with you. I have a house and beautiful bride now, I didn't have last winter. I want to clear more land and farm. Build more house. Maybe someday I'll have you a real *gudbrandsdal*."

"A what?" she asked.

"*Gudbrandsdal*," he laughed. "In Norway, that is a rich farmer house with a courtyard for people inside. Animals and creatures outside."

"Do you think your corn is going to come back, Andrew?"

He looked out the window and shook his head grimly. It wasn't something he liked to think about. "Papa and Uncle Ira went with me today to look at it. They say no use to wait; I should plant something else before too late."

"But what could it be this late?"

"Papa said buckwheat, it's not too late for that. Uncle Ira say why not put in some cabbage and turnips."

"But those are garden vegetables," Susan frowned.

"He thinks being close to the canal, maybe we can ship some east to port along the way or maybe even New York." Andrew did not sound confident. "If not, he say they make good stock feed, and sauerkraut."

"Ten barrels of sauerkraut lined up along the house this fall. Phe-ewe!" She held her nose and they both laughed.

"Whatever I plant this time, I'll keep my hat on like good Norske."

"What difference will that make?"

"Sowing seed in ground iss-iss like praying..."

"Sacred?"

He nodded. "Maybe I should have remembered that when I planted the corn."

"I doubt if that is the reason it hailed," she said, going for more coffee from the new blue coffeepot on the stove.

"We'll soon have milk of our own now anyway," Andrew announced. "The calf is almost old enough to eat grass away from her mama. Next year we'll have two cows."

"And I've got 30 baby chickens, six little turkeys and two brooding hens on goose eggs," added Susan proudly.

"I want to get some lambs now to grow up for wool and more lambs."

"No goats though," said Susan.

"You don't think you like to straddle a goat backwards to milk her like little Norske milkmaid?" Susan emphatically shook her head. "All right, I keep on getting goat cheese from Bertha and Daniel."

"Are they one of the families planning to move West next spring?"

"I think so," Andrew replied. "Just about all of them are thinking about it, but waiting for Cleng to get back with more..."

"Details," Susan put in. "Do you wish you were going?"

It was a question, even in his own mind, which always made him uncomfortable. "Not without my beautiful wife," he said evasively, but smiling.

"I doubt if I'd make a very good pioneer."

"Then we stay here beside your mama and papa. If we change our minds later, there is time for that."

Andrew's last comment troubled Susan as she cleared the table after he'd gone to shut up the animals for the night. Did he really want to move West, or was he reluctant to see the colony move away without him? With a heavy heart, she thought about leaving her home and moving somewhere where they'd be surrounded only by Norwegians. Not now, or ever, she hoped.

Andrew's replanted field grew even better than he'd expected. There was ample rain in July, the cabbages grew in bulbous rows and the buckwheat shot up until bushy heads appeared. Some of the Norwegians offered to trade some of their corn, when it was ready, for enough buckwheat flour for breakfast cakes. They laughed at his huge garden of cabbage and Andrew laughed with them, but hoped something good would come of it.

One day he rode the horse down to the canal in Albion. There was a barge docked and the captain, identified by his cap, was just coming ashore. In his halting English, Andrew asked him if he thought there was a market for cabbage anywhere along his route.

"Cabbage!" the captain scoffed. "Who in hell would want to buy cabbage?"

Andrew was embarrassed, but stumbled on. "I...I just thought maybe eating places or factory...where they make sauerkraut."

The captain looked at him, studying him for a few moments. "Well, now it could be. Since you're a furriner, I don't mind helping you out. Let me do some askin' around." Then he lowered his voice to a confidential pitch, "I'll tell you, Norske, where you could make some real money. Get you together some apples, any kind'l do. Make you some cider and let it get hard. Or better yet, cook up some whiskey. Find somebody that knows how to put together a still, make some good likker. Now that's what sells. I could make you a rich man quick and a healthy profit for myself."

Andrew began shaking his head before the man had even finished speaking. "No...no. This Norske doesn't drink whiskey or deal in hard drink. We have Quaker beliefs, no strong drink."

The captain shrugged. "Well then, cabbage it is, I guess. Tell you what. I'll see what I can find out and leave a message for you with Lemuel at the store here. Check with him in a couple of weeks."

Andrew was exuberant as he rode home on the dappled gray horse named Dolly. He didn't want to tell anyone yet about the possibility of a New York market. Surprise them, even Susan.

Susan spent most of her days at her mother's, where Andrew often joined them for dinners at noon. There were days when he'd rather pick up something to eat in their own house, but he didn't want to seem ungrateful, so he'd trudge over for dinner, then walk back again for a few minutes' rest before returning to the fields. Today she was again at her mother's when Andrew got home.

Two weeks after Andrew met with the barge captain, he invited Susan to go with him on a trip to Albion. He said they would make a pleasure trip of it and stop at the Village Inn on Ridge Road for dinner. Susan was ecstatic. "Oh, I've always wanted to eat there. But it will cost so much!"

"We'll use the wedding money my mother sent."

Susan wore her wedding dress and Andrew dressed in his best also. Then riding grandly in the buggy behind Dolly, they arrived at the large and impressive Cobblestone Inn. Andrew felt like a king, escorting his wife to a table near the large stone fireplace now filled with ferns for the summer.

Susan looked around excitedly at the rich velvet curtains, white damask tablecloths, shining silver and crystal. It had been hot and dusty on the road, but it was cool and pleasant inside.

Andrew was shocked at the prices on the menu. He saw Susan frown and reached for her hand. "This is present from my mother. She wants us to have the best."

Susan nodded. They ordered beef steak.

While they were waiting for their dinner, Susan said, "Andrew, if I write a letter to your mother and tell her about this nice place and our dinner and...and how much I love you, would you write it in Norwegian for me?"

Andrew nodded with a fullness in his heart.

Before their dinner was finished, the proprietor came to the dining room and stopped a minute at each table, including theirs. Susan did most of the talking, explaining that Andrew was Norwegian and that they had just been married a couple of months. She mentioned that her former name was Cary.

"Cary? Any relation to Ira Cary?"

"He's my uncle," answered Susan.

"You don't say! Why, I've known Ira for years. My wife and I are quite often with him and Helen in New York. We spend our winters there like they do." He looked more closely at Andrew. "I remember now. He helped you build your house, didn't he?"

"Yes. He helped very big...much," Andrew stammered. He had been trying to understand all of the rapid conversation.

"He thought you had some pretty clever ideas about things. Well, well, this calls for a celebration. I think I have something for you two." He winked at Andrew and walked toward the kitchen.

They watched him, wondering. Susan whispered, "What if he brings us some wine?"

Andrew shrugged, "I guess we have to try and drink some of it."

They finished their meal, but he did not return. "He must have forgotten about it, thank goodness," said Susan.

The friendly serving girl in black dress with starched white frill in her hair came to pick up the dishes. "You wait now, Mr. Fuller has ordered something special for you," she said, moving away.

Susan looked around. "Maybe it's the cakes. I see other people eating them."

The waitress returned with a silver tray, two small plates upon it. She set before each of them a cake and beside it a satiny mound of what Andrew thought was a molded pudding.

"Ice cream!" Susan exclaimed.

"Is it really?" Andrew touched it lightly with a finger. "I've never tasted it before, have you?"

"Yes, a few times when I visited Uncle Ira and Aunt Helen in New York. But I didn't know they had it here. Isn't this just perfect?"

"It is so cold and...flat?" Andrew said after tasting it.

"Smooth," Susan corrected.

"When I was little boy, we used to put sugar in cream and set it outdoors in winter to freeze, then stir and eat it. But it was never like this."

"Sometimes in winter we make snow ice cream, the little boys and I. We pour cream and sugar over fresh snow, but it isn't thick, just soupy."

Before they finished the cake and ice cream, Mr. Fuller returned.

"How do you like the ice cream?" he asked.

"Very good, thank you."

"Delicious. Do you always have it?" Susan asked.

"No, we can't always get ice to freeze it. But we have some friends visiting from New York and I made a special trip to the ice house in Albion to get some. It was left over from last night, packed in ice and salt."

When they had finished every melted drop of ice cream and crumb of cake, Susan smiled at Andrew. "Thank you, Mama Stangeland and Mr. Fuller. I feel full and pampered."

Andrew paid the bill and again thanked Mr. Fuller before returning to the buggy.

In Albion, Andrew went to Lemuel's store to see if the captain had left a message. Sure enough, there was a sealed envelope crudely addressed to "The Norwegian". The cabbage was to be at the dock on September 3. Price for shipping would be $12 and would have to be paid in advance.

Andrew was pleased and proud. He had sold his cabbage. The shipping charge seemed high and he didn't see why it couldn't come out of the sale but maybe that was the way they did things in America. He wouldn't even tell Susan. It might worry her.

To further celebrate, he purchased an assortment of penny candy, then went back to the buggy where Susan had already returned from her bit of shopping and window-looking.

At first she was excited about the good fortune, but wondered, "Why didn't he say who he sold it to?"

"Like me, I guess he doesn't write so good."

They ate their candy, peppermint sticks, molasses taffy and horehound drops one after the other as Dolly jogged along Ridge Road. Laughing, talking, cuddling and kissing, they regained their decorum only to greet the few passersby in buggy, wagon or on foot.

It was late when they reached home. Susan helped with the chores, then they tumbled into bed. Andrew sighed contentedly. What a fine day it had been! He reached out his arm to draw Susan close to him.

"Andrew, I'm sorry...it...well, there won't be any – any baby starting this month either."

"Oh." He knew he must not show the disappointment he felt. "No matter. Maybe we're expecting things too soon."

Susan sighed and was silent. Then she turned to face him. "Maybe you should start wearing your hat to bed."

He raised his head from the pillow. "You say – my hat?"

She giggled. "Like a proper Norwegian sowing his seed. It made the cabbage and buckwheat grow." He spanked her playfully and they laughed as she cuddled against him in her lace-trimmed nightgown.

On the first of September, Susan invited her family over for supper and the birthday cake she had baked for Andrew. They squeezed around the little table and ate the first fried chicken of the summer, the biggest young rooster. Susan gave Andrew wool socks she had knitted and Mrs. Cary gave him a muffler.

The next day Andrew and Susan spent cutting and packing the cabbage, keeping split or imperfect heads for themselves to store in the sod hut or for sauerkraut. Early the next morning, Andrew borrowed Mr. Cary's wagon to haul the cabbage to the dock and await the barge. Without knowing the details, John Cary rejoiced with Andrew that he had sold his cabbage crop. "Might be the beginning of a steady market," he remarked. "Cabbage is easy to grow."

The barge docked about noon and the captain looked almost surprised to find Andrew waiting, "Oh, yes, the Norwegian with the cabbage," he grinned. "Well, load it on right along the rail there anyplace." Andrew was disappointed that he didn't so much as take a look inside one sack of the fine, solid cabbage.

"Where did you sell it?" Andrew asked.

"In Syracuse," he said, "at a wholesale place there. You got the price of the freight with you?"

Andrew took the money from his pocket and carefully counted out 12 dollars into the captain's hand. Then he began stacking the sacks of cabbage along the rail. He waited for the captain to return from the tavern where he said he was going to eat his dinner. The steersman, as well as the tow boys, lay asleep on the deck. Andrew sat in the sun waiting, almost to fall asleep himself, when the captain finally reappeared. He muttered, "You still here?"

"Forgot to ask when to pick up my money from the cabbage."

"Oh, two weeks or so, my next trip back. I'll leave it with Lemuel again."

Andrew reached out his hand, "Thanks very much. Hope we do business next year, too." The captain nodded, and took his hand.

On the way home, Andrew tried to figure in his head how much the cabbage would bring and how best they could spend it. He must save some of it for seed next season, It was seed money he'd spent on the freight bill, but there should be enough to buy a churn and some other things Susan wanted. He really needed new boots before winter and now he could take his order to the cobbler in Kendall.

Two days short of the two weeks, Andrew had to take his small crop of wheat to Bascom's mill to be ground. While waiting for the flour, he drove to the dock at Albion to see if, by chance, his money was in yet. There was a barge docked and it looked like the same boat. What luck! Seeing no one on deck, he hurried to the store. Lemuel wasn't in, but the young man in charge could find nothing for him in the drawer where messages were kept. Andrew went excitedly to find the captain. He didn't find him any place around the dock so he supposed he was in the tavern.

He entered and looked along the bar, searching the faces of the few men standing there. They turned their heads to see who had come in. One of them was the captain, who quickly turned his attention back to the mug in front of him. For the first time, suspicion seized Andrew. Haltingly, he went up behind the captain and tapped his shoulder. When he turned, Andrew looked carefully at the face to be sure it was the same man. "I came to get the money for sale of my cabbage."

"Cabbage! What are you talking about?"

"Cabbage you took to Syracuse for me last trip," insisted Andrew.

"You've got the wrong man, I'm afraid. I don't haul any perishable freight."

"You did, you know, for price of twelve dollars."

"What was the man's name who took your cabbage?"

"I don't know your name, but we shook hands to make the deal," said Andrew, his voice trembling.

The captain nudged the man beside him. "Shook hands, he says." Then he turned back to Andrew. "Let me see your receipt, mebby I kin help you figure which barge you put your cabbage on."

Andrew felt the blood rush to his face as he opened and closed his fists helplessly. The man shrugged, and turned again to the bar. Andrew's first impulse was to grab him by the coat collar, drag him out into the middle of the floor and put all his strength behind one good punch. But he turned and hurried out before he could follow through.

As he strode down the street toward his wagon, his anger turned to shame and anguish. He stood clutching the edge of the wagon rack, not knowing what to do next. Without any evidence to show, there was nothing he could do. He climbed on and slowly began the trip back to Bascom's Mill. Tears stung at his eyes, a man he'd trusted, an American, had treated him sinfully. Even made fun of his trust because he was a foreigner. Then he thought of how he had let Susan down. And then there were his new boots, already made and waiting to be paid for.

He was not only out the whole profit of his crop, but the 12 dollars as well, which could have bought staples for the winter and seed for spring. What would they do.? To let the Carys give them more than they had already given, would be humiliating. What kind of husband was he that couldn't provide for their daughter, he asked himself. And finally he thought about all his beautiful and carefully tended cabbage. Was it dumped somewhere along the canal? Or had the captain actually sold it and pocketed the money?

CHAPTER 20

A Strange
Encounter

J OHN CARY HAD JUST BROUGHT Susan home with baked goods and an assortment of vegetables from the garden when Andrew arrived home. Not detecting his dark mood, Mr. Cary said cheerfully, "Glad you got back before I left, now I can help unload the flour and take my wagon home; save you a trip and give me a ride."

Susan emerged from the house, smiling and eager to hear the good news.

All the way home Andrew had dreaded facing these two; now he must tell them. "I...I lost all my cabbage," he quavered.

"You what?" Mr. Cary dropped the sack of flour back on the wagon.

"What do you mean?" Susan cried, alarmed.

"The barge captain dumped the cabbage or something, I don't know what. He wouldn't admit he ever saw the cabbage, or me."

"What about the freight money?" Susan frowned.

"Lost that too."

"Didn't you have a receipt?" Susan asked, "a piece of paper with his signature?"

"No, we yust shake hands."

"Oh, Andrew," Susan exclaimed, near tears, "that isn't the way things are done in America."

"If he had a receipt, Susan," Mr. Cary said, "a crooked captain might have found some other way to gyp him." He turned to the silent, chastised Andrew. "I should have warned you, all the stories I've heard about the swindlers and drifters that seem to have come with that canal." John Cary said disgusted as he grabbed a sack of flour, "Well, it's a big loss, but you'll find some way around it." Susan went silently back into the house.

Later, when Andrew went in where Susan was preparing supper, he said, "I'm so sorry, so sorry, dear Susan. I'm going to think of some way to get the things you wanted."

Susan sighed, "It isn't just my things, you need those boots and they're already made."

"I'll get by with these for awhile yet," Andrew looked down at his shoes, coming apart at the soles.

"We'll both get by," Susan said and gave her downcast husband a hug. But she turned quickly back to the stove.

"I'll find some work somewhere to pay for the boots so he won't think I broke my promise to him, too," thought Andrew miserably.

Later that week, Cleng returned from his summer-long travels. The first Andrew knew of it was when he came to the door as they were finishing breakfast. After a warm exchange of greetings, Cleng handed Andrew a letter.

"With this new mail route on Ridge Road, I guess they haven't got all the names straightened out yet."

"It's from my mother," Andrew exclaimed eagerly. "I haven't heard from her in a long time. I'll save it to read later; we'll visit now."

After Cleng and Susan exchanged greetings, the two men lapsed into Norwegian and she began clearing the table. Unable to understand but an occasional word, she had no idea what they were discussing. She was afraid Cleng was trying to persuade Andrew that they should move West with the group. After the setback on the cabbage, she was afraid he might be easily swayed.

"Did Cleng convince you that we should go West with your friends?" she asked after their visitor had left.

"Oh, no, Susan, we hardly talk about that. He tell me about his travels and I tell him about the cabbage. I promised you we won't move unless some day you want to."

She kissed him on the cheek. "And I know I don't need a receipt for that," she laughed. "When will the colony leave?"

"They plan now to go right after sugar season in the spring."

"Read your letter now." She patted him on the shoulder.

After he looked at everything on the outside of the envelope, he paused again, holding it lovingly, anticipating the news from home. Then he tore a neat narrow strip from one end, carefully unfolded the thick packet and an American ten dollar bill fell out. "Look at that!" he exclaimed, holding it up to Susan as he read the first of the letter. "For my birthday even if it's late getting here, she says." He looked happily at Susan, "Now I can get your churn and something else you most want."

"Oh no, Andrew, that's your birthday present and will pay for the boots. My mother will lend me her churn as long as I need it."

Andrew was soon lost in the closely written letter, devouring every word of news from home. When he finished the first reading, he placed the letter on the mantel to await several more readings and to share with his Norwegian friends.

"If you say I should get the boots, will you ride with me to get them this afternoon? I want to buy you a little something anyway, maybe some candy, or a fancy cake from the bakery?"

"All right, I accept. Let's each have a fried cake or something from the bakery with some tea or coffee."

"Tomorrow I go hunting," Andrew said in a much brightened mood, "and get something to put in that new smokehouse." He had recently completed the little structure from crooked and odd logs not suitable for the barn he was building. With a barn, new livestock could be added and one end would be sectioned off for the chickens where the new pullets could lay their eggs.

The next morning as Andrew left to go hunting, Susan asked, "Are you going to wear your new boots?"

"No, my old ones will hold together for that much more and be more easy on my feet."

"I think I'll walk over to Mama's today; it's such a nice fall day. We're going to cut corn off the cob to dry for next winter."

As Andrew walked along, rifle at his side, deeper and deeper into the forest, he was keenly aware of the richness it offered on this autumn day. The air had an October nip that coaxed down gold and crimson leaves ahead and beside him. He looked skyward to see the sun glinting through breaks in the trees, and wondered how Heaven could be more glorious.

After an hour of walking, waiting and listening, he saw a yearling doe and decided against taking it. Since he'd have to take the time to clean, dress and drag it home, he wanted enough meat to be worth the haul. Instead, he stood for a few moments to enjoy watching the graceful animal browse.

Suddenly, something whizzed over the deer and past his own head, making the deer leap for safety into the nearby brush. It wasn't a bullet, could it have been an arrow? He immediately remembered the times he'd sensed there was something near him in the woods just out of his vision. And the time Anne Marie had been frightened by a man, not one of them. Surely the arrow was meant for the deer, not him, but he still didn't want to encounter a band of Indians, or even one. Should he be prepared to shoot? He couldn't shoot another human being unless it was to protect Susan, who should be at her mother's by now.

Nevertheless, for the rest of the morning Andrew moved cautiously, looking for both man and beast. By the time the sun was directly overhead he had not seen another deer and began to wish he'd taken the small one.

He had not seen any other hunters either. On such a nice fall day, he rather expected to run into one of his Norwegian friends.

He sat on a log near what he figured must be a branch of Sandy Creek. The water he drank was clear and cold. He pulled the bread and cheese from his pocket and ate hungrily. When he had finished and was just about ready to begin on the apple, he heard motion behind him, someone or something coming through the brush not far away. Making no quick moves, he cautiously peered around the tree where he had been resting his back. A huge buck deer, well within shooting range, had his head down, reaching for the green grass beneath a vine maple. Guarding every motion and staying behind the big tree, Andrew drew on his trigger, then carefully aimed for the left shoulder and fired. At the explosion of the muzzle-loader, the buck leaped to clear the area. But the hunter's aim was true and the ball struck home.

Rushing over to the stilled animal, he forgot everything else in his excitement. It was the finest buck he'd ever shot, a real hat rack, with five long and evenly matched antlers to the side. In his keyed-up state, he had little trouble dragging the five pointer a few yards to a clean, leafy area where he began the gutting chores.

He was concentrating on the task at hand when suddenly a shadow fell across the white underside of the deer where the entrails were beginning to spill out. Andrew slowly looked up, heart thumping, to see a tall, gaunt man in dirty buckskins. His tangled black hair fell around the copper colored face, and an irregular, welted scar slanted downward across one cheek from hairline to under his chin. One end of his bow rested on the ground near Andrew.

The Indian stood quietly. There seemed to be nothing aggressive about him. Andrew nodded and said, "Hello...god dag," suspecting that one language made no more sense to him than the other.

Without acknowledging the greeting, the visitor rapped the deer's belly and pointed to himself. He wants the deer, thought Andrew. Well, I'll certainly give it up without a fight, he thought. There are other deer, but a dead husband wouldn't be much good to Susan.

Andrew spread his hands in resignation and moved to stand. But the Indian shook his head and tapped the same spot on the upper part of the deer. There must be something inside he wanted, probably the heart. As Andrew went on slitting with his knife just under the tough hide, the Indian began making strange sounds in his throat as he squatted and bounced up and down on his heels. As the rich mahogany of the liver showed, the Indian grabbed at it in a frenzy. Andrew quickly cut it loose. The scar-faced Indian snatched it and began taking huge bites of it, fresh blood dripping from his mouth as he disappeared into the thicket. Andrew shuddered and swallowed hard.

But he finished the dressing, trussed the deer for towing, and started home with his heavy burden. After a short distance, the Indian appeared in front of him again, for the rest of the deer, Andrew was certain. But the

Indian thumped the deer, then his own shoulders and pointed towards Andrew's house. He must already know where they lived. And he wanted to carry it for him.

Andrew protested with a shake of his head. But the Indian threw up his arms, pounded his chest and danced up and down. The liver had evidently made him strong. So Andrew helped load the deer across the Indian's shoulders and then led the way, getting as many branches out of his path as possible.

When they reached the clearing, the Indian dropped his load where Andrew indicated in front of the smokehouse. Without hesitation the native turned to go. Andrew called to him, took his knife and pretended to slash off a piece of the deer for him, but the Indian shook his head.

"Well, thanks, then." Andrew smiled and raised his hand. As an afterthought, Andrew took the apple from his pocket and held it out. The scar-faced Indian took it, but not as eagerly as he had the liver, and disappeared into the forest.

Andrew stood staring after him and shaking his head in disbelief. Would anyone believe this story! Susan apparently wasn't home yet; he could hardly wait to tell her.

CHAPTER 21

A Profitable Visit
To Rochester

"YES, THERE STILL ARE A FEW Indians around," John Cary laughed when he heard Andrew's strange account. "Somebody will see one every once in awhile. They're usually old bucks living alone in caves or brush lean-tos somewhere deep in the woods – too independent to follow the tribe, except maybe in winter. I've never heard of one doing any harm. He probably carried your deer to show off his strength and to have human company for awhile."

"I feel sorry now I didn't try harder to talk to him," said Andrew. "I know how lonesome it is without knowing someone's language."

"Anyway, you won't get any fried liver out of that deer, will you?" Mr. Cary examined the piece of meat Andrew had brought them. "Looks like good venison. We'll enjoy having some fresh meat, haven't had any for awhile."

Susan had listened to the incredible story when she returned from her mother's the night of the hunt. She shuddered when he told about the raw liver. Then she sat on his lap and put her head on his shoulder, her arms around his neck. "What if he had been a dangerous Indian? You might not be here. I could never live without you."

"I'll be here for you a long time," Andrew said, holding her tightly and gently stroking her. "I'll be right here with all the love this Norwegian heart can hold."

From the Cary's, Andrew went to Gudmund's house. His cousin had brought them some fresh steaks from his deer; now Andrew would share some of his with them. Gudmund was splitting wood and the two men sat on upended chunks to visit.

"Did you decide yet if you're going to join the group going West next spring?" Andrew asked.

174

"Gurene and I have been talking about it and we've just about decided we will. Mother Madland doesn't want to be separated from the group, and Gurene doesn't want her mother and Serene to go without us. I don't care much whether we go or stay. Farming is farming wherever there's a place to put in the seeds, way I figure it. How about you, Andreas, any chance you'll change your mind?"

"No, I won't be going." Andrew tried to sound both cheerful and confident. "We're getting settled and making progress here. And Susan needs to be close to her mother for awhile yet, too. She's pretty young."

"I can understand that. Well, we'll go see what's out there and let you know how it is. Maybe you can come later."

When Andrew got home, he didn't have an opportunity to report on his visits; Susan was in tears. She was trying to hide them, but his first words of concern brought her from the dishes she was drying to the table. She slumped down and rested her chin on her folded arms. "No baby again this month," she announced glumly.

Andrew was relieved; so that's all it was. Still, wanting children as she did, it was devastating enough for her. He wanted children, too, especially sons to help with the farming, and both sons and daughters to whom he could pass on the Norwegian ways and tell the Norwegian stories. But he knew how Susan ached for a child of her own, he had watched her cuddling other women's babies and talking to someone else's toddlers.

As he held her hand, he forced himself to say what had sometimes been on his mind. "Maybe Norwegian father and American mother don't mix? Maybe you need...an American husband?"

"Don't even say such a thing!" She was almost angry now. But she took his hand and held it against her cheek. "No, Mama says it's likely because I'm so young. She says just be patient. And if...if we never have a child of our own, there are always little orphans to – to take in." She burst into tears, obviously not happy at the prospect.

Andrew sighed. What a child she was sometimes! "Your mama is maybe right. Wait and trust. Maybe we worry too much."

The winter that followed was mild. Andrew had more opportunity than he expected to clear land further into the forest, using the logs to finish his barn. Whenever he talked with a group of his friends, the conversation soon turned to their plans for leaving for the West early in the spring.

In spite of what Andrew felt was a steadfast decision, he couldn't help having times of doubt. Maybe he was passing up a great opportunity. Even Joseph Fellows, the Quaker land agent who had helped them secure their present farm sites, was negotiating deals in which their mortgaged farms would be exchanged for land sites, similar in size, in Illinois. The Quakers were eager to get a stronghold in the new Western frontier.

"Better change your mind and go along with us, Andro-o-o," said Big Nels as he bored into a big maple to tap for his last sugar season. "We can't get along without you, and you certainly can't get along without us!"

Andrew never lingered long at the colony after they began urging him to join them for the westward trek. He'd go home and work with a vengeance to console himself that what he had was more important than leaving for the unpredictable. These were thoughts he never shared with Susan. She had no idea there was so much pressure on him to change his mind, or such confusion in his own mind.

Maple sugar season over, the Norwegian colony was like a swarm of bees; the excitement of anticipation, sorting and packing, and finishing their business in New York. Andrew felt the need for a visit to Lars and Martha, who would become more important than ever to him now. He thought such a trip and visit would also be good for Susan who was depressed over the most recent disappointment. He broached it while waiting at the table for breakfast.

"I think the spring plowing can wait a few days. Let's put our maple syrup crop in the buggy and take it with us on a trip to Rochester for a visit with Lars and Martha and Nils and Carolyn. I don't think syrup sells for any less there and maybe even more."

"Oh, Andrew, let's do!" Susan's face lighted up with the first enthusiasm he'd seen in days. He didn't want her ever to lose that little-girl playfulness he loved so much.

She turned back to the stove and neatly flipped over the buckwheat cakes with the tool he had given her for Christmas. It was made just for that, a novelty to all who saw it. While waiting for the pancakes to cook, she held it up to her face like a hand mirror, pretending to see herself as she pushed and twisted wisps of hair.

"When shall we go? I want to wash my hair and my pink dress, get all prettied up for the city. Won't that be fun, Andrew? Our first long trip together!"

The following week on an April day of gentle breezes, when the trees were pale green with buds, they began their journey to Rochester along the canal. Wooly white clouds sailed in a blue, blue sky. Every minute was precious. They turned the road over to Dolly and sang and laughed. They talked of future plans and how, someday, they would go West on the canal to its very end.

"Maybe we can even visit the Norwegians' new homes," Susan said, a thought that just occurred to her. "And James, living up there in the wild Michigan Territory." His letters back to the family told of the bright prospects in that part of the country. That information had given Andrew encouragement that there were other places to be considered.

As they approached Rochester, they could see a large gathering as though a sight-seeing boat had just docked. Many well-dressed people were milling around the nearby streets. "Let's go by and watch for a little while," Susan urged. "It's still early."

Andrew turned Dolly into the fringes of the crowd and drove up under the shade of a large tree. After a few minutes, a man in a high silk hat walked over to the buggy. "What you got to sell there, farmer?" he asked jovially.

Andrew started to shake his head in reply when he thought of the maple syrup. "I just got maple syrup."

The man looked into the buggy. "How much is it?"

Andrew hesitated, trying to decide, and cast a glance at Susan.

"My husband doesn't speak English very well." She peered around Andrew. "It's two dollars a gallon, freshly made this spring from our own trees." Andrew was embarrassed. He was going to ask a dollar and thought that was high.

The stranger lost no time in taking out his purse. "I'll take two gallons." He carried it back to his circle of friends, held it up smiling as they exclaimed and looked toward the buggy. Wives began hurriedly hunting husbands, talking excitedly, pointing toward the buggy. Two more men came over, followed shortly by others. Andrew had hopped out of the buggy and was handing out the jugs, bowing deeply as he accepted the money. Susan was making change in her lap.

Finally Andrew spread his empty hands and shook his head, "Sorry, no more this year. Only one for my friends left."

One of the men said, "I'll give you $2.50 for that gallon."

Without hesitation Andrew said, "Sorry, for my friends."

"Three dollars?"

Andrew got in the buggy, and picked up the reins. Smiling and shaking his head, he slapped the horse's flank and they moved slowly away from the crowd.

"Whee," Susan murmured, bundling the money and tying it in a dish towel to tuck into their lunch basket, "my head is swimming!"

When they were well away from the crowd, Andrew threw back his head and laughed, "I think you should be with me when I try to sell cabbages."

They squeezed hands joyfully. "What will we do with so much money?"

At the Larson home, Martha and Siri greeted them with the warmest kind of welcome. Martha sent Andrew to the boat works to tell Lars and Nils that they were in town and that Nils should bring Carolyn and the girls over for supper. She then showed Susan around the grand new house. Two full stories and an attic. Rooms were large and high ceilinged, like a palace, Susan thought. The comfortable furnishings showed evidence of Lars' carpentry skill.

In the long, narrow dining room, Siri began spreading the table for the evening meal. As the three of them worked, Martha commented, "I thought sure you and Andrew would have a fat little Norwegian-American baby on the way by now. You not look like it."

"We keep hoping, but nothing..."

"I'm sorry, Susan. I should not ask. You just be patient and trust in the Lord. Some fine day...you'll see, just wait."

"Thank you, Martha. That's what my mother says, too. She thinks I might be too young for a year or two yet."

"Once they get started, you might have trouble shutting them off," Martha laughed.

At the supper table, loaded with many heaping bowls and platters, some of which Carolyn had brought, long and heartfelt blessings were expressed for the privilege of being together again. The three women murmured amens.

When the dishes started going around the table, Susan realized the conversation was in their halting English for her sake.

She said, "Go ahead and talk Norwegian, be comfortable. You don't get together very often. I don't mind, really I don't. I'll break in when I want to." Andrew reached over and gratefully patted her hand. She turned her attention to Carolyn's two little girls who sat, wide-eyed and adoring, near their former teacher. They now spoke English almost as well as Norwegian. Susan looked up occasionally and smiled warmly at Siri, who had insisted on waiting table and helping the two little Larson children in the kitchen.

Later Susan read and told stories to all the children in front of the dining room fireplace until the little ones were whisked off to bed and Anne and Sara fell asleep on the rugs in front of the fireplace. Finally, Susan went to Martha in the parlor, where the reminiscing and laughing still went on.

"I'm sorry, I can't stay awake any longer. May I go to bed?" Andrew rose to go with her.

"No, Andrew, you stay. Visit as long as you can. It might be awhile before you get together again." She patted him lightly on the shoulder, he looked fondly up at her. She was sleeping soundly when Andrew finally went up to bed. He slipped in beside her and fell asleep.

Towards morning, near the time they usually got up, Susan, half asleep, murmured, then threw her arm across his chest, pulled herself to him and nestled into the hollow of his arm. He responded immediately and they soared to heights they had never known before. With a blending of body, soul and mind, they seemed to ascend to the very brink of Heaven. "That was beautiful," she whispered and fell asleep again in his arms.

May brought an early surge of warm weather that year and by the second week the earth seemed to explode with green and growing things. The fragile corn blades were already darkening to a sturdy green as Andrew hoed around them. He straightened to rub his back and heard the sound of Susan's singing.

She was coming down the path from a day at her mother's, carrying stems of lilacs in one arm. A bird darted in front of her and Susan stopped, surprised and laughing. Then she broke into a little dance of her own making and came on down the path. Andrew shook his head in amusement, but his heart swelled with gladness and love.

"Oh, Andrew, what a beautiful day!" she cried as she glimpsed him. She picked her way between the corn shoots to stand before him. Her pink cheeks glowed. Sometimes, Andrew thought, this girl's brown eyes shone like the stars in Heaven.

"And what did you do today to make you so happy?"

She looked at him as if debating something. Then she dropped the lilacs and, ignoring the precious corn shoots, stepped closer and threw her arms around his neck.

"Oh, Andrew, I was going to wait until tonight to tell you, but I can't. We're going to have a baby! Mama is as sure of it as I am!"

CHAPTER 22

Eleazer
Cary

I T WAS SHORTLY AFTER SUSAN'S happy announcement to Andrew that the Norwegians set their date for departure to the Fox River area in Illinois. They were more than eager to leave the grim, difficult land of the Black North and move to where, as Cleng described it to them, there were only enough trees for their use and acres of wide open prairie land to be cultivated.

Some of the men thought they should have gone earlier to get crops in, but Cleng warned that the weather there could be unpredictable until June; they'd better wait since they would have to camp out until buildings could be put up. Each family now owned and would travel in a wagon, knowing it might be necessary to live on or under it for awhile.

The two families, besides the Stangelands, who decided to remain with their farms in New York were the Henrik Herviks and the Thompsons, Nils and Carolyn. Ole Olsen had returned from Norway to his house in Rochester bringing his bride, a widow, and her seven-year-old son. Nils and Carolyn decided they wanted to return to their farm rather than to follow the group to far-off Illinois.

The Herviks had just built a new house and, like Andrew, were well on the way to having a good farm.

Andrew and Susan were at the settlement to see the travelers depart. For Susan it was difficult to see her former school children leave, knowing she would probably never see them again. But she knew it was far more heart-breaking for her husband to bid his friends a last goodbye – Big Nels and Betsy, Cornelius and Kari, Daniel and Bertha, but especially Gudmund. Andrew was as sober and near tears as Susan had ever seen him.

After the travelers had wheeled out of sight, she held his hand as they went from one deserted cabin to another, piling on their wagon things that had been left behind for them, sugaring kettle, a small cart and some hand tools. Andrew absently picked up and discarded a broken stool, a leaky bucket, a bent washboard. Then he put his fingers through the crumbled chinking in the poorly constructed cabins.

Finally, he felt the need to say something. "I hope their next houses will be better built than these were."

"Let's go home, Andrew." Susan urged. "This loneliness is eating you up." Tears ran down her face as she put an arm around him.

"I don't think I'll be spending much time here," he said. "I just pray they are headed for a better life ahead. It wasn't easy here. I was lucky and met the Cary family." He smiled faintly at her.

Andrew's newly-cleared ground to work up and plant kept him busy during the summer of his friends' departure.

Susan's morning sickness lasted into mid-summer. Andrew worried about her, but she laughed it off as part of having that baby they so much wanted.

Most of their social life was spent with the Carys and their friends and relatives, but occasionally the three Norwegian families got together for a supper or Sunday dinner. July Fourth was celebrated, like the years before, at their favorite spot beside Lake Ontario. For this get-together the Lars Larsen family and the Ole Olsens came from Rochester. It was not only America's Independence Day, but their independence from Norway as well, their day of departure. It would probably be celebrated in Illinois as well.

When the Norwegians got together, Susan still encouraged them to talk in their native language, even though she silently felt left out and ended up talking to or playing with the children.

Fall arrived with cooler weather and a good harvest. Susan was rolly polly, rosy and happily waiting out her time.

Christmas Day, Susan and Andrew spent with the Carys. Also invited were Susan's cousin, Angela (Ira's daughter), her husband Frank and their two children.

After the blessing for the bountiful Christmas dinner, all eyes were turned on Andrew, who was about to perform magic.

"Ready, everybody?" Susan called.

"I'd better keep a glass of water handy in case it lights something besides the candle," Mr. Cary laughed.

Andrew cautiously drew the blue and orange tip of the little stick across the side of the box. A flame burst forth and flared up. Andrew jerked slightly, but held on to the match, moved it to the candle and lit the wick. There were exclamations all around the table. "Look't that!"

"It's still burning!"

"Fire out of nothing, like flint."

"Won't it be wonderful when we can all have some of those?"

It had become a tradition for Andrew to buy Susan something each Christmas that was new, a novelty. First the slate, then the kitchen tool for turning pancakes and now the matches.

When everyone had eaten their fill right down to the spicy raisin Christmas pudding, Susan needed Andrew's arm to lift herself from the chair. Others were stretching and complaining that they had eaten too much.

Alexander, who had sat next to Susan, commented, "You are so fat! You must eat all day."

His mother hushed him, "You just never mind, young man."

Susan put a loving arm around her outspoken little brother. "You better not insult me or I'll make you start calling me 'Miss Cary' again. Only now it would be Mrs. Stangeland."
"How do you like your new teacher?" Andrew asked the boys.

"Mr. Wood? Oh, he's all right, but we'd rather have you and Susan."

"He plays with us sometimes out in the yard at recess," Leander added.

"He doesn't tell as good stories as Miss Cary...I mean Susan," their cousin Angie said. She was a little older than the twins, round-faced and chubby like her mother.

"Susan, did you ever get over to the school to help like you planned?" Angela asked.

"Very little, I never seemed to have time. Now I know why married women don't teach." Susan began clearing dishes from the table.

"Shoo. You go sit down," Angela said, "I'll help Aunt Lydia with the dishes."

"Today I won't object," Susan said.

"We should be getting home to the chores."

"If you want to stay, I'll go do chores and come back for you," Andrew offered.

"No, I'm ready to go, too. From the looks of the weather, you might have to get out the sleigh by morning."

A few snowflakes were already falling as they went into the cold winter evening. Bearing a basket of leftovers, throwing kisses, waving, and with a final "Merry Christmas," they rode home behind Dolly, a sheepskin robe tucked around Susan's legs.

When Andrew returned from his chores, the house was cozy and warm. Susan smiled from where she lay on the bed. Andrew looked at her solicitously. "You think we might have a Christmas baby?"

"No, I think I just ate too much. Mama says these little pains are just warnings that it won't be long."

Andrew sat on the steps beside the bed and rubbed his hand around her bulging stomach, "I don't see how all that come out without hurting you so much."

"Oh, Andrew," she chided, laying her arm along his, "women have been having babies for thousands of years; now it's my turn."

"Yes, but all those women are not my Susan."

The baby was due the middle of January, but it was a long wait during the cold days after Christmas and Susan became impatient. Mrs. Cary had talked to Mrs. Tillman, the midwife, and Mr. Cary would go for her as soon as Andrew brought word that she was needed.

Several inches of snow, frozen solid, stayed on the ground. Susan didn't dare venture outdoors without help. Andrew planned work near the house within hearing distance of her call. He wondered if he could make it faster to the Cary's on foot or in the sleigh. The sleigh was one Uncle Ira had loaned them when he went to New York for the winter.

New Years Day, 1829, was cold but clear. By afternoon, the sun sparkled on the snow and Andrew suggested they take a sleigh ride.

"I'd love that," Susan said. "I feel so restless and cooped up when I can't get out and walk anywhere."

Andrew carried her to the sleigh waiting out front and tucked her in with warmed robes. Then with bells jingling and Dolly's colt, Cloud, prancing alongside, the two Stangelands went past the Carys, waved but did not stop, past the schoolhouse and the church, then back home again. Andrew didn't want to get too far away or let Susan get cold.

"Just think," Susan said, "next sleigh ride there will be three of us."

"I think you will be easier to carry in two parts," Andrew laughed as he set her outside the door.

On Friday night, January 9, the little heifer had her first calf. Never had Andrew been so interested in every detail of the birth process, and wondered how much it paralleled a human mother's experience. But the young cow came through in fine shape and now they had a bull calf to sell in the spring.

Two days later, Andrew awakened in the cold pre-dawn. He enjoyed a few more luxurious moments before rising. Because it was Sunday, he could do only what he must. He missed going to Meeting with his Norwegian friends, but he would not admit to Susan that he preferred it to the fiery sermons at her church.

Susan groaned in her sleep, then awakened with, "Oh-h-h." Andrew got up immediately, stirred the fire, added wood, then lighted a candle. "The pain in my back is terrible," she said. "Mama says that's where it starts, but I'm not sure it's like this. Maybe I just slept in one spot too long."

"We better not take any chances. Mrs. Tillman said to call her even if we're not real sure." He quickly slipped into his pants, new boots, the woolen shirt Susan and Mrs. Cary had made him for Christmas, then grabbed his coat, cap and mittens.

By this time Susan was in enough pain to be sure something was going on. "Hurry back, Andrew, will you?" she pleaded.

"I'll hurry," said Andrew shakily. "Stay right where you are." He hesitated one second at the door before deciding that by foot was fastest. Hitting the familiar path by leaps, he found his way lighted only by the pre-dawn light on the snow.

Mr. Cary, just coming out of the house, heard, then saw Andrew's long strides toward him. "Is it Susan?" he called.

"Susuun, yes," Andrew answered. Mr. Cary hesitated only long enough to call back to his wife, then ran to the barn for King and the sleigh. Andrew retraced his steps as fast as he came.

Short, chubby Mrs. Tillman, apple cheeked and jolly, loved babies above all else, and young first-time mothers second best. Her voice rose and fell in pleasant crescendo, assuring the apprehensive Susan that this was one of the happiest occasions of her life. "We'll have that little old fat baby in the basket for the papa to see before you can count to one hundred backwards." She turned to Andrew, who was poking a fire that didn't need attention. "This will be my first little Norwegian baby."

From the bed, Susan called proudly, "It's the first Norwegian-American baby anywhere that we know of."

"Oh, how exciting," the midwife trilled. "Do women in Norway have an easy time with their babies?" she asked Andrew, who had finally set the poker down. "Of course you wouldn't know, would you, this being your first? Well, I can tell you little Susan will be all right. I never delivered a Cary yet that was difficult, even when her mother had those little twin boys. Wasn't that fun, Lydia?" She spoke to Mrs. Cary, who was sitting on the steps by her daughter, smoothing hair from her brow. Lydia Cary rolled her eyes and said nothing.

Lena Tillman was laying out things from her basket onto the table. Susan twisted, grimaced and rubbed her feet together through another pain. Andrew watched her anxiously. Mrs. Tillman said, "It sounds like things are warming up. If you men have some wood to chop or something, check back in a couple of hours to see how things are going."

John Cary, who had just come in, said, "Come on over to our house, Andrew, when you get your chores done."

Andrew went about his chores mechanically but hurriedly. Carrying milk to the cellar to pour into pans, he lifted the outside cellar doors and tried to hear what he could as he went down the steps. There was still just a pleasant mingle of voices until he started to leave, then he heard Susan's loud, "Oh-h-h...oh-h-h." His heart knotted.

Then he heard Mrs. Tillman's calm voice saying, "Count, Susan, count 100, 99..." He heard the pain in Susan's voice as she counted along with her. He clenched his fists and hurried back to the barn, where he quickly finished his chores. He didn't want to leave, but Mr. Cary was expecting him, and there was no place else to go. He walked over the familiar path, his mind still in their cabin.

Mr. Cary had a pot of mush on the stove and the boys were eating. They wondered what was going on. Why was their mother at Susan's so early in the morning while Andrew was at their house? Why were they going to Angela's instead of to church?

The two men tried to make conversation. "What do you think about that railroad they're talking about putting through near here?" Mr. Cary asked. Andrew hadn't heard about it and shook his head absently. "It's like a buggy or a wagon, maybe more like a sled sliding along on a metal track."

"Oh, boy, can we ride on it, Papa?" Alex asked, showing far more interest at the moment than Andrew.

"Not as long as I'm around," his father answered. "None of my family is going to ride on something faster than a horse can run. And that steam engine business, why it could blow the whole thing sky high. I just don't believe it's God's will for man to be inventin' things like that."

Without Andrew contributing to the conversation it soon came to an end and Mr. Cary got the boys ready to go and visit their cousins for the day. Andrew decided to go back home and chop wood so he'd be close by. Chopping wood on Sunday surely couldn't be a sin when Susan had to work even harder.

He went to the wood pile near the house and paused often, trying to hear what was going on inside. The counting went on. He wondered how many times she had started over at 100. Finally, he heard her shout, "I can't count anymore, I can't remember where I am."

"That's all right," Lena soothed, "you're too busy pushing now. Once more...once more..." The words echoed through Andrew until he realized that he, too, was straining, wanting so desperately to help her.

"Oh, God, God up in Heaven help her," he prayed. Why, oh, why had they wanted a baby so much? Maybe Norwegian babies didn't come so easy in American mothers, or not at all! What could be done then? Surely Mrs. Tillman could not handle that. The axe forgotten, he paced in wretched agony.

Finally, there was a very loud, merciless groan. Andrew sobbed as everything inside became strangely silent. Then he heard Mrs. Tillman's delighted voice, "There you go, just like that! Here's your, let me see here..." Andrew held his breath, "boy...it's a fine fat boy!" Andrew heard the wail of his firstborn and wept.

Then he heard Susan's shrill voice, half-crying, half-laughing, "Oh, Mama, get Andrew, get Andrew."

"Give us just a couple of minutes here to get finished up and ready for visitors. Here, Grandma Lydia, you take this little fella'. You know as well as I do what to do with him. Isn't he a beauty?"

Andrew's emotions had switched so quickly from anguish to pride, he found it difficult to breathe. Then Mrs. Cary came to the door. "Andrew," she called, "you've got a fine son!" Mr. Cary was approaching in the sleigh and the news was repeated to him.

The new father hurried in and, with a long glance at the baby in the basket beside the fire, he went to Susan and sat down beside her, but was afraid to touch her until she reached out for his hand.

"It's over, Andrew, and we have a baby boy!" Lydia Cary brought the little bundle which was squirming and making little sucking sounds. He lay on the bed between Susan and Andrew.

Andrew stared in wonder. "He looks like a fine boy to me." Then he noticed the tired grin on Susan's face, the little-girl grin after what she'd been through.

"Isn't he a little miracle?" she asked.

Mr. Cary came over and bent to have a look. After a few moments he said, "Do you know, that little feller looks like his great grandfather.

188

Eleazer Cary, sure as the world. Lydia...look at that mouth and the brow...L'l Leazer."

Susan smiled, "You named me right off, so maybe you've named him. But don't you want us to name him John?" It was to be John if a boy or Lydia if it was a girl.

"No-o, enough Johns in the family. If you want to name him after our side, call him Eleazer Cary. He was a good looking man." Susan looked at Andrew, he nodded and the new baby was named.

"The next boy will look just like his father and be a Norwegian baby," Susan declared.

"Maybe they'll all be better off to look like Carys," Andrew said, finally daring to put a forefinger on the baby's soft cheek.

"All right, you proud men folks," Mrs. Tillman said from the background. "You clear out again while we give that fat little baby something to suck on and see how he takes to that."

Andrew walked out into the foggy cold of that Sunday afternoon, bade his father-in-law goodbye, then wandered toward the barn and fell to his knees on a pile of straw. He poured out a heart full of thanks to God, who had sent him this wonderful son and permitted him to become the father of a first Norwegian-American baby.

After the prayer, Andrew lay in the straw thinking about his family in Norway. How very much he wished that by some magic he could let them know, this very day, about the new grandson, nephew and cousin over here in America. It would take weeks for a letter to reach them. Mrs. Tillman said she was going right to the newspaper with the news. When it was printed, he would send that to them.

CHAPTER 23

Hugh
Samuelson

"LOOK AT THIS," Andrew said and handed a folded newspaper to Susan. He had just come from the Carys with clothes Susan's mother had washed for them. "Your mama sent it along."

Susan was sitting with Leazer beside the fire in the mammy chair. The unique chair was Mrs. Cary's. All her children had slept in it, the twins only briefly since they didn't fit for long. It was a cradle on one end, a rocker on the other, so the mother or nursemaid could rock her baby as she knitted, darned or patched.

Susan laid down her mending and read aloud the front page item of the Albion newspaper.

" 'A son was born to Andrew Stangeland from Norway and his wife, Susan (formerly Susan Cary of Holley) on January 11. Named Eleazer, the baby is the first recorded half-American, half-Norwegian child born in America. Mr. Stangeland came over with the immigration of Norwegian families who landed in New York Harbor October of 1825. Mr. and Mrs. Stangeland and their new baby live on a farm near Holley.' "

Andrew was smiling broadly as Susan looked up at him. "I wish I could send that piece of paper to my mother," he said. "I wonder if she got my letter yet about little Leazer."

"Of course you should send it to her," Susan said. "I'll get another paper for us from one of the neighbors."

Leazer thrived on Susan's milk and doting care. He grew plump and rosy and smiled almost from his first week. As Andrew watched Susan nursing him, talking to him, playing with his hands and feet, he realized she was wife, mother and teacher that no Norwegian girl could have bettered.

By late February, the warming days foretold that sugar season was about to begin, even though there was still snow on the ground. Andrew had now been through enough sugar seasons to recognize the signs, as he examined the new little fruit orchard he had planted the previous fall on new ground cleared near the house. There were only six fruit trees so far, purchased from a peddler who came through in October. He and Susan had planted the two apple trees, two cherry trees, a pear and a plum with pride and reverence. Andrew had made sure to keep his hat on.

The apples the Carys had given them a year ago lasted far into the winter inside the sod hut, but it would be nice to have their own fruit in a few years. He wanted to become more independent of his in-laws as soon as possible. Probably there would always be cooperation between them for work and for tools as long as they lived there, but it must not always be in his favor.

It was becoming quite a chore to move Susan and the baby and the washing, or whatever the project for the day, to her mother's each morning and then go after them in the evening. But she still needed her mother's help plus the wash tubs, churn and other things they did not yet have, so he didn't resent it. He hoped they would be able to have these things as well as a garden of their own this year so she could work at home and watch the baby.

Andrew was going to plant more buckwheat this year, along with wheat and corn and potatoes instead of cabbage, which he was certain he would never raise again as a crop. To sell his potatoes, Lars suggested that Susan write a letter to Francis Thompson. "You know, he's one of the owners of the Black Ball shipping line and helped us when we ran into trouble at the harbor. He's a devoted brother in the Society of Friends. I saw him at the yearly Meeting here in Rochester last fall. Contact him and see if his company would buy potatoes direct from you. Maybe they would help pay your fare to see them direct to New York."

The conversation with Lars gave Andrew cause for thought and planning, but he was into the sugar season before he had time to act on finding a market for his fall crop of potatoes.

It was about this time that he saw the Indian again. Apparently he traveled a wide area and only came to the Kendall forests occasionally.

THE BECKONING

Andrew had watched for anything that looked like a temporary dwelling, such as his own sod hut, but never ran across anything; however, while hunting the previous autumn, he did see what looked like an overnight camp. Just a mashed-down place in a shelter of trees with the remains of a fire and a few scraps of deer hide left by coyotes. Perhaps this was the only shelter he had and returned to the tribe for the winters. Andrew wondered if he still lived on raw livers.

Andrew had spent several evenings whittling and hollowing out pegs to drive into the maple trees and on an early March day began to bore them into the trees. Suddenly, the Indian appeared before him. Andrew was not as startled as he had been previously upon the stranger's sudden approach. "Hello," Andrew grinned.

The Indian nodded and grunted, then stood watching him for awhile before pulling something from the pocket of his deerskin tunic. He showed it to Andrew. It was a spout made from some kind of branch, already hollowed out. Andrew looked questioningly at the Indian, who motioned for him to follow. The Indian located a bushlike tree nearby and with his knife cut through a branch about an inch thick. After making another cut, a piece about six inches long remained. With a small twig, he poked into the soft center of the stick, hollowing it out. In all it had taken him about five minutes.

Andrew examined the stick which the Indian handed him. Then he shook his head and clapped his hand to his forehead. He showed the Indian all the spouts he had so painstakingly whittled. The Indian's expression didn't change; he just nodded and strode off into the woods. Andrew looked at the bush carefully so that he could identify it again. Later, when he told Mr. Cary about the encounter and showed him the stick, the older man exclaimed, "Why, that's elderberry. I never knew about that. Here I've been making my spouts all these years."

A week or so later when the sap was running good and was boiling briskly in the big kettle over a fire near the house, the Indian appeared again. He followed Andrew with a pail of sap. Susan was watching the kettle and the baby was in a basket nearby. She and Alex, who was helping, eyed the native curiously as he stood silently by the fire after his pail was emptied. Aside to Andrew, Susan said, "I think he's hungry. Alex, go gather up what's left from supper and offer it to him."

The scar-faced Indian didn't refuse. The sidemeat, cold biscuits and boiled potatoes were devoured in a few gulps. He handed back the plate with a jerk of his head, and went back to carry more pails of sap. Another evening when Susan fed him, the Indian began trying to tell them something. He picked up the piece of venison on his plate and pretended to drop it in the kettle of boiling sap, then made out-and-away motions in the steam, tapped the meat again and nodded his head. Andrew shook his head in bewilderment and looked at Susan.

Susan's face brightened with understanding. "I think he means to boil a piece of meat in some sap until the syrup thickens, then the meat will be tender. That sounds good. I'm going to try it." She smiled at the Indian and said, "Thank you!" For the first time, Andrew saw his facial expression change to almost a smile.

Andrew and Susan looked forward to another trip to Rochester to sell the syrup, hoping they could repeat their good luck of the year before. Baby Leazer would be with them this time, so they waited for a spell of warm weather. Andrew didn't want to take the time from his crops, but if they left on Friday and came home Sunday, it would really be only two working days. They would take along the Bible and Susan could read from it on the way home for their own private Sabbath day service.

When they arrived at the dock there were not many people around since no boat was docked as before. Little Leazer was fussing and they decided that Andrew should take Susan and the baby to Larsons, then come back and sit with the syrup. It might take that evening and the next day to sell it all.

They were preparing to leave when a man by the water's edge, who had seemed to be eyeing them, came their way. He carried a valise in one hand, his coat over the other arm.

"Isn't he a grand looking man?" Susan said quietly to Andrew.

"He doesn't look very comfortable," Andrew whispered back, "warm as it is today." He had on a high-crowned fur hat and broad satin stock around his neck, high-standing linen collar inside it. With his coat off, the suspenders showed over the starched white shirt and were hooked to tight-legged black trousers.

He approached the buggy, and nodded a greeting. "Is that whiskey or maple syrup you got there?"

"Maple syrup from our farm," Andrew answered.

"I figured that's what it was. How much are you asking for it?"

Since it had sold so easily last year for $2, they had decided to ask $2.25 this year. The man counted the jugs, looked back at the dock, and stood as though considering, "Would you take $2 a jug for all of it?"

"Yes, sir!" Andrew said and Susan nodded as she held the baby over her shoulder and patted him to keep him from crying.

"Well, if you'll move it over there near the dock and unload it, I'll write you a bank check." Without hesitation, Andrew picked up the reins to move the buggy.

Susan placed a restraining hand on his knee, and bent over to speak to the man, "I'm sorry but we can only take cash money."

"I can understand that," the stranger said politely. "There are so many dishonest people along the canal these days. Let me see how much I've got. I have to buy my passage back to New York yet." He counted his money. "No, I'm short. Let me hurry over to the store, there. He knows me, maybe he'll take my check. There comes my boat now, but he'll be docked for awhile."

"I'll move it over and wait to load it right on boat for you."

"Thanks, I'll be right back."

"Now I feel bad," Susan said. "He's an honest businessman."

Andrew patted her knee. "I think you're just good American businesswoman."

The man returned as the packet boat was docking, counted out the money into Andrew's hand, then tucked a silver coin into the fold of the baby's blanket. "That's for the little one. Boy or girl?"

"Thank you!" Susan said. "It's a boy. His first money and all he did to earn it was cry." She laughed lightly and blushed under the stranger's steady gaze.

"Then maybe I'll be buying maple syrup from him someday." He turned away and talked to the captain, and paid for his fare and the freight. The captain indicated the spot where Andrew should load the jugs of syrup.

When he had finished, the man pulled a card from his pocket. "My name is Samuelson, Hugh Samuelson. I'm a wholesale broker from New York and come West to buy a variety of merchandise. This is my address. Would you let me know when the maple syrup is ready next year and where to meet you? Do you write English?"

"Not good," Andrew shook his head. "But my wife is a good writer. She was a schoolteacher."

"Very well," he glanced again at Susan. "What else have you got out there on the farm? Maybe we could get together on other things."

"I expect to have big crop of potatoes this fall."

"Good, good. Your name is...?"

"Andrew Stangeland."

"Standart?"

Andrew spelled out his name slowly as the broker wrote it on the back of another card.

"Stangeland. Norwegian, aren't you?" Andrew nodded. "Do you live in that settlement near Kendall?" Andrew again nodded.

"I hear they are fine, hard-working, honest people, but you are the first I've met."

Andrew said proudly, "My wife American. My son, first Norwegian-American baby."

"Is that right! Seems to me I read that in the paper. And now I've met you."

The captain was calling, "All 'board!"

Mr. Samuelson took out another coin, and laid it in Andrew's hand as he shook it. "Thanks for loading the syrup onto the boat. I'll see you next year." He turned back to where Susan waited in the buggy, tipped his hat and bowed.

THE BECKONING

As Andrew walked back to the buggy, he felt a glow of great satisfaction. Not only had he sold the syrup so easily, but maybe his potatoes too. It was a successful business deal with a smart, sophisticated man from New York which might prove fruitful for the future. Futhermore, he had heard warm praise from a stranger about his countrymen. He climbed in the buggy, put an arm around Susan, and pulled her and his baby son closer to him, smiling. "What a lucky man I am," he thought.

They drove on to the Larson house which seemed to be extremely busy, with people going in and coming out, carrying possessions, minding children and babies. By dress and demeanor, Andrew suspected they were Norwegians, but strangers to him.

"More immigrants must have arrived," he said to Susan as he jumped down and took up the jug of syrup again saved out for the Larsons. "I'll go in and see what's going on."

After several minutes he returned. "A group that arrived last fall has come to Lars and Martha for help and advice about finding jobs and getting settled somewhere. But Martha said they still can find a bed for us. We might go back tomorrow, though, instead of Sunday since they're crowded and we sold the syrup so easy."

"I think we should. If I can just bathe the baby and make him feel more comfortable and have a night's sleep, I'll be ready to start back early tomorrow."

Andrew spent an enjoyable evening visiting with the new-to-America Norwegians. They weren't from Stavanger, but some had been there recently and had even stopped at the Stangeland bakery. Andrew was eager for every word of his hometown or anything else they could think of to tell him.

Susan, with the baby, retired early in Siri's room; Siri volunteered to sleep in the kitchen. But Andrew lay awake for a long time after he joined his family. Selling to the New York buyer, then talking with the new immigrants had made him realize how Americanized he had become. On the other hand, hearing Lars' advice to the newcomers to move on west or north renewed the stirrings within Andrew to make such a move himself. His farm, improved as it was now, would bring a good price. The few

196

letters that had come back to them from the Fox River settlement in Illinois were favorable about the situation there. But he couldn't resist the thought that when he made the change it wouldn't be to follow the others, but rather to go to a place he'd chosen for himself.

He looked over at Susan and the baby sleeping soundly, sighed, turned toward them and waited for sleep.

CHAPTER 24

Help!

EPTEMBER 1 WAS ANDREW'S 30th birthday but, it went uncelebrated because Susan was sick in bed all day. He worried about her, afraid it was malarial fever. Mr. and Mrs. Cary had gone to Farmington so Andrew stayed around the house and yard to care for her and Leazer, who was fat and smiling and pure joy. He was too big for the mammy chair now; Andrew realized that before winter, he'd have to build a shelf with box bed for him. It would be at the foot of their bed.

Susan laughed at the idea at first, but Martha assured her that it was where all Norwegian babies slept. So she decided it was a nice cozy arrangement and more comfortable than keeping him in bed with them.

The day after Andrew's birthday, Susan felt better but not up to doing much, so he set the mammy chair out in the warm September sunshine for her and Leazer while he split wood. Andrew watched how she played "This Little Piggy" with him. Leazer laughed and squealed. Then she sang to him as she returned to her knitting.

Finally, Andrew gave up the chopping and came to sit on the ground near them. Leazer had just drifted off to sleep. Susan stopped rocking and felt of her breasts, first one and then the other as she did when trying to decide which was the fullest for nursing. She frowned and looked at Andrew, "Do you suppose I could be with child again?"

Andrew looked incredulous. "You don't think already? Not from Lars and Martha's house this time."

"No," she laughed. "I'm not sure, and I haven't spoken to Mama about it. But I've missed the second month, which I guess isn't very unusual while I'm nursing, but being sick yesterday and the way I've felt lately..."

Andrew looked worried. "Will it be too soon? When will Leazer quit nursing?" He was thinking about cows who dried up several months before calving.

"I'm not sure, but I guess I'd better talk to Mama and Mrs. Tillman about it. Think of it, Andrew, maybe a little girl this time, or a little boy who looks like you."

He took her hand to hold against his face. "If you're glad, and it's not too soon for Leazer, I'm happy."

It was true. Susan was expecting again and the date was set for early in April. After those first few weeks when she felt sick most of the time, the rest of the fall and winter was spent quite comfortably.

Since it was Leazer's first Christmas, Andrew wanted to observe some of the Norwegian customs for the holiday. He made and set out a bowl of cream porridge for the trolls so they wouldn't play tricks on them through the coming year. Susan listened, as she washed the dishes, to the tale he told Leazer about the trolls.

"Once," he began, "there was a girl who was very lazy and selfish. She didn't put out cream porridge on Christmas Eve night. And you know what? When she went to milk the cow next day, that troll stood behind a post and dangled a big-g-g spider from a stick in front of her face. She got so scared, she jumped up and spilled a whole pail of milk, and nobody had cream porridge for Christmas."

Susan smiled, but Leazer was only interested in pulling his father's beard and poking fingers in his ears.

For Susan's Christmas present, Andrew bought a book of Alfred Lord Tennyson poems. She loved the writings of the new young poet and often read his verses to Andrew.

On Saturday, the 20th of February, an unseasonably warm day arrived. Snow was melting rapidly by late morning. They could hear the much-needed water running into the cistern in the cellar. There had been deep snow right after Christmas with little chance to melt until now.

"This will loosen up the sap for sure," Andrew said to Susan as he came in from getting poles ready for the frame to the new addition. With

Leazer's things taking up so much space, Susan scarcely had room to set up the churn on buttermaking days. Now with the new baby less than two months away, it would soon be even more crowded. She was tired of packing things to her mother's to wash once a week. With two babies it would be almost impossible.

Andrew sat for a few minutes to talk to and play with Leazer, who was banging a spoon on a tin plate. The high stump stool the baby sat in had been made to keep him off the drafty floor. The stump had been cut and hollowed out to form back and sides made comfortable with a small blanket. A wide strip of cloth held him in until he found he could slide under, so Susan put another strip between his legs, over his shoulders and hooked it to the back. Leazer didn't much like the confinement, but Susan dared not let him on the cold floor.

When they took him to his grandparents, he was allowed to crawl the length of their big table, usually with one of the twin uncles at each end watching him. Sometimes Susan let him stand on his feet, but not often enough to make him bowlegged. How nice it will be, Susan thought, when he can toddle about on the floor. She hoped it would be before the new baby came.

"I'm going out to check the maple trees and maybe cut some elderberry sprouts for sugar season," Andrew announced as he picked up the spoon for Leazer one last time. "Need anything before I go?"

"No, I don't think so. Wish I could go along," she said wistfully. "If you find any pussy willows, will you bring some?"

He nodded, drew a hand across Leazer's soft brown hair, turned to Susan's lifted face for a kiss, then patted her rounding belly, "You, too, whichever you are."

Susan went on churning and after the butter turned, she drained off the buttermilk, and gave a little of it to Leazer, who shook his head in protest and reached for her breast. "No, no, you have to drink cow milk and save this for the new baby."

He cried so pitifully she picked him up to nurse for a few moments on the nearly dry breasts. But it put him to sleep and since she would be right with him when he awakened, she laid him in the mammy chair even though it was too small for him and without sides.

She finished pressing the butter into the mold which she had received as a wedding present and took it to the cellar. She hesitated for a moment in the warm sunshine on her way back; it was so good to be out in fresh air again! She breathed deeply. This would be a good day to air the feather tick, she thought. The boards Andrew had put down led past the clothesline and he had scooped them off. Leazer was asleep.

First she took out the blankets and quilt and spread them over the line, grunting with each effort. She should have had Andrew take out the feather tick, but it wasn't heavy, just bulky. And what a nice fresh bed they would have tonight! She walked carefully on the narrow boards with her top heavy burden. She got one end over the line, but the weight at the other end pulled it down and it dropped in the wet snow. She grabbed it up and gave one mighty heave over the line. The bed tick stuck, but her feet slipped out from under her. She went down with a hard thud on the slippery board. Sitting very still, she tried to feel what was going on inside of her. Did she break anything?

Her back hurt, but nothing alarming. Surely it wouldn't hurt the baby if it didn't hurt her. Her mother had warned her so often about going outdoors where she could slip and fall. She wouldn't even tell her about it, nor Andrew either.

Leazer was alone in the house in the little bed, she must get back to him. She started getting up, her heavy stomach a burden to lift, and since she was already wet from the melted snow, she turned over to rise from her knees. A terrific pain shot down her spine and hips. "Oh, no, no..." she cried. "Dear God, don't let the baby come yet. It can't be alive!"

Unable to rise against the pain, she turned her head toward the woods and cried out in anguish, "Andrew...Andrew!" No sound, but the creaking of trees letting go of their snowy burden. Crying and sobbing and shaking, she finally managed to rise when the pain subsided. Dragging her wet skirts through the snow, water sloshing in her shoes, she crept over closer to the woods. "Andrew, Andrew..." she screamed again and again. Still no human sound. Another pain bent her over. Without stifling her moans and groans she cried out again. There was motion in the bushes and she was ready to fall into Andrew's arms. But it was not Andrew who appeared, but the scar-faced Indian.

"Go get Andrew," she screamed in pain, "Oh please, please hurry." She pointed into the woods. He took only a moment to locate the tracks then went, not running but leaping into the forest.

Andrew had gone farther and farther into the woods cutting elderberry sprouts and finally searching for pussy willows which he hadn't yet found. He heard something crashing up behind him. Thinking it was an animal, he grabbed his gun from beside a nearby tree, then heard strange gutteral human sounds, "Drew...Drew," it seemed to be calling..."Drew...elp."

The Indian came into view. Thinking he might need help with a deer he'd killed, Andrew came slowly toward him, then saw the frantic look on his scarred, twisted face. The Indian bent over hugging his belly, repeating, "Un...Un," then swung his arms like rocking a baby. Andrew was perplexed, what could have gotten him so excited? Was it something about a baby fawn. He wasn't as good as Susan at figuring out such motions. He began following the Indian who kept urging him on faster and pointing toward his house.

"Oh, God, does he mean Sus-un?" When the Indian heard the name, he nodded excitedly. Andrew sped wildly round him. Was it her or had something happened to Leazer? Something about a baby. It couldn't be the new baby already – unless she was losing it.

As he sprang into the clearing near the house, he saw the bedding on the line, but he couldn't see Susan. "Susan!" he shouted. The Indian was still behind him, but turned to go as Andrew dashed towards the house. Thinking he might need a messenger, Andrew motioned for the Indian to wait.

At the door Andrew saw Susan in the bare box of the bed with Leazer beside her, soberly watching his mother writhing in pain. "What happened?" he shouted.

"Oh, Andrew, the baby's coming. Get Mama, get Lena, get somebody!" she sobbed. "Don't leave me, don't leave me," she cried, going into another pain.

Andrew was so frightened he could hardly move, let alone decide what to do. He snatched a scrap of paper and the pencil always kept on top of the mantel, began scribbling in Norwegian, then hastily crossed it out and tried to think of the right words in English and how to spell them. Then he took it to the Indian, and pointed to the smoke rising above the trees at the Carys.

John Cary was walking from barn to house when the Indian came bolting into the yard. He immediately recognized him as the lone Indian about whom Andrew and Susan had told so many tales. The bedraggled messenger, long tangled hair swinging about his scarred face, handed the paper to Mr. Cary and pointed back toward where he had come. John looked at it, the scrawled writing: "babe com kick." He knew it meant something important but...what? He ran to the house, "Lydia, what do you make of this? The Indian brought it."

His wife hurried from her seat at the spinning wheel, and studied the paper. "It's Andrew's writing, he began in Norwegian," she said with alarm. "Bab-e com...QUICK. He means quick, John. Something has happened to Eleazer," she shouted. "Get the buggy or sleigh or something!"

"I'll get King. We'll both ride him."

As they entered, Leazer was screaming, Susan was sobbing and moaning. Andrew had taken off her shoes and stockings and had her dress up across her chest trying to find the strings to her soaked, stained drawers and get them off.

Lydia bounced over to them, "What in the world happened?"

"Oh, Mama, the baby's coming. The water already broke!"

"John...get Lena!"

"No, Mama, there isn't time. I feel it coming. Don't leave me."

"Oh, honey, I won't leave you!" Lydia Cary's usual calm was shaken, but she was resolute.

"Papa, take Leazer," Susan wailed. "I'm scaring him to death."

With one long arm, John Cary scooped up his grandson. Leazer screamed for his mother, but Grandpa Cary threw a coat around him and carried him outside.

"I don't know how these come off." Andrew said in anguish, his face red and perspiring. "Do they tie in back or in front?"

"Here, let me. You get her dress and petticoat off."

He was shakily fumbling with the buttons at her breast.

They had to pause as another pain wrenched through her. Lydia placed her hand on Susan's bare abdomen and felt the strong contraction and winced. "It's coming all right," she said nervously to Andrew.

"It's going to be dead, I know it is!" wailed Susan.

"Well, dear child," her mother said shakily, "we'll do our best. I'll try to follow what I saw Mrs. Tillman doing last time. Do you feel like pushing?"

"I don't know...I don't know..."

Lydia stripped down the winter underwear as soon as Andrew had the outer garments off and Susan lay naked before them, only one thin blanket between her and the boards of the hard wooden bunk.

"Find some blankets, quilts, tablecloths...anything!" Mrs. Cary said to Andrew. "John!" she shouted to her husband pacing around outside the door with his grandson. "Get some covers from the line."

Andrew brought what he could find. "Now get some warm water and a cloth so I can clean her up a little." She spread a baby blanket beneath Susan's hips and could see the head emerging.

Susan was pulling against the cross piece at the head of the bed. Then with one scream of pain, she felt her baby slip into the world. Lydia and Andrew stood aghast looking at the tiny doll-like creature. Susan, exhausted, lay with her eyes closed, panting.

Then they all heard a little mewing sound. Susan grabbed Andrew's arm. "It's alive! What is it?"

Lydia was looking closely. "It's so tiny and bony...It's a girl. Sure it is, it's a girl and kicking lively. Maybe we can save her. Get another warm blanket, Andrew." Lydia was gingerly dealing with the cord as she had seen Mrs. Tillman do. Then she wrapped the baby, handed it to Andrew, and turned back to Susan.

He held the tiny wrapped mortal, his daughter. She was so little she could fit into one of his broad hands. But her features showed clearly. "Susan, she looks like you." His voice trembled with emotion.

"Oh, bring her here," Susan cried. Andrew laid her down on the bed beside Susan's breast. Tears fell on the blanket as she cuddled the tiny infant. "My little girl...God didn't let you die!"

"Mama...Andrew...how very much I love you both...when I saw in my misery...both of you bending over me...caring about nothing but helping me...It's something I'll always remember. I'm so sorry I went out and fell down...both of you warned me so many times."

"Did you fall?" her mother asked, "When I saw the mud on your clothes, I was afraid you had."

Mr. Cary stood quietly by, still holding Leazer. "Oh, Papa, come here." He handed Leazer to Andrew and went to her. She hugged him tightly, "I love you, too – so much."

When she released him, she had a small grin on her face. "But you don't get to name this one, I do. She's Lydia Andrea." Then she suddenly remembered something that seemed hours ago. "Where is the Indian? He's the one I should be thanking. We probably owe her life to him. I don't dare think what might have happened if he hadn't heard me."

"You cook him a good dinner when you feel better. I bet he'll be thanked." Andrew, his knees suddenly weak, sank down on a chair, his son in his arms.

CHAPTER 25

A Guest
For Dinner

USAN WAS TIRED. Not just evenings as she was before the baby was born, but all day long. One or the other of her babies demanded attention constantly. Little Lydia was so tiny and fragile, even her cry was a weak wail, rather than the lusty demands from Leazer. Occasionally, Susan nursed them both at once, Lydia taking only a few intermittent sips before going back to sleep. Leazer emptied a breast in a few gulps, pushing and pummeling like a baby lamb. When a cup of milk was offered, he'd thrust it away. But he was eating potatoes mashed with cream or broth and bread soaked in milk, and for breakfast he ate mush.

"It won't be long until he gives up the breast," Susan's mother assured her. "He'll be so busy learning to walk he won't think about it, especially if you can nurse the baby when he doesn't see you."

Mrs. Cary helped her daughter even more now, taking over much of the washing, baking and churning. She'd take home cream, and by Leander or Alex, send back butter along with fresh baked loaves of bread and often mincemeat or dried apple tarts.

But Susan craved the fresh greens of spring, and longed for the time when wild berries would ripen. One afternoon in early spring when Mrs. Cary was there to watch the babies, Susan asked, "Would you stay awhile so I can go out and look for greens? I'm so hungry for them."

"Why, yes, it will do you good to get out in the spring sunshine. Stay as long as you want." Mrs. Cary sat in the mammy chair rocking her granddaughter and darning one of John's socks. Little Lydia was wide awake, eyes that were turning brown, looked out of the blanket.

Susan bent over her before leaving and the little face lighted up with a slight smile that dimpled her chin, now beginning to flesh out. "When

Mama Stangeland wrote to us," said Susan, "she wanted to know if either of the babies had a dimple in its chin like Andrew has, under the beard."

"Well, right there it is," Mrs. Cary said caressing the tiny cheek.

"Oh, Mama, I love her so much. It's hard to leave her even for a little while."

"Yes, I think you were born to love children. But you must get your strength back, so get out and away for an hour or so."

"You do so much for me, Mama. How can I ever pay you back?"

"I probably don't do any more for you than most mothers with young married daughters. It will be your turn to help little Lydia someday when she needs it, or some other daughter down the line."

Susan sighed. "Right now I don't feel like I ever want another baby, and I always thought I wanted a dozen."

"With all the nursing you probably won't have another for quite awhile."

"We try to keep from...you know...but, Mama, we love each other so much."

"Of course, that's what God intended."

After Susan left, Mrs. Cary watched her daughter for a few minutes as she strolled along towards the woods. She could hardly realize that her little daughter now had two children of her own. She then turned her attention back to baby Lydia, her namesake. The child was rolling her eyes up so that the pupils were out of sight in the way new babies do. Mrs. Cary took one tiny hand out of the blanket, letting the fingers wind around her own as she continued the rocking.

"Poor little darling," she murmured. She worried more about this baby than she'd ever let on to Susan. To the experienced grandmother the baby seemed so delicate, any little sickness could steal her away. Dear God, she prayed, take care of this precious baby.

Susan walked along with her pail and knife toward the edge of the woods, not wanting to venture very far into them alone. Much as she wanted greens she couldn't help from looking up instead of down; the birds were singing and the trees beginning to leaf out. She wanted the children to get old enough to go out with her on walks. She would explain things to them. Or would she always be too busy and too tired for walks?

There seemed to be no greens to be found in the woods and she was headed for the bank along the creek when the Indian appeared before her. She recognized him instantly and wasn't afraid. He hadn't shown up during the sugaring season as Andrew had hoped, since she had not been able to help. He and Nils, Mr. Cary and the twins worked together, sharing help as best they could.

The Indian seemed to be waiting for some kind of explanation and Susan thought it might be about the baby. He'd certainly earned the right to know. She rocked her arms and nodded, pointing to herself. "Girl...like me." She pointed back to the house.

She detected a twitch beneath the scar of his stoic face. Slowly he lifted his arms and rocked them and pointed to himself. Something about his baby son? He cupped his hands and made the outline of a woman, laid his head to one side and closed his eyes, then gestured along the ground.

"Oh, I'm so sorry," Susan said, pain showing on her face. She wondered whether mother and baby had died recently or long ago. She had no idea how old the Indian was. Perhaps it might have been during sugaring season, the reason he didn't show up. But she suspected it was longer ago or he wouldn't have been roaming around alone everytime they saw him. He seemed to have more to tell her. Lifting his coppery fingers to his face he jabbed rapidly all over his cheeks, his neck and his chest.

For a few moments she frowned trying to interpret. "Smallpox! Was it small...pox?" He nodded and she shook her head sadly. He pointed to himself and shook his head. He apparently didn't get them. Had they been banished from the tribe when smallpox struck, Susan wondered.

Finally she smiled again, pointed to the house, and made motions like eating. He indicated the couple of small greens in her pail, then waved a hand out along the creek bank behind him. Then he turned and vanished as silently as he had come. She guessed he meant that there were more greens back in the woods, but she wasn't about to go look for them and chance meeting up with a wild animal.

She looked a little farther finding only a few more and was so tired she started back. Just like a mother cat, she thought, who never strays far from her nest of new kittens. But there was none of her former exuberance, no desire to skip or run.

Late the next afternoon, Susan was nursing Lydia while Leazer slept. There was a thump at the door. Thinking it was Andrew, she didn't investigate until she had laid down the sleeping baby. Then, looking out, she saw a massive bundle of greens tied together with a vine. Laughing with delight, she knew immediately where they had come from. She looked around for the Indian and saw him sitting on a log just inside the clearing. He had come to supper.

Doing something for someone outside her family again, even so minor as fixing a meal herself, gave Susan incentive to forget her tiredness. She plunged the greens into the old wooden bucket filled with water. As she anticipated having all the greens she wanted to eat, she cut smoked side pork to season them. She didn't know what Indians liked, but he had always eaten all they gave him before, so she'd fix as though for themselves; slices of ham from the smokehouse, fried eggs, the fish Andrew had caught that were cleaned and waiting in cold water. Of course there would be the greens, also boiled potatoes and sauerkraut. She doubted if an Indian ever tasted sauerkraut and smiled at what he might think of it. She'd also bake some cornbread to eat with fresh butter and maple syrup. And there were the dried apple tarts her mother had brought over.

Fortunately the babies were cooperative. Lydia slept, awakening for a few sips at the breast, then back to sleep again. The April day was warm enough for Leazer to be on the floor and needed only to be kept away from the fire, as he practiced standing and taking his first few steps from table to bench to stool. Susan was teaching him the word "hot" by placing his hand on a very warm stone near the fire. So now he'd look at the fire and say, "Ha...ha."

For company and her sheer joy in them, Susan talked constantly to her babies, even though they couldn't understand. In her heart she knew there was a special love for Lydia, without taking anything away from Leazer. Her mother and father often remarked how much she was like their baby, Susan, only she had been fat and robust, and like Leazer, always letting her wants be known. Private tears were often shed by Susan, wishing the baby could have stayed in her little nest until time to come, so that she too, could have arrived vigorous and strong.

When Andrew came to the house after a day of plowing, he did not see the Indian who had fallen asleep sitting on the log in a patch of late afternoon sunshine.

With a smile, Susan pointed him out to Andrew. Then she lifted the lid on the simmering pot of greens. "He dumped all these on the doorstep and just went over there and sat down to wait. I'm having a good time fixing a real feast for him."

"Am I invited or is this just for two of you?"

"I think there's enough for three," she teased. "Do you think he'll come in and sit with us?"

Andrew shrugged. "We'll ask him."

"Can we eat before you do your chores? Things are nearly ready, Leazer is hungry and the Indian has waited a long time."

Andrew went to bring the guest, who had awakened and was again watching the house. Andrew motioned for him to come. He followed slowly and hesitantly. Susan came smiling to the door to welcome him in, but he stopped at the doorstep and shook his head.

"Let me show you the baby," Susan said, rocking her arms, then went to pick up Lydia. For a moment the Indian looked in the blanket at the heart-shaped face surrounded by soft dark hair, then nodded. Pointing to himself, he then swung a finger toward Leazer, who stood by watching the Indian with curiosity. "His baby that died must have been nearer Leazer's age," Susan interpreted to Andrew.

"I'll fix your plate," she said, laying the baby down and taking out her biggest platter, the one she served turkey on at Thanksgiving. She filled it well, laid on a large buttered slice of cornbread with maple syrup poured into its yellow center. On top of that she placed the apple tart. She gave him a fork, a spoon and a pint cup of coffee with plenty of cream. He took it and hurried back to his place on the log.

Through the little window, Susan and Andrew watched him before they sat down to eat. He picked up the tart, turned it over and over, pushed his thumb through it, then ate it first. Then he began working his way hungrily across the plate from one side to the other.

"Let's eat," said Andrew, "I'm hungry."

"I'm waiting for him to get to the sauerkraut."

"After raw liver, he should be able to handle it."

"Hush, I don't want to think about it."

Before they had finished eating, there was a light tap at the door. Andrew opened it. The Indian handed him the completely empty platter, the cup, fork and spoon on top. Again without smiling he nodded slowly three times, looking past Andrew to Susan. She smiled and held up her hand. "Come again," she said.

After the door was closed, Andrew showed her the plate. "Not even sauerkraut left."

"I wonder how much he dumped behind the log," she laughed.

"When are you going to teach him English like you did me?"

She wrinkled her nose. "It wouldn't be so much fun sitting close to him."

Andrew put an arm around her, remembering the excitement and wonder of those first lessons side by side on a bench by the fire. "Now we got each other all the time and two babies, too."

"Oh, I almost forgot to tell you," Susan said. "Mama and Papa got a letter from James, and guess what?"

"They're coming back to New York?" Andrew asked.

"No, they're doing fine there in the Michigan Territory. But they have a baby boy! James Junior."

"Already they have a baby? Married just a year. They did better than we did," Andrew laughed.

"And I'm an aunt, finally."

CHAPTER 26

Gift From
New York

L ATER THAT SPRING a letter came from the New York merchant Susan and Andrew had sold their syrup to in Rochester. It was in answer to the letter Susan had painstakingly written, as requested, about the 1830 spring crop of maple syrup. They hadn't believed it would actually reach Mr. Samuelson, but already here was a reply. Susan unfolded the single sheet to read it to Andrew. For a moment they reveled in the importance of the fine paper with the business heading across the top and "Hugh Samuelson" signed in flowing script.

He informed them that he did want the syrup, but couldn't predict the day, let alone the hour when he would be coming through the area. But before May 15, could Andrew leave the syrup with the boat builder in Albion, who lived near the canal and was an honest man? As soon as he picked it up, Mr. Samuelson would immediately mail them a check from the office. He asked about the potato crop and assured them he was still interested in it if they would let him know when it was ready. The letter ended with a request to "Extend my greetings to your lovely wife and baby son."

Susan flushed, remembering, as she often did, the suave, handsome New Yorker. But to Andrew she only remarked, "He doesn't know that now we also have a daughter."

Taking the maple syrup to market had become a special and anticipated trip. Busy as he was, Andrew would take a full day off for it. After all, they must celebrate the good fortune Mr. Samuelson had brought to them.

"Shall I pack our dinner in a basket?" Susan asked at breakfast, realizing how much had to be done before she would be ready to go.

"No, we'll stop at the Village Inn. I have a dollar saved special for this trip."

"Oh, I wish we could...but I don't know if we should take two babies in there."

"Would you rather get something from the store to eat cold?"

"Let's do. I hear they have a new bakery in town. You ought to know your way around in that."

"Yah," Andrew laughed, "maybe I can get a job."

So they leisurely made their way to Albion behind Cloud along the newly-named High Prairie Road. The colt had grown into a fine horse, broken to pull plow as well as buggy. After being bred to Mr. Cary's King, Dolly was expecting another colt any day.

The sweet moist smell of spring was all about them. Wild flowers spread their abundance along the wayside. Lazy white clouds drifted by the horizon of Lake Ontario, cobalt blue beneath the lighter blue sky.

Susan was beginning to regain her strength and looked better. Andrew noticed, some of the color had come back in her cheeks and the dark circles under her eyes were nearly gone.

Mr. Sloan, the boat builder in Albion, had already heard that they would be leaving syrup with him, and he was glad to oblige, especially when Andrew insisted he take a pail of the syrup for his trouble. Pails were now being used instead of jugs to hold the syrup. Susan had written out a receipt for Mr. Sloan to sign, indicating the number of containers left with him. The two men talked of Lars Larson, whom Mr. Sloan, being in the same business, saw frequently. He went to Rochester by canal for materials unavailable in the small village of Albion.

When Andrew finally returned to the buggy, Susan was beside herself trying to keep the children quiet. Both of them were hungry and Leazer was feeling much too confined. "What took so long?" Susan asked with irritation.

"We'll go right now to the store and bakery. I talked too long with Mr. Sloan about Lars Larson. He goes to Rochester sometimes and sees Lars."

THE BECKONING

When they stopped in front of the store, Susan asked Andrew to take Lydia while she went to the privy; when she returned she asked him to take Leazer with him to the bakery so she would have an opportunity to nurse the baby.

She watched father and son walking toward the bakery. How she'd like to go see it too. Maybe after the children had eaten and quieted she could look in the store windows. She gazed longingly toward the millinery shop, but couldn't see what was in the window.

Andrew and Leazer emerged from the bakery empty-handed and turned into the store beside it. When they appeared, Leazer was munching on a little brown cookie.

"They didn't have bread today at the bakery." Andrew explained, "because the oven was shut down for fixing. So I got these little brown cookies to eat with our sausage." They had splurged a couple of times before on a ring of the already cooked sausage in a casing and found it delicious.

"Cookies with meat?" Susan peered in at them doubtfully.

"Only thing I could think of," Andrew said, then grinning, reached into his pocket and pulled out two bright yellow bananas.

"Oh, Andrew, bananas!" She did so crave fruits and vegetables at this time of year when they were almost never to be found. "Did you have enough money for all that?"

"It took few more pennies more than the dollar, but I had enough and I thought you would enjoy. They just came in on the canal boat."

He took the coarse gray blanket from behind them and spread it in a sunny spot near a grove of budding trees.

"Will you pull Cloud over closer and tie him so I can leave Lydia in the buggy? She's already asleep."

So the little family had their first town picnic, Lydia sleeping and Cloud waiting patiently, intermittently switching his tail, stomping his feet or dozing. Andrew got out his pocket knife, the last gift his father gave him, sliced off a piece of sausage, skinned it and handed it to Leazer. The meat was new and strange; questioningly he held it up to his mother.

"Good. Good."

He licked it, then began eating. Without the burden of either child on her lap, the tired mother began to relax and enjoy her own dinner.

Andrew munched on a cookie. "He called them ginger...ginger breaks or something like that. Ginger snaps, that's what it was. Something new. He got a whole keg of them."

"And bananas!" Susan drew the peel back slowly. "My what a feast."

Andrew was delighted to see the pleasure it was bringing to his wife. "You eat all that one. Leazer and I eat this one."

"Oh, no," Susan protested, "I'll share with Leazer." But Andrew insisted, saying he'd finish the sausage and they'd still have a few cookies to eat on the way home.

They took turns going to the town pump for a drink of water, and laughed at Leazer trying to drink from under the spout like his father had done. Then Andrew took down the tin cup from the wire hook and offered him a drink from that.

Their pleasant little picnic ended. Susan went to look in a couple of store windows before leaving for home.

As they again approached Mr. Sloan's place of business, he came hurrying out carrying a fancy box and waved for them to stop. "I was watching for you to come back. I plumb forgot this package that was left for you from the canal boat this morning. Must be something you ordered from New York."

Andrew and Susan looked at each other shaking their heads in bewilderment. "Must be a mistake," Susan said.

"Well, it says for Mrs. Stangeland on it," Mr. Sloan said, looking again. "Not a very common name around here."

"For me?" Susan said with astonishment. Mr. Sloan handed it to her. She read her name on top of the box, quickly broke the seals, and took off the lid. Her eyes grew wide, as she lifted out a straw colored bonnet with sprigs of dainty purple violets around the brim.

"A letter inside," Andrew pointed out.

THE BECKONING

Susan opened it, noted that it was from Hugh Samuelson, as she suspected, then read it to Andrew. "A little gift for your kindness in writing to let me know about the maple syrup. Also in hopes you will keep me informed about your husband's potato crop and any other good produce in quantity that you may know of. All due respects and best regards."

"What a generous gift!" Susan flushed with pleasure. Leazer grabbed for the purple ribbons, so she quickly, carefully replaced it in the box.

"Aren't you going to wear it home?" Andrew asked, concealing his jealousy.

"No, I want to show it to Mama and Papa just the way it was in the box. Can we stop there on the way home?"

"We go right past."

Susan chattered on about other things, pointing out to Leazer sights along the way. The warmth and pleasantness of the day added to her soaring spirits as she kept thinking: The latest spring bonnet from New York City and from a polished, well-dressed businessman! He must have been as attracted to me as I was to him, she thought.

Finally, she realized that Andrew sat silent and hadn't spoken for several minutes. She reached across the now-sleeping Leazer to pat her husband's knee. "He only sent it to me, you know, to be sure he gets the potatoes and more maple syrup. I guess that is the way they do business in New York."

"I think he remember how beautiful you are, too. No man could not see that." He moved the reins to his other hand and squeezed hers with his broad palm.

For the next few days, when Andrew wasn't around, Susan took the hat from the box and modeled it for Leazer, then looked at herself from every angle in the small mirror. Leazer soon learned to say hat (which sounded like his word for hot) and pointed to it on the high shelf where she kept it.

On Sunday, she wore it to church, winning the admiring glances and comments of nearly every woman. Andrew, with his quaker leanings, inwardly thought it too ostentatious and was slightly embarrassed, but he could never bring himself to forbid her to wear it.

It was the day of the monthly carry-in basket dinner with a short service afterwards, which Mr. Cary laughingly referred to as naptime for babies and old men. "I get a little drowsy myself," he confided to Andrew as they stood outside in the spring sunshine discussing Andrew's good fortune with Mr. Samuelson. "I might put potatoes in that west patch beside yours. If he wants all he can get, might as well add mine to yours, if it's all right?"

"Of course it's all right. Maybe a little pay back for all the favors you do to me."

Monday morning Susan felt so good she determined to do her own washing rather than taking it to her mother's as usual. She and her mother had made the summer's supply of soap the week before and the large unwashed kettle still sat in the yard. She could boil the clothes in it outside and do two jobs at once. It meant a lot of lifting and carrying because Andrew was taking advantage of the good weather, using every daylight hour to get in as much plowing and planting as possible.

By evening Susan was proud to have gotten all the clothes boiled, scrubbed on the board, rinsed and dried on the line by supper time. But she was so tired that getting supper ready seemed like a real chore, so she made do with leftovers.

Soon after, she got Leazer asleep in his little shelf bed, then decided to crawl in bed herself even though her dishes were not done and Andrew had not come in from his chores. Her back ached and she hadn't nursed Lydia yet. So, rather than sitting down with her in the mammy chair, she took her to bed to nurse. They were all sound asleep when Andrew came in to lay his weary self beside them.

Sometime in the night Lydia began fussing. Grogged with sleep, Susan unbuttoned her gown, removed a breast and nudged the nipple into the baby's mouth, cuddling her close and away from the hard rail of the bed. For a moment of awareness she basked in the warmth and secure feeling of her family surrounding her. Andrew breathed deeply as he slept; Leazer stirred and turned in his bed. She nosed around for Lydia's little head and softly kissed the top of it, murmuring her love, then fell asleep again.

In the morning it was already light when Susan awakened. Andrew had gone to his chores and neither child was yet awake. Her breast still lay by Lydia. She slid away from her to get out of bed as quietly as possible to get dressed before Leazer awakened to demand his breakfast.

After she dressed and had the mush bubbling on the stove, she heard Leazer awake, chattering to himself as usual, then finally calling, "Ma...ma."

She dressed and fed him, put side meat on to fry for herself and Andrew, thankful that Lydia had not yet wakened. But as usual, she could not stay away from her very long without at least looking at her. She went over to the quiet bundle at the back of the bed, and gently pulled her forward, but the baby did not stir. As light fell on the child's face, Susan noticed the strange gray cast to her skin. Alarmed, she began unwrapping her, and curled her finger around the tiny hand. It was cold. With rising panic she lifted the hand...the arm. It was rigid.

In one breathless moment she flung the rest of the covers off the quiet little form, grasped a foot, then jumped back with a scream. Startled, Leazer began to cry. Continuing one shrieking scream after another, Susan ran from the cabin, took a few steps toward the Cary house, then ran toward the barn, where Andrew met her, his face white with fear.

She sprung on him, still screaming. "What iss it...Susuun?" She could not answer as scream followed scream. He looked toward the house and saw Leazer lustily crying at the door and assumed he was all right. "Was it an animal? Indian? Did you hurt yourself?"

Finally, like the last gasp for help before going down for the last time she forced out, "Baby...dead."

Unbelieving and knowing how sensitive Susan was to every ailment which beset the children, he soothed, "No-o...she's all right. We get back to her." But Susan loosened her grasp, shook free from him, turned quickly and ran wildly up the path toward her parents' house.

Andrew ran frantically to the house. He latched the door behind him so Leazer wouldn't try to follow his mother. Seeing the skillet of burning meat smoking on the stove, he grabbed a towel and pushed it to the cooler side. Then he looked around for the baby, and went to where she lay uncovered on the bed. He had only to touch one cold arm to know. Falling on his knees at the side of the bed he wept in anguish, "Gud...Gud nei hva er dette! Sorg...sorg."

CHAPTER 27

Visit From Carolyn

FTER A FEW MOMENTS of empty despair, Andrew rose heavily and went to Leazer who was still pitifully crying at the door and calling for his mother. Without a word, father lifted son, and pulled him to his shoulder, where the small boy lay sobbing and trembling. Tears rolled down Andrew's cheeks as the two clung to each other for comfort.

To Andrew, the death of his baby daughter was painful enough, but foremost in his mind was the wild look in Susan's eyes when she fled. He knew the special bond between her and the baby and worried for her sanity. Presently he heard the rapid pounding of horse's hoofs; it would be John Cary on King.

"Oh, God bless you, son." The older man entered and gripped Andrew's hand, then cast a sidelong glance at the baby's body on the bed. Andrew knew the grandfather's grief was as great as his own.

"Is Susan with her mother?" Andrew asked brokenly.

Mr. Cary nodded. "She's quieted some, but can't tell us what happened. Said the baby was all right in the night when she nursed her...but gone this morning."

"How could that be?" Andrew asked in anguish.

John Cary shook his head sorrowfully as they moved hesitantly toward the bed and began examining the tiny form. "If it was from a bite or sting there surely would be a mark somewhere."

But they found nothing. Andrew lovingly smoothed down the soft brown hair, and covered her over with a blanket. Leazer, who was now content to toddle about, came over and began climbing steps to the bed.

"Baby's asleep," Andrew said, lifting him down.

"Ba–bee s'eep," Leazer repeated.

"I must go to Susan," Andrew whispered.

"I'll stay here, then," said Mr. Cary.

But upon Andrew's arrival at the Cary house, Susan did not so much as acknowledge his presence. Her outburst of terror spent, she sat beside her mother on a bench by the fire as though she did not see nor hear nor distinguish one family member from another. Andrew sat down on the other side of her. Mrs. Cary rose, stifled a sob and went to the kitchen.

Tears running into his beard, Andrew put his arm around Susan, but she was like a cold lump of clay. He took her hand, it was limp. He kissed it, and pressed it to his face. No response.

Mrs. Cary came back in, eyes red, tears streaming. She went to Susan and put a hand on her shoulder. "Honey, I'm going back up to be with Papa and...and dress the baby. Do you want to go?" Susan shook her head slightly. "Is there a special dress you want her to wear?"

Susan dropped her head with more violent weeping, moaning through the sobs, "My baby, my baby, my baby..."

Mrs. Cary spoke through her tears: "When Uncle Ira gets there, we'll go past Angela's to tell them and leave Leazer." She gently rubbed Susan's shoulders. "People will be coming, honey. They'll all want to help in some way."

People did come, all that day and the next and before the burial on Thursday. They brought food, kind words, offers of assistance, anything at all they could do. Norwegian neighbors helped Andrew with his chores, and urged him to spend the nights with them. He tried to appreciate all such generous offers. But his well-spring of emotions had frozen over. Nothing mattered.

Susan had little to do with Leazer. He'd come to her and try to climb on her lap, but she'd only lay a limp hand on him and say, "Mama's too tired" or "Not now, Leazer." Then Angela or Angie or one of the twins would lure him away with a cookie or other sweet. If that failed, they would drag him away to quiet him out of her sight.

Although there was plenty of tempting food around, Susan ate none of it. Once in awhile her mother could get her to drink a little milk or broth.

She made no effort to go home or to touch the baby after it had been prepared for burial. People, in well-meaning kindness, would say to her, "She looks like a little doll, just sleeping." But it would send Susan into spasms of weeping, gasping and shuddering...."my baby, my baby, my baby." At night in her parents' house, her mother or father sat by her side until she fell asleep from exhaustion.

The baby's little burial box was made by Uncle Ira, then lovingly padded and lined by Aunt Helen and some of the neighbors. Andrew asked Susan if she would like her buried in the little spot they enjoyed at the edge of the woods where wild flowers grew in all colors. Without looking at him, she nodded her head.

Thursday morning relatives and friends gathered around the burial spot, and baby Lydia was lowered into the freshly-dug black earth between two stately maple trees. Andrew and Mr. Cary supported Susan, hardly able to walk, almost too weak to even cry. After the short ceremony, as they were leaving, they overheard a small cluster of women talking together. "Poor little thing, she is so young..."

Andrew tightened his grip on Susan's arm.

Mr. Cary urged Andrew to spend the night at their place, but he used the excuse that he must stay where he could hear the livestock in case wolves or coyotes invaded. He knew that he had to get back to work in the fields, chores, anyplace to help ease his tormented mind. Everything he did took such effort. Like dragging a plow everywhere he went, Andrew thought bleakly.

For the next two days, he worked until the sweat dripped and his strength gave out. He avoided people as much as possible. When he could go no longer and darkness came, he ate a little food and fell exhausted on the bed, fully clothed, and slept as though in a drunken stupor. Arising as soon as he awakened on Saturday morning, he realized he must do away with the bed. He would go talk with Nils and Henrik to see if they could find time to help put on the addition to the house which he and Susan had been planning. He had expected to use maple sugar money on the lumber and work on it himself throughout the summer. But now it could not take that long.

He went first to Nils and Carolyn's house. She met him at the door. They had been at the burial but had only spoke briefly. Now that they were alone and could speak Norwegian, she clasped Andrew's hand again and again, "My heart just cries for you and poor little Susan. I know so well all she is going through. I wish there was something I could do, anything." Andrew recalled the image of Carolyn as she stared vacantly into space from her bed for days after her sickness, devastated by the death of her baby daughter, then her husband, all in one week.

He told of his plan to add the new bedroom to relieve the horror of the present bed.

"I know Nils will help, we'll all help. I'll invite other neighbors, too. There is that new family of Norwegians moved in south of us, you know. They have a couple of big boys. I'll tell Nils as soon as he gets back from Kendall."

As Andrew started to leave, he hesitated, and turned back. "Carrie, would you go visit Susan at her mother's house? Maybe tell her...how you felt?" His voice broke in a sob. "I might lose her. She and Leazer are my whole world. If I lose them, I'll have to go back to Norway. I couldn't stand it here."

Carolyn came to him, and lovingly stroked his arm, crying also. "Andreas, dear friend, I speak so little English, I'm afraid I would do more harm than good."

"She...I'm afraid she thinks she smothered the baby," Andrew faltered. "I don't know if that is true, but what else could have happened?"

"I'll go see her this afternoon, Andreas, I think God will help me with the words."

"If she doesn't respond to you, please don't feel hurt. She is so grieved, she can't help what she does."

"Of course I know. Nothing could ever hurt our friendship. And don't even think of going back to Norway. She'll come around, just give her time. Look how happy I am with Nils now, and once I thought I could not go on living."

After visiting Henrik and getting a prompt offer of his and Martha's help, Andrew took a detour through the woods, thinking that its silence and density might give him some peace of mind. Its survival depended on death and regrowth.

He sat on a log trying to concentrate on the greening of the trees, the happy songs of the birds. But it only made him more lonesome for Susan, their way of life, their contentment before this happened. What did the future hold? "Susan...Susan, don't leave me," he murmured. "We'll move away, anything!" He dropped his head in his hands in tormented weeping. After awhile he heard the slight stir of brush underfoot nearby. Almost before he looked up, he knew it would be the Indian.

The disheveled native stood before him, arms folded. He nodded slowly then placed his hand over his heart and nodded again.

Andrew was deeply touched by the simple message. He had long suspected that events at the Stangeland farm, and now this tragedy, were known to him. Andrew rose unsteadily to his feet, and extended his hand. The Indian hesitated for a few seconds, then slowly reached out and took it lightly for an instant, then as usual, quickly disappeared into the woods.

Andrew trudged on home, but decided not to go to the field. Instead, he would tear out the bed and get ready to work on the new room.

That afternoon, Carolyn, in her best dress, walked slowly toward the Cary house, dreading the encounter with Susan and praying she could find some words of comfort for her. Mrs. Cary met her at the door, clasped her hand and said, "So nice of you to come. Susan is in her room, I'll tell her you are here."

"T'ank you," Carolyn murmured.

After several minutes, during which Carolyn knew Mrs. Cary had to talk her daughter into coming out, Susan emerged and acknowledged her visitor with a slight nod. "I'm going out to feed the chickens," her mother said quietly to Susan. "There's tea in the pot if you two would like some."

Susan made no move to get it, merely sat down heavily in a chair opposite. "I'm afraid I'm not much good for visiting, Carolyn, I'm sorry."

"Please...not be sorry. I know ever...feel you have. Andrew maybe tell you...I once lose...baby and...husband same week?"

"Yes, I know."

"I lay in bed. Could not get up. People tell me do this...do that, I feel better. But they not know...big stone on my...(she laid a hand on her breast) could not move off."

Susan looked up at her, fresh tears in her eyes.

"They say to me, you got more...other girls to t'ink about. But I t'ink of no thing but sweet baby I never see again...and her papa...I luff so much. And I never see them...till Heaven. I yust want to go home to Norway...and be a little girl again." Tears ran down the Norwegian woman's face.

"Oh, Carolyn, you do know how I feel," Susan said with more feeling than she had shown since the morning of the tragedy. "But you didn't...smother...your baby." Her head fell as great shaking sobs overwhelmed her.

Carolyn waited, then said gently, "I don't t'ink you smother your baby. So close to you, you hear her or feel her...kick, or somet'ing."

Susan looked up startled. "I know it too, Carolyn. When I woke up, the baby was on her back several inches away from my breast. She couldn't have been underneath. I know I would have felt her struggle."

"Woman I know in Norway lost baby...little time old. He born too early, like your Lydia. He die in cradle in night. No sound. Not'ing. We t'ink God take him back...born too soon. Somet'ing only God know."

Susan rose quickly, came over and dropped on her knees in front of Carolyn. "Oh, Carrie, do you think so, too? I think that is why God woke me up in the night to say goodbye to her. For that moment I felt such a rush of love for her. But I can't explain it to anyone else."

"I t'ink that be true, yes. I tell all I see, I t'ink this and they say, 'maybe so'." She paused as she stroked Susan's hair. "Andrew, my friend long time. He hurt much, too."

"Oh, I know. But I can't go home to him. I feel so ashamed or something. Like I could never sleep with him again."

"Don't be afraid to go home. He know how you hurt. I see him this morning. He tear out old bed. We going to help him build a bedroom. All Norske neighbors come to help."

Susan clasped Carolyn's hands in hers, "Oh, Carrie, you're so good. He knew who to send to me. Will you walk home with me?"

As they approached the Stangeland house, they could see Andrew carrying boards from house to barn. "I go home now," Carolyn said and Susan turned with a slight shudder to face the house she had left in such wild frenzy.

Andrew saw her hesitant approach, quickly dropped the boards and came to meet her. She put her arms around his neck, crying softly, "Andrew, Andrew." His arms went tight around her and without further words, they cried together as they had not yet been able to do. Finally she said, "Take me in the house, will you? I must get used to it again. I hear we're going to have a bedroom."

They walked slowly to the door. Andrew went in first, and holding her hand, brought her in. He had moved the table to where the bed used to be. She looked around them. "What a lot of room we're going to have. But where are you going to sleep tonight?"

"I cleaned out the hut, some, and will sleep out there."

"Alone?"

"I'd rather not."

"We'll go down to Mama's for supper and bring back my things. Tomorrow we'll get Leazer. Poor little boy without his Mama or Papa. She went over and gave the mammy chair a last rock with her finger.

"Shall I store it in the cellar?" Andrew asked.

"Not in the cellar, I have to go there too often. Could you put it safely somewhere in the barn?" Andrew nodded. She stood looking around a few more minutes then reached up on the shelf and took down the fancy hat box. "There is one more thing I must do." Without so much as looking in it, she thrust it into the blazing fire and slowly turned away.

"Oh, Susan, are you sure?" Andrew asked.

"I'm sure. I must never again permit such vanity."

Andrew stood solemnly watching the flames curl the box apart to get at the dainty straw hat with the purple violets. It vanished with one whoosh.

Is this the time, he asked himself. Is it time now to move West, away from the site of this tragedy?

CHAPTER 28

Cleng
Brings News

THE NEW BEDROOM ADDITION was completed in two days with the help of the Norwegian friends and other neighbors. Then the iron bedstead that Susan had formerly slept on was brought over from the Carys and set up. The dresser, as well. Even the washstand and the bowl-and-pitcher set with the hand painted pink roses now graced the new bedroom. Susan's former room had become a guest room, but now the boys wanted to move down from the loft which previously was their brother James' sleeping space. So Mr. Cary had made bunks to hold straw ticks and they were happy without all the "fancy junk," as Leander described it.

Susan was thankful for the extra space and the privacy of a bedroom. Leazer's little trumble bed was pushed under the bed during the day.

After a month Susan was able to go through part of a day and sometimes all night without those hauntingly painful memories, without seeing the dear, sweet little face of baby Lydia everywhere she looked. Sometimes she couldn't recall that image and she'd panic. But soon it would come back again. She tried over and over to imagine her as a little angel with wings, happily flitting about Heaven, not missing her mama as much as her mama sorely missed her.

She went at least twice a week to visit and tend the little grave, sometimes in the evening or on Sunday with Andrew. Sometimes she took Leazer, letting him walk as far as he could, then carrying him. Together they would look for and listen to the birds, find wild strawberries, and pick flowers. Paying extra attention to him usually kept her from the overpowering grief and tears she didn't want him to see.

Andrew proposed a trip to Rochester for Susan's July birthday, since they hadn't been away from home since the tragedy.

As usual, the Larson house was filled with newly arrived immigrants. Lars and Martha's second baby girl was named Lydia and everyone was careful not to call the little girl by name when Susan was around, an omission of which Susan was sorely aware. Martha was now expecting again.

"Better be a son this time," Lars told Andrew. "Got to have one boy at least to leave my boat works to."

Martha had received a letter from Cleng's sister, and was anxious to share it with Andrew and Susan. Kari reported that the Norwegians at the Fox River settlement were working hard, long days carving their place in the Illinois prairie frontier. Livestock constantly had to be protected from wolves and horse thieves. She told of the great danger from fires in the tall, dry prairie grass; Indians sometimes deliberately set fires for their own amusement. But in spite of those difficulties, farming was much easier than it had been in the Black North. There were births, some deaths; a few had moved with new immigrants to the north in Wisconsin territory and others further west to Iowa territory.

Cleng was on the road most of the time, she wrote, exploring, helping others, finding homes for orphaned children. All the things he loved and did best.

On the ride home, as Andrew and Susan discussed the news, Andrew said, "You know, I keep thinking about Cleng, I wouldn't be surprised if he didn't show up on our doorstep one of these days."

"Maybe he'll come in time to help dig potatoes," Susan said.

"I doubt that," Andrew laughed.

Back in April, before the baby's death, a check for the maple syrup had arrived from Hugh Samuelson. Susan had carefully written a letter of thanks for it and an extra special thank you for the hat (which now she tried never to think about) and informed him of approximately how many potatoes Andrew would have.

Promptly came back a reply asking for all the good potatoes he could get in one lot and to let him know when they were ready.

It was late in August when Andrew decided his potatoes were ready to dig. Mr. Cary told him the boys could help pick them up because he wouldn't be working on his for a few more days.

THE BECKONING

On the day Andrew opened the field and began digging the big, white potatoes, he came home at noon for dinner and was met by the boys carrying something.

"You got a big, heavy package from Norway," nine-year-old Alexander shouted, brother Leander not far behind.

Andrew knew the package would be from his mother and for his birthday. "Come on in the house and we'll open it," Andrew told the two eager boys.

Andrew washed the dirt off his hands and arms at the pump and dried them on the towel Susan kept there. He took the package, feeling of it, turning it over and over, noting the carefully copied address in his mother's hand.

Susan had dinner already on the table so the package was placed on the bench, the four on-lookers eagerly standing by. Leazer clawed at the wrappings to hurry his dad and see what was inside. "Feels like a blanket," Andrew said.

The thick black fold appeared and Andrew held it up. "Why it's a coat," Susan exclaimed. "And look at those silver buttons! It's beautiful."

"Sure looks warm," Andrew said trying to hide some of his pride.

"Put it on," Alex said. Andrew looked down doubtfully at his dirty clothes, then carefully slipped into it.

Susan nodded, smiling. "She hasn't forgotten your size. My don't you look handsome."

Running his hand into the pockets, Andrew brought forth a letter and happily held it up. He slipped off the coat. "It will feel better in November than it does in August," he laughed. "Let's eat. I'll read my letter later. Are you going to stay for dinner, boys?"

"No, we already ate," Alex said.

"Can we have a cookie anyway, Susan?" Leander asked.

"You may have a cookie," she passed them the plate.

A cookie in each hand, they bounced out the door. "We'll be back in a little while to pick up spuds," Alex called back.

They heard Leander say, "I get to tell Mama and Papa about Andrew's coat."

"No, I do," Alex said. They began racing each other.

"If I know those two, they will both tell it at once," Susan laughed.

After dinner, when Andrew had read his letter, he reported to Susan, "Ole is making the bakery bigger and his son, Sevve, has my job now. Tollak's Oscar helps some too. The farm is going good. She has...what you call it here when legs and arms ache?"

"Rheumatism?"

"Must be. She doesn't get around so good. Said she wanted to buy me something nice to last while she could still get out into the stores. She says they are still enjoying the maple syrup we sent with Ole."

He sat for several minutes lost in thought, holding the letter in one hand, staring ahead of him, looking very sober. Susan's heart ached for him, so far from his beloved family. And she was so close to hers. She went over and hugged him, but Andrew, like most Norwegians, was not one to share emotion when it concerned himself.

The combined potato crops were too much for one wagon so Henrik brought his *kubberulle* to help haul the load to Albion. They would then unload Henrik's wagon so he could return home and Andrew would stay to wait for the freighter. Then he would help load the potatoes on the boat for passage to New York to be received by one of Samuelson's men.

Andrew slept on the wagon with the sacks of potatoes, a September moon overhead. It reminded him of the other times he'd slept on freight – on the ocean and on the canal barge, and the cold, miserable night in the rain near Holley with Gudmund as they waited with the immigrants' possessions before they were hauled to that first crowded cabin. Then he turned to a warmer memory: The night he had proposed to Susan.

He thought about her, wanting her warm, eager body against his. She had finally returned to him as though her body was willing, but her mind was not. "I don't want another baby just yet," she'd cried.

"I'll be careful," he promised. She was, at 20, a much more mature Susan than she had been before the tragedy. Extra cautious about so many things: that Leazer was safe, that she didn't go away and leave a candle or lamp burning. When she went to skim the yellow cream from the milk pans in the cellar, she walked cautiously down the steps.

Even though quieter and more often sober, she was his beloved Susan, who, with Leazer, his home and the farm, were everything to him. Sometimes when he'd been gone until after dark and came home towards the lighted candle in the window and puffs of smoke from the chimney, he felt the blessing of a man with a good wife and child. It was like a dream come true. No matter how poor they were, no man on wealthy Strand Street in Stavanger could ever have felt richer.

The next day when he returned home, he had another gift for Susan from Hugh Samuelson. She took it hesitantly, remembering the beautiful bonnet and its consequences. She was relieved it was a box of candy. Though a luxury, it was something to share with the family.

In September, Andrew was just starting to husk his corn when from deep in the field he heard far-off a familiar whistle. Before he so much as looked out, he knew it would be Cleng. Andrew waved and shouted, then hurried to the edge of the field where Cleng stood waiting. "Got a cold drink of water for a wayfaring friend?"

They gripped and shook hands for a full half minute. "How glad I am to see you, Cleng! Did you stop by the house?"

"No, I saw the corn stalks waving and I knew you'd be out here." He looked around him. "What wonders you have wrought here, Andreas. You've got a farm almost equal to the Carys."

"We've sure been working at it. Had some good luck and some bad."

"Not too bad, I hope." Then Andrew told him about their little Lydia. He had written the news to his friends at Fox River, but Cleng had not been there since early spring. He was just now headed home.

"Come on up to the house. We'll tell Susan you're here, then we'll walk on down to Nils' house, have them and Henriks up for supper."

Cleng hugged Susan warmly, and told her how sorry he was about the baby. "May our Heavenly Father continue to strengthen you both in your sorrow," he said with sympathy.

Susan brought grape juice from the spring house for them to enjoy with sugar cookies from her stone crock. Then she offered to take the news of Cleng's arrival to Nils and Carolyn and on to Henriks. She and Carolyn had become close friends after that day almost four months ago when Carolyn helped free Susan from some of her doubts and feelings of guilt. Carolyn and Nils' two-year-old daughter, Serena, sometimes stayed with Susan, and Eleazer was often tended by Carolyn and the older girls. She had recently confided to Susan that she expected another confinement in December, hoping for a son for Nils this time.

Carolyn suggested the supper be held at their house since they were midway between the Stangelands and the Herviks. It was a festive evening with lots of food from all three homes. After supper, Susan spent most of the evening with Anne and Sara Thompson, helping them keep up with Leazer and little Christopher Hervik, whose mother was also expecting another baby before year's end.

While Susan had always been willing for the Norwegians to talk in their native language when they were together, this evening she wondered, with chagrin, if it must always include her caring for the children as well. She was the youngest, yes, and a former teacher, but she did understand a little Norwegian and could keep up with most of the conversation. Now, for example, they were discussing the railroad coming West through the area which would provide another mode of transportation for their produce.

Finally, Susan quietly suggested to Andrew that since Leazer was getting awfully tired they should be going home. She was glad when Nils urged Cleng to stay overnight with them.

Andrew was so full of the evenings' conversation, he didn't realize Susan was unusually quiet.

After a day of rest, Cleng was on the road again, since he wanted to return to Fox River before the cold and snow caught up with him. He would get a ride on a canal freighter as far as Rochester and spend some time visiting his friends there, and doing what he could to advise and help new immigrants looking for jobs or a permanent place to settle.

In the evenings for several days following Cleng's visit, Andrew looked at maps in one of Susan's books, locating places Cleng had talked about.

THE BECKONING

After watching her husband concentrate over the maps for several silent minutes one evening, Susan asked, "If we were ever to move on West, which of those places would you like to go to?"

Andrew looked up, surprised that she had brought up the subject. "And if we did move," Susan continued, "would you want to move where there are other Norwegians?"

"I'm not ready to move anyplace just yet, are you?" Andrew replied.

Susan thought of the little nearby grave, which she would have to leave behind. Her answer was a single word, "No."

CHAPTER 29

New
Additions

USAN STOPPED KNITTING and rested her arms on her bulging stomach. "Andrew, in the five years we've been married, you've never explained why the Norwegians from Stavanger have darker hair and eyes than the other Norwegians coming over." They were sitting by the fire on a cold night in January of the year1832. Susan was knitting a new pair of woolen stockings for herself. The pair she had were darned in too many places to last the winter.

Andrew concentrated on his carving, a toy he'd worked on many evenings and intended for Leazer's third birthday. When finished it would represent two billy goats bunting each other head-on when a lever was pressed. It was like a toy Andrew remembered from his childhood.

"I wish I knew to tell you why all Norwegians don't have straw-colored hair and blue eyes. God didn't want us all alike, I guess." He held the little wooden goat closer to the firelight to correct the curve of the horns. "Maybe someday we'll have enough money to visit Norway and see my mother and brothers – all my family."

I'd love to see them...of course. But I can't imagine crossing that ocean, no matter how much money we have." She shuddered. "I think you'll just have to keep telling me about them. Who were your grandparents? I used to wonder about them, but I didn't dare ask too many questions when you couldn't speak much English."

"I'll tell you love story about my grandmother."

"I like love stories."

"Well, her name was Inger Stokka who lived in Høyland *sogn*..."

"Sogn means county, doesn't it?"

"Yes, and the name of the village was Stokka like her name. She was very pretty..."

233

"Of course." Susan arched her brows above a smile.

"Well...pretty enough she had two suitors courting her. She like Tollak Bergsen, but he was so poor. His father had only enough land to raise one cow..."

"But not a daughter-in-law?" Susan broke in.

Andrew grinned. "How can I tell you a love story if you keep laughing?"

"I'm sorry. Go on."

"Soon we get to the sad part. Her family thought she should marry Torsen Godeset. His father had big *gard*, or farm, for him to inherit. Finally, she gave in and agreed to marry Torsen. His father had a betrothal feast for them. Many relatives and friends were invited. Torsen lived just across the lake from my grandmother, so he and his family began to row the boat across to Stokka for the feast. Their dog swam after them and they stopped to take him in. But the boat turned over and Torsen drowned before he could be rescued."

"Oh, how awful! Didn't he know how to swim?"

"I don't know that. Maybe he let others be rescued first, or he hit his head or something. Anyway, grandmother and some of her friends had gone down to the lake to meet them and saw it happen. She was so sorry with grief, she threw her engagement ring in the lake also."

"Then she went back to the other suitor?"

"She did. After awhile she began to see Tollak again. And when my great-grandfather see how much they love together, he said all right for them to marry and even gave over his farm to him." Andrew smiled at Susan. "Just like your father say all right to marry you before your seventeenth birthday."

"Did they have many children?"

"Only two. My mama and Aunt Katrine. But my grandmother died when she was thirty-eight."

Susan sighed. "I wonder how many children I'll have by the time I'm thirty-eight. If they are all as big as this little fellow, I hope not too many more."

Andrew looked at her with concern. "I hope he'll not give you too much trouble?"

"I just hope he won't wait too much longer. I want to get it over with."

"Do you want me to get the rocking chair cradle out yet?"

"Not yet. I don't want it to sit empty. I just want Lena Tillman to get here in plenty of time."

"She says she's keeping her clothes right by at bedtimes. I want her here, too. No more like last time..." he caught himself and wished he hadn't said it.

Susan was silent, then suddenly laughed. "I can only vaguely remember that you were trying to get my wet drawers off."

"I couldn't find the tie. I was ready to cut the string when your mama came to help."

"I wonder what ever happened to the old Indian. Suppose we'll ever see him again?"

"Last time I saw him was in the woods...after little Lydia."

"That took a lot of courage, to take your hand." For several minutes she gazed into the fire, lost in thought. "I wonder if he got killed by some white farmer who didn't know how good he was?"

"Maybe he went back to the tribe and got a new woman," said Andrew.

"I hope so. I miss him and I'll always be grateful to him."

February 14 came with bright sunshine and a lacy paper Valentine from Andrew to Susan. He had bought it on a trip to Kendall.

"Oh, Andrew," she exclaimed. "I'm getting too old for such frivolous things! But I love it just the same."

Big and uncomfortable as she was, Susan could do little beyond absolute necessities. Andrew stayed near, going no further than the woodpile or the barn.

Late that morning Susan said, "I think before the day is over I'll have a Valentine for you."

"The baby? I'll hurry and tell Papa to bring Mrs. Tillman."

"I don't think there is a big hurry, but I'd feel better if you did. You can take Leazer to Carolyn's when you get back."

It was a painful delivery, but not particularly difficult. Andrew agonized with every sound that came from the bedroom. Then he heard the first lusty cry of his second son. At the door, Andrew and Mr. Cary, who had just come, heard Lena say, "You great big lunker Norwegian, you, you'll be chopping wood by the time you're five years old."

Andrew's first look was for Susan, who lay pale and exhausted, furrows of pain still lingering on her face. He hurried over to her and took one of her hands. She said weakly, "Bring him over. Let's have a look at that Valentine."

As he took the bundle from Lena, Andrew said, "He feels like quite a chunk."

"Ten pounds if he's an ounce," declared Lena.

Andrew laid him carefully in the crook of Susan's arm and pulled the blanket away from his face. She said, "You little scamp, you'd better amount to something, coming into the world with all that pain." She raised her head slightly and peered at him. "Little Andrew!"

Mrs. Cary, bending over the bed, said, "That was my first thought, too."

Andrew's throat tightened as he, too, saw the resemblance to himself. He touched the small forehead crowned with a whisper of dark hair above a face of squarish proportions. He lifted a little hand, comparing it to his own. The short fingers curled around one of his own.

On seeing the new grandson, John Cary smiled. "Now you got a li'l Leazer and a li'l Andrew."

Finally Andrew spoke, "I'd rather name him Tollak. It was my grandfather's name."

Susan nodded agreement, then closed her eyes and drifted off to sleep.

Andrew was proud that now he had two sons. He was doubly inspired to finish clearing his 48 acres. He'd have sons to help farm it and to leave it to if they stayed on here. But in the meantime, he needed help. Mr. Cary needed his boys at home, Susan wouldn't be able to help during the sugar season; he decided to hire help for the first time.

Several new immigrants were coming through the area since a stagecoach began making regular stops at Sandy Creek on Ridge Road. Most of them were enroute to the government land out West which they heard was selling for a dollar an acre, but some of them settled down on farms near Kendall or Morton. Perhaps one of them would be willing to work for the small amount he could pay.

Nils told him about a Norwegian living alone in the woods to the east of them. He'd come to their house asking for food a few days before. "He's a rough looking fellow, but maybe he's down on his luck and is a good worker," Nils said.

Andrew approached the makeshift shack put together with assorted boards, leftover logs and canvas. Just outside the curtained entry, Andrew called, "*God dag.*" A man about Andrew's age sleepily thrust his head out from the canvas.

"I'm looking for a man to help me during the maple sugar season," Andrew explained. "Nils Thompson thought you might be interested even though I can't pay very well."

"I don't know what kind of work that might be," the dirty, grizzled man said, "but I'm getting mighty low on grub so I'll work for you."

Andrew began having doubts about the man as soon as he smelled the foul odor of him and the interior of the shack. Did he want this man carrying and handling his sugar sap? But it was too late now to reconsider.

Thore Johansen didn't show up the following day until after sun-up. Andrew thought this might be because he had no time piece. He patiently explained what he wanted him to do. The man seemed bright enough and understood directions, but moved with exasperating slowness and took time out to stand against the tree and rest his back after each trip.

At noon he ate everything Susan offered him and asked for more. After he'd gone outside Susan burst out, "Where did you find that poor excuse for a man? My whole house stinks of him. I don't want him to even touch Leazer or the baby."

"I'm sorry I hired him. He's not only dirty, he won't work," Andrew said with disgust. "There's nothing much worse than a lazy Norwegian."

Susan's anger turned to slight amusement. It was the first time she'd heard her husband say one word against his people. Perhaps he was becoming more Americanized than she thought.

That evening, badly as he hated to do it, Andrew paid Thore 50 cents and told him he'd come get him if he was needed again. The man seemed relieved. Andrew went out that evening and hired a couple of 12 and 13-year-old boys from the new Norwegian family that had moved in near Henriks.

The following year, in September, another son was born – Bela. Lena declared he was the most beautiful baby she'd ever delivered. He had the same angular shape to his face as his brother, Tollak, but the features were decidedly like Susan's. The bit of brown hair clung close to his head, too short to curl.

When Susan first realized she was pregnant again so soon after Tollak, she remarked to her mother, "At least this time I'll be confined in the summer when I can eat greens and lettuce and berries and apples." She was only mildly disappointed that it wasn't a girl and agreed with Andrew that a farmer needs sons.

A third room had been added to their house so that all activity wasn't in the kitchen, a state which Susan had found almost unbearable, especially with a new baby. Andrew had used part of the proceeds from his potato crop shipped to Hugh Samuelson for the addition and had help from Nils and Henrik, just as he had helped add extra space to their houses.

It wasn't until Bela was almost three that Susan became pregnant again.

On the morning Susan knew that birth was imminent, she called Leazer who was stacking chopped wood against the house as Andrew had instructed. "Go to the barn and get Papa. Tell him I need to see him."

"What for Mama?" He asked with earnest concern. He was so grown up for a seven-year-old, she wanted to tell him what was going on, but of course she must not.

"I've changed my mind about what I'm going to do today. You boys will get to walk over to Carolyn's all by yourselves. Run now."

Leazer obediently dropped the sticks of wood from his arms and hurried towards the barn. He loved going to Carolyn's house, and he'd get to take his little brothers all by himself.

When Lena laid baby Rosetta (a name Susan had been saving since Bela was born) beside her mother, she said, "Now there's a little bundle who's going to be a big help to her mama." The newborn was robust and strong-boned like her brothers, not at all like the tiny Lydia had been.

Susan beamed at her new daughter and asked Andrew to wait a couple of hours before going after the boys. "I want to see their faces when they first hear about their baby sister. But I want to sleep awhile first.

Grandma Cary stayed days with Susan and the children until her daughter was able to take over again. Susan hoped it would be by Thanksgiving time. The boys had eagerly looked forward to helping stuff and roast the gobbler they were fattening. Leazer showed a real interest in cooking and wanted to learn to bake bread, especially after he found out that his father had once been a baker.

Chores about the farm and in the fields he was not so eager to do. One night after a day of digging potatoes, Andrew had said to Susan, "I don't know if I ever make a farmer out of Leazer. He picks up potatoes for awhile, then he runs across a spider and wonders if it's a Norwegian bug, then he watches the edge of the woods for trolls and nissen."

"Well, who told him all those Norwegian fairy tales?" Susan reminded him.

"They never scared me."

"Leazer seems to be sensitive and easy to frighten. But he's smart. Mr. Kettering told me last week that Leazer learns so fast he can hardly keep up to him."

Andrew chuckled. "Like his Mama. I don't know if Tollak is as smart, but he sure can pick up potatoes for a five-year-old."

"Well, now there's your farmer! For awhile I'm really going to need Leazer's help around the house."

"They're brothers and so different," Andrew mused.

So now there were three little boys and a new baby girl. When Leazer wasn't in school, he took over as though Rosetta were his own responsibility, talking to her, covering her, rocking her in the now battered mammy chair.

On a Saturday evening Andrew came home after a visit at the Herviks. He sat down in the kitchen as Susan worked around him. She was not in a good mood. They had induced Andrew to stay for supper while Susan was holding the meal for him at home. Finally she and the children went ahead and ate. Now she was clearing the table, and had eight loaves of bread baking in two big pans in the fireplace ovens. Tomorrow was Sunday, church to be ready for. Bath night, which meant heating big kettles of water for the washtubs for each in turn to bathe in a corner of the kitchen before putting on clean underwear. And Andrew wanted to tell about his visit to the Herviks.

"Henriks haf a Norwegian family staying with them now. Yust arrived."

Susan flinched. After a visit to his Norwegian friends, Andrew always came home with a deepened accent. It was all she could do to keep from lashing out at him, but the children's presence restrained her.

"Are the new people going to stay with Herviks all winter?" Susan asked. "If they do, it will be awfully crowded, won't it?"

"Henrik say he can..."

"Says, Andrew, *says* he can," Susan broke in.

Andrew nodded, "Henrik says he can use Olaf this winter to cut trees and pull more stumps."

"Well, I still feel sorry for Martha having to put up with an extra family all winter. How many children are there?"

"Just one little girl and a boy about Leazer's age."

At the mention of his name, Leazer stopped playing school with his brothers and came to lean against his father's knee.

"Word seems to keep going back to Norway about the opportunities over here," Andrew continued. "Olaf told us about a rich farmer from

Numedal who expects to bring twenty Norske over with him next spring. He's going to buy a very large farm in the West and let the twenty work out their passage money on it."

"He sounds more like a businessman than a farmer," Susan commented dryly. "I hope those twenty people know what they're getting into." She looked into the oven full of bread, tapped the tops with a knife and decided they weren't yet done.

Leazer pulled at his father's sleeve. "May I go play with the new boy about my age sometime?"

Andrew put an arm around his son. "You would have to teach him to speak English."

"Mama taught you to speak English."

"Eleven years ago," Susan sighed. "Can it really be that long? Life was so simple then."

"Tell me about it again, Papa. About the Thanksgiving when you scared Mama and she dropped the eggs in the snow and fell down."

Anticipating a story, Bela and Tollak came over. Andrew looked at the big clock which had been a Christmas present from Susan. Almost chore time. "If I tell you a story, you have to come help me feed and milk old Boss and Cherry."

"I will!" said Leazer.

"I will," said pudgy Tollak.

"I will, too," Bela insisted.

Susan sighed with relief. They would be out from underfoot for awhile.

Andrew took off his good coat and hung it on a peg. It was the coat with the silver buttons his mother had sent him five years before, but it showed little wear. Soon two boys were on his lap and another pressing in. As usual, their Papa mixed in several Norwegian words. He didn't get very far into the story before Tollak pulled on his sleeve, "What does that mean, Da?"

Andrew paused, waiting for Leazer to answer.

"That means chicken, Tollak."

"What does *sno* mean?" Andrew asked.

"I know, I know," Tollak said eagerly, "It means snow."

"Tell me one, Da," Bela said.

"All right. What does egg mean?"

"What chickens lay," he answered disappointed. "But I mean a 'wegian word."

"That is Norwegian. Norwegian and American both, just like you boys and Rosie," Andrew said.

Susan, ironing at the table, set the flat iron back on the stove. She picked up her slate, sketched a picture, and handed it to Andrew. "What's that?"

He looked up and they laughed together. For a moment there were only the two of them.

Leazer said, "Ah, Mama, that's two different kinds of ears!"

"When your Mama taught me to speak American," chuckled Andrew, "she drew me many funny pictures. It helped me remember. I'm not so good to draw so I tell stories."

"Tell us about the old Indian who carried your deer," Leazer pleaded, "the big buck with the horns that hang in the barn."

Susan listened as she guided the iron over her pink dress. Leazer probably knows more Norwegian than I do, she thought. Why had she been so reluctant to learn the language? Was it because Andrew never asked her to learn it or offered to teach her?

The last few times they'd been with his friends, she wanted to say: I know it's the schoolteacher in me, but I think, for the sake of the children, you ought to be talking English instead of leaving it all up to them.

But she never said it. Speaking together in Norwegian seemed to heighten their joy in each other. And they were so far from their homeland and other relatives....Was she being selfish? Or was being American essential for the proper upbringing of the children? She was too tired now to think about such a weighty problem.

CHAPTER 30

Love
Story

O N A SUNNY DAY in late March of 1838, Susan was airing the feather tick and drying the boys' straw tick over the line outdoors. She hoped the bed-wetting was almost over, at least for the three boys. Of course there was Rosetta yet, and how many more? She had bundled up the little girl and tied her to a chair outside in the sun, where she sat babbling happily while watching the barn cats, the chickens and her brothers.

The boys were playing with stick horses which their grandmother had made for them. Each head, made from an old sock, was different. Mr. Cary had attached reins and Susan had lettered on the names: Brownie, Blacky and Old Gray. The boys played with them daily, stroking the wool manes, feeding and riding them and sleeping with them reined to the bedposts.

Grandmother Stangeland did not always send Christmas presents, but the past year she had sent two very special gifts. To the children she had sent a silver locket with a tiny ribbon-tied wisp of Andrew's baby hair. She sent Andrew and Susan a mechanical pencil, the first either of them had seen.

From the clothesline, Susan could hear Leazer trying to explain to his little brothers some new adventure too complicated for little boys of five and six to understand. He never got angry with them when they gave up listening and drifted off to play by themselves. Leazer would then just turn his attention to some solitary pursuit. Usually it was taking something apart to see inside, a pod, last year's bird nest, an ant hill.

Susan remembered that she must remind the boys their father had told them to haul up more wood to be split. They could use the little wagon Andrew had made them for Christmas. Father and sons referred to it as the little *kubberulle*.

THE BECKONING

Her Christmas present from Andrew had been a home medical book, a "doctor book," as she called it. It was one of the first anyone in the community had seen. It was borrowed so often Susan hardly had time to read it herself. Some of the diagrams and information in it made her blush. Although discussed in whispers and giggles by young married women, it was scorned by the old as trash to be kept away from unmarried girls.

One evening the book had been left lying on the table after Carolyn returned it. Susan was getting supper and Leazer was supposed to be doing sums on the little slate. He suddenly asked, "What does w-o-m-b spell?"

"What! What are you reading?"

"This big ol' book," he said innocently. "It's got pictures of peoples' insides in it."

"You go pump me another pail of water and never mind that book." She rescued the "doctor book" and put it high up and far back in the kitchen cupboard.

Holding a clothespin in her mouth as she slipped a sheet over the line, Susan noticed that her oldest son had now abandoned his brothers to their own pursuits and was whistling to get a response from a redbird hidden somewhere in the nearby woods. He was so smart, she hoped he could get lots of education. Maybe even go to college. Wouldn't that be great if they could send a son to college?

But the crops would have to be better than they were this spring. The 1838 maple supar season yielded the smallest harvest the Stangelands or Carys had gathered. The spring thaw was too gradual and the nights not cold enough for a good flow of sap. There wasn't even enough to ship to Hugh Samuelson, who now owned the wholesale business in New York. Lars bought what little syrup they had for people he knew in Rochester. Mr. Sloan, the boat builder in Albion, would take it to him on his next trip.

Lars and Martha now had six children, one of them a boy, Elias. Nils and Carolyn had a son, Abraham, as well as another girl, who was named for her mother.

Andrew found Susan in the kitchen preparing supper when he arrived home from Kendall. "We heard in town that there is to be a total eclipse of the sun next Sunday," he announced.

Susan looked startled. "There is? Do you suppose it will cause any trouble?"

"Some say it to be a bad year for all crops, like the syrup. Also a lot of sickness." Andrew looked very sober. "But Pastor Haines and some of the elders say it's a sure sign of the end of the world, so maybe we won't have to worry about either one."

At this point the boys discovered their father was home and came riding in, little bells jangling, manes flying.

"Did you bring us anything, Papa?"

"Not this time, Bela. But you know what?" Three sets of eager brown eyes leaped to his face. "On the first day of April a show is coming to town. A man will bring a dancing bear and a pig that does tricks."

"Oh boy, Papa, can we go?" Leazer asked.

"A dancing bear!" Bela laughed.

"And a pig that does tricks!" Tollak almost fell down giggling.

"I tell you what," Andrew began stroking each dark head in turn, "You be good boys and help your mama and papa until then and maybe we'll hitch up Old Cloud and take Mama and Rosie with us to see that bear and the funny pig."

"Can we have a picnic with gingersnaps and baloney and a banana?" Leazer asked eagerly.

"Might have to wait and see if we can afford all that."

Susan smiled at them. "If we can't buy anything, I'll pack a nice dinner for us to eat on a blanket or in the wagon." Six people were too many for the single seated buggy when all of them went, so they took the wagon, referred to as the BIG *kubberulle*.

The following afternoon, as she was throwing out the dish washing water, Susan saw her father walking up the path, and noticed how gray and stooped he was getting. Since his brother Ira died a year ago, he seemed to have aged. But he loved those grandsons. Rosetta too, but she'd have to be older before he could talk to her and take her with him on short jaunts like he did the boys. Susan wished he could see his other gransons, James' two boys in Michigan. Seemingly they were getting along well.

The three boys "rode" to meet their grandfather, Bela and Tollak each grabbing a thumb to tow him toward the house while Leazer led the way, walking backwards, talking. "Grampa, when are we going to make those hoe cakes?"

"The hoe cakes. That's right, we never did get to them, did we? Well, how about this evening? We'll ask your mama if you can go home with me, then we'll build a nice little fire in the syrup pit and fry them suckers."

Tollak danced along with delight. "We have to scrub the shovel off good."

"Then we have to grease it with a big ol' piece of sidemeat," Bela remembered.

"The hoe has to be good and hot," Leazer added. "May I mix up the cornmeal and water?"

"We better let Grandma do that. She puts in some other stuff, I don't know what all. But you can each fry one for yourself."

After getting permission from their mother, Mr Cary told the boys, "You run over and tell Grandma what we're going to do and I'll be along in a little bit. Watch them now, Leazer. Don't let them get off into the woods where a bear can eat them up or an Indian will scalp them."

Eleazer looked soberly at his mother. "Oh, Papa, don't scare the daylight out of them," Susan laughed. She nodded to her son. "It's all right. Just go straight over there."

The boys trooped out and John Cary asked, "Where's Andrew working today?"

"He's getting that field next to Nils ready to plant sorghum. Or else he's visiting Nils and Carolyn. He went in that direction."

"Is he getting serious about a move on West?"

"I'm really not sure. Some days he's all ready to sell out and go, other times he thinks we're pretty well off where we are and shouldn't make a move."

"What do you think? You want to go on out there?"

There was a long pause, then Susan sat down at the kitchen table and wearily cupped her chin in her hands. "Papa, I don't know what to do. I think with any encouragement from me he'd sell and move on. But if I did agree to it, it would be for a reason he doesn't suspect." She looked down at the table and fingered the glass sugar bowl in the center of the table.

"What's that?"

Hesitantly Susan answered, "To get him away from the other Norwegians."

If John Cary was surprised he didn't show it. "But wouldn't he move to that settlement in Illinois?"

"That's what I'm afraid of although he's hinted at going someplace near James."

"Do the few families of Norwegians living around here give you trouble?"

Susan looked distressed. "No, not trouble, that's why I feel so guilty thinking the way I do. They're very nice and kind to me, but they treat me like an outsider." She paused again, her fingers lining up the spoons in the spoon holder.

"Andrew's birthday party last fall made me realize how left out I am. I thought I should invite his friends for a change rather than you and Mama and the boys so I worked all day fixing a nice supper and a birthday cake. I'd also saved my egg money and bought him that new book of just words, *Webster's Dictionary*." Susan was close to tears.

"Well, after supper they started looking at the book, laughing and discussing it in Norwegian. The children got tired of it, too, and begged me to come into the other room and talk to them in English, and the parents didn't say anything to them about it. Just like I was supposed to be a...a nursemaid. And that's all I had to talk to all day, just children."

Deeply troubled himself over his daughter's dilemma, John Cary wondered what advice he could give. "Did Andrew say anything about it after they left?"

"He seems to think that as long as he tells me all that was said, it's all right." She dried her tears on her apron. "When I have my family so close to me, I don't feel right asking them to change their ways for me. Even the children are learning more and more Norwegian, even sometimes talking to each other in Norwegian. I can't defy Andrew and forbid it. I don't know anymore what's right or what's wrong or if I'm just being selfish. I do so want the children to grow up being good, educated Americans."

John Cary looked aside solemnly. "Of course we don't want to see you leave. But then we didn't want James to leave either, and he seems to be making good in that new state of Michigan. So it isn't for us to say. I suspect your mother would be the one to suffer most. But she left her mother back in Vermont, so that's the way of life."

"Just don't make the big decision when you're upset or discouraged," he advised. "Wait till things even out a little. It might take quite awhile to sell the place anyway."

"Maybe after this weekend and the eclipse, we won't have to worry about it," Susan sighed.

"That's so. But we're all God's children so we'll be together with nothing to worry about. You know about the prayer vigil at the church, early till late?"

"Yes. Of course we're going, unless the Norwegians convince Andrew that we should meet with them."

"Well, I better get on over there with those boys. Want to come over and eat hoe cakes covered with ashes?"

"No, thanks," Susan laughed, remembering those she used to make. "It isn't often Andrew and I get to eat alone."

"Bundle up Rosie and I'll take her too."

"Oh, no, Papa, you'll have enough to watch with those boys."

"Pshaw. She'll be good company for Grandma." John Cary picked up his only granddaughter, and raised her high over his head, bringing delighted giggles.

Susan watched her father leave, Rosetta peeking back over his shoulder, and was glad she'd shared her concerns with him. She felt better and began looking forward to the peace of an evening alone with Andrew.

The house was so quiet and she felt free from responsibility. She began to sing and the hymns reminded her of what Sunday, just two days away, might bring. What could the end of the world be like, she wondered. The Bible said it would end in fire. But how would it start, just one big blast or like a grass fire? Surely God wouldn't make them suffer long before meeting them on the other side. She shuddered and resolved not to let her children or Andrew out of her sight on Sunday, not even for a minute.

When Andrew returned, he was carrying his hat full of mushrooms which he'd found on the way home. She received them eagerly. "I'll cook some for our supper. There is no one here but you and me."

"Just us? Where are the children?"

She told him about the hoe cakes. "We were invited to join them, but I thought we'd have fun eating alone once again."

Andrew went out to his chores while Susan prepared their supper. Since it was a lovely evening, she pushed the pans of food to the back of the stove and went to the barn to join Andrew. For this one hour, she wanted to feel young again. She began skipping. But after a few steps, she felt awkward and self-conscious. She was a woman now and the mother of five, a girl no longer.

After the cows were let out to graze and the chickens locked in for the night, Andrew put his arm around Susan and drew her to his side. They walked silently, the shimmering spring evening surrounding them. Nearby meadowlarks sang to their mates. At the doorstep Andrew took her in his arms, and held his face against hers. "My Susan, my own little Susuun. She work so hard for so little."

But Susan couldn't reply because he was kissing her before he swept her off to the lush grass beneath the blossoming apple trees in the orchard. Supper could wait.

CHAPTER 31

Bag Of
Coins

ONDAY MORNING, THE DAY after the total eclipse, Andrew awakened and realized he was still in his own house. He reached out to Susan. She stirred and awakened. "We're still here, aren't we?" she whispered.

"God didn't want us yet, looks like." He pulled her to him and they lay in blissful comfort for a few moments before arising.

It had been a strange and awesome Sunday. They went early to church, taking a cold, meager lunch to eat with the rest of the congregation. As the wagon pulled away from the house, they turned back, expecting it might be the last look at their earthly home. Leazer sensed their half-hidden anxiety, but was afraid to ask questions.

At the churchyard, people talked in hushed voices and kept casting fearful glances around the horizon, not really knowing what they were looking for. But once inside, there was the solace of being together in God's house. Older children watched the faces of their parents for reassurance; smaller children were more fretful and restless than usual.

At midday the eerie darkness began dropping its strange mantle and the prayers, amens and praise-the-Lords grew louder and more fervent. The blot on the sun began centering with beaming rays around it. The elders watching from the door, gestured to the pastor and he bade the congregation to file out. Heads were bowed as they moved onto the damp, chilly churchyard.

The haze surrounding them was different from anything they had ever seen. Unlike the approach of nightfall, it confused bird and beast alike. Chickens and turkeys at the nearby parsonage were hurrying, with squawks and gobbles, toward their roosts. Birds in the trees had stopped singing and were flitting from one place to another. Howls of wolves and coyotes came from the depth of the woods. Then the dark circle began to glide from the sun and the brightness of midday returned. The prayers ended, and people looked about with a sober confusion almost akin to disappointment.

Dishes were quietly brought out for a solemn lunch. More prayers and readings from the Bible followed. Near chore time, the congregation was dismissed with admonitions to keep up the vigil for the rest of the day.

The world did not end that March 26, 1838, but the following summer brought one hardship after another to the Stangeland family, as well as to most other farmers in the area. Following the light maple sugar season came the ruin of Andrew's corn crop.

The weather caused the corn to sprout early and Andrew was hopeful of a good year. But one day in early June, after the boys had gone out to play while Andrew and Susan lingered over dinner, Leazer came running toward the house. "Papa...Mama...look!"

They hurried out. A darkness like a heavy cloud waved overhead. There was a cacophony of honking, squawking and flapping of wings. With a great deal of jockeying for position, the mass headed downward and the birds settled in the cornfield.

"Canadian geese!" Andrew shouted running for the field, sons following. Susan hesitated long enough to snatch up Rosetta. When she came panting up to where Andrew stood in dejection, the last goose was departing. The dark look of desperation on her husband's face told of the devastation even before she saw the beheaded spikes of green, clipped clean from one side of the field to the other.

"Will it grow back?" She ventured to ask.

"No, I don't think so. Your papa said it happened to his crop one or two times. Just have to plant over, if I can get the seed."

The boys came running back to them. Bela's eyes were big with wonderment. "Lots of big birds!"

"They're naughty birds, Bela. They ate up all of Papa's corn," Tollak frowned.

Leazer asked, "They are such pretty birds. Why do they have to be so bad?"

THE BECKONING

Andrew sighed, and laid a hand on his son's head, "They are not really bad. They are God's creatures. They only know to eat when hungry and what looks good. Maybe we'll plant potatoes next. May be too late for corn."

But the potato crop was not much better. After the spring rains came a summer of drought. Even the gardens around Kendall produced little in spite of hand watering. In the fields, wheat headed early and contained little grain. Andrew and the other farmers were discouraged and wondered how they could get their families through the coming winter. They might have to eat what should be saved for seeding crops the following spring.

Hard times was about all the men talked about when they got together. Some declared the eclipse was responsible. Others said it was the beginning of lean years to follow the fruitful years – a warning form the Lord that they had not been frugal enough, or that God wanted to remind them to be humble and grateful for these good years when developed farm land was selling for as much as ten dollars an acre.

On a day late in July, as Susan sat on a bench by the door snapping green beans for supper, a fancy-looking trap hitched to a pure white horse drove into the yard and went toward the barn, where Andrew was flailing his meager wheat crop on the wide canvas in a frame. Andrew greeted the man in English, then they began speaking Norwegian. After awhile, he got into the buggy with the stranger, told the boys that, no, they couldn't go along, and to tell Mama he would be back soon. Susan could see Andrew and the visitor getting in and out of the buggy here and there around their farm. She had a good idea what it was all about, and she felt both anticipation and sorrow.

During supper, Andrew seemed to be consumed with thoughts of his own. She knew he didn't want to speak of them until the boys were asleep. Finally, when it was almost dark, Leazer drifted off beside his two little brothers.

Andrew took a deep breath, and leaned his head on his hands behind his head as he and Susan sat on the bench beside the house. "That was Ole Orsland here today."

"About buying the place?"

Andrew nodded. "He's the man Nils and Olaf told about who brought over twenty Norwegians to work for him on a six-hundred acre farm out West. But the workers didn't last long. Some didn't even get their passage money paid back before they left him or died of sickness. He doesn't want to live on that big place anymore. He's looking for a smaller farm for just himself and wife."

"Did he make you an offer?"

"No. Today he's just looking at several places."

There was a long pause between them as night settled in and the whippoorwills made their last calls of the day. A buggy went past their house towards the Carys on the road now known as the Norway Road. The evening was so still the dust took a long time to settle.

Andrew took Susan's hand, rubbed the back of it with his thumb, looked absently at it, then held it more firmly, "What do you think, Susan? If he wants, should we sell?"

She didn't answer immediately. Then in a steady voice she said, "Andrew...wither thou goest, I will go." She laid her head on his shoulder, and spread an arm across his chest.

He held her close. "But I don't want to decide alone. I want you to be happy, too."

"You know it would be hard for me to leave Mama and Papa and the twins, where I've lived all my life, even if we moved just twenty miles away. But I'm a grown woman, a wife and a mother. We must do what's best for us. All I ask is that we move *to* something." She pleaded, "I don't want us to start out not knowing where we're going and have to camp until we get something built."

"Oh, no, I don't want us to do that either. If I sell, I make him give me time to find a farm somewhere else."

They sat in silence again. Susan asked hesitantly, "What if we found a place not close to your Norwegian friends? Would you be content without them?"

"That wouldn't bother me. Fourteen years out of Norway, I guess I must be at least half American, like the children." He lifted her face and kissed her lightly. "And I'm sure you would be glad not to have to talk to only children while the rest of us talk so fast in Norwegian you can't understand."

Tears stung at Susan's eyes. He did know how she felt!

"I was thinking maybe James could find us a place," Andrew ventured.

Susan sat up quickly. "Oh, I'd like that! Then Mama and Papa could come see us both."

"Well...we see what happens, we leave it to the Lord. Maybe Orsland has his eyes for another place by now. He was going to some other farms tomorrow."

For the next couple of weeks, Susan made a point of doing more things with her mother than she had done in a long time. They made hominy together outdoors in the big black syrup kettle. They canned applesauce from early apples in the Stangelands' now-flourishing orchard. With the boys' help, they picked gallons of blackberries while Rosie sat in a box nearby. They made jar after jar of jam and as many cobblers and pies as they could eat. They boiled some of the juice with sugar to make syrup or to be thickened into a pudding. Andrew, like all Norwegians, loved this dessert which was close to the traditional lingonberry pudding. Mother and daughter also canned the few peaches from the Cary orchard, small because of the drought. They took an afternoon off work and drove the buggy down County Line Road to visit Mrs. Ose Webster, a longtime friend of Lydia Cary.

Two or three times a week, the families ate dinner or supper together. The children loved being so often with Grandma and Grandpa.

Seeing the love between grandparents and grandchildren gave Susan's heart an extra tug. The closeness would have to end if they moved, but surely they could visit for the twins were soon 18 and doing much of the farm work at home. Anyway, Orsland had never been back; apparently he wasn't impressed with their farm. It might take a long time to sell, maybe not at all. Andrew would have a hard time getting seed and starting up next spring unless the maple sugar season was a lot better than this one had been.

Following several weeks of dry weather, there was a good rain in late August, washing everything clean and beginning to soak into the dry, caked earth. Mr. Cary came over early in the morning to ask Susan if she wanted to make apple butter from the early fall apples.

"Sure, I wanted an excuse to get outdoors today. Tell Mama I'll be up to help peel apples just as soon as I can get things put away here and Rosetta ready."

"I'll take the boys with me then, and you can bring the buggy."

The boys were within hearing distance. Leazer hesitated a minute then said, "Grampa, you go on with the little boys. I'll stay to hitch up the buggy for Mama and help with Rosie."

Susan's face softened into a smile as she looked with pride at her son, then at her father. He grinned and nodded, putting an arm around his oldest grandson. "You're all right, young man, you are. Maybe you can even help Grandpa with the cider press and the big copper kettle so Alex or Leander won't have to come in from the field to help."

Susan saw Andrew coming from the barn with a last pail of milk. "Where is Leazer?" he asked with irritation. "He was supposed to come back and finish some chores."

"He must have forgotten." Then she repeated the conversation between Leazer and his grandfather.

Andrew shook his head. "I don't know what that boy will be when he grows up, but it won't be farmer."

"Maybe a schoolteacher," Susan laughed. She told Andrew to come over to her mother's for supper; they'd have the traditional apple butter-making-day dinner of pork chops and fresh-baked bread.

By early evening the apple butter was proclaimed done by the experienced Lydia Cary. The big kettle was carried by the twins on an iron rod thrust beneath the bail, to just outside the kitchen door, where Susan and her mother dipped it into jars and sealed it for use throughout the winter.

The bread was out of the oven. Grandma cut off a heel for each of the boys to test the new made spread. Finally supper was ready. But Andrew still had not come. As usual, Susan began to worry when he was late. So many things could have happened to him.

"Let's go ahead and eat," she said. "The boys are hungry and so is everyone else. If he doesn't come soon, Leazer and I will take the buggy and see what's keeping him." She sounded more calm than she felt. She fed Rosetta and helped the little boys, but had lost her own appetite.

"Here he comes," Alex said.

Susan sighed with relief. "He must have stopped to pick mushrooms; he's got a bag in his hands."

As Andrew entered, the whole room seemed to light up with his broad smile. He strode over to Susan, rattled the coins and put the cloth bag in front of her.

"I traded the farm to Orsland for his whole 600 acres and two hundred dollars to boot."

Susan sat speechless, unconvinced. The others began asking questions.

Mr. Cary whistled, "Six hundred acres! That's a lot of land for just forty eight."

"Orsland says he's too old to be a pioneer. Wants to come back East on a settled farm just big enough for him and his wife."

"Are you sure it's good land?" Mr. Cary asked again.

"He says, it's rich black soil next to a small lake. Not all drained yet. Has to have some more ditches dug."

"Where is it?" Alex asked.

"State of Indiana, not far from where James is in Michigan. He showed me on a map."

Finally Susan asked, "Does it have a house on it?"

"He drew me a picture of the house." Andrew dug in his pocket and brought out a folded piece of paper. Susan spread it over her plate and looked at it as Andrew slid into a chair beside her and reached for a thick slice of bread. "It isn't large house, but it's on a pleasant knoll, he said, with close neighbors, a church and school, too. So it's not just wild country."

"How far away is Indiana, Mama?" Leazer asked.

"A long, long way," Susan sighed.

"Will we take the *kubberulle* or ride on the train?" he asked his father.

"We have to talk it over and decide what's best. You and I might have to take the *kubberulle* with a load on it while Mama and the others take the train or a canal boat."

"I want to go on the *kubberulle* too," Tollak said, distressed.

"Me, too," Bela said. They all laughed.

"You won't leave yet this fall, will you?" Lydia asked.

"No, I said to him we'll stay here until spring. We'll share next season's maple sugar crop so I can help him get the hang of it, then we'll leave right after. I tell him he can come into the fields to clear or cut wood or do anything he wants to do this fall and winter after I get my crops off. They live in a house in Kendall now."

A little later, supper finished, the men and boys sat in the other room talking over the new development. Rosie, surrounded by her brothers, was on a blanket on the floor. Susan and Mrs. Cary began slowly, silently picking up the dishes. Mrs. Cary noticed tears running down her daughter's face. "Is it leaving baby Lydia behind that's the hardest? You know, dear, there will always be a Cary around to tend the grave."

"It's partly that..." she paused, "...but Mama," she whispered, "I'm expecting another baby next February. I haven't even told Andrew yet."

Lydia Cary stopped abruptly. Finally, her frown changed to a smile and she put an arm around her daughter.

"Remember those days when you worried so that you'd never have any children?" A pale smile and slight nod from Susan. "You must, of course, stay here until the baby is born and you're well again before leaving. But it will work out. You'll see. It's part of God's plan for you and Andrew."

On a sunny morning in early April of 1839, the Stangelands and Carys clustered around a wagon well-loaded with essential possessions. The newest member, two-month-old Maria, comfortably cradled in the arms of her big brother Leazer, resembled little Lydia but was already robust and plump.

Andrew had wanted Susan to take the two little girls on a canal boat as far as they could, then he and the three boys would meet them. She considered it, but turned down the idea. What if they didn't make connections or what if Andrew had trouble with the wagon and needed her to stay with the boys while he went for a new wheel or something? But she knew the truth was she didn't want the family to be separated for so long. She'd worry too much.

"Camping along the way won't be so bad," she said, "And just think of the baloney and gingersnaps and banana picnics we can have." The boys didn't need encouraging. They were ecstatic.

Susan and Andrew had received a letter from the Abraham Ott family, who would be their closest neighbors in Indiana. Mr. Orsland, on his last trip back to the farm, had given them the Stangeland's address. Sarah Ott welcomed them to the community and insisted they stay with them for a few days until they could get their own house organized. The Orslands had left several pieces of furniture for Susan and Andrew.

Grandma Cary, tears streaming, was hurrying form one beloved grandchild to another with extra kisses and admonitions. "Now, write me a letter, Leazer, I know you can. Tollak and Bela, you're big boys, now, you can help Mama and Papa a lot."

She and Susan had said their goodbyes in a last, quick tour through the empty house. There had been few words. The memories within those walls spoke for them both.

John Cary watched his wife, bemoaning her loss even more than his own. He pumped Andrew's hand. "Tell you what, fill an extra straw tick next summer and we'll be out to see you on that great big farm."

Andrew nodded, trying desperately to hold back the tears. He groped for words, but they would not come. What could he say to this man who had been like a father to him? Impulsively, as with one thought, the two

Susan hugged each of her brothers, who were now handsome young men. "Don't you two get married now, until you find the right girls, and without letting me know."

Alex said, "Leander's got his eye on a little Norwegian gal up the road." Light laughter broke the tension as Leander gave his brother a playful shove. Then the two of them helped Susan onto the wagon.

"Everybody ready?" Andrew called as his family settled into their appointed places. Cloud and Misty tossed their heads impatiently. He slapped the reins and the creaking wagon lurched down Norway Road. The sun, just breaking over the woods, glistened on the silver buttons of his Norwegian overcoat.

EPILOGUE

I FELT I HAD FOUND an answer to my leading question: Why did my generation know so little about our Norwegian grandfather?

Great Grandmother Susan, in the mode of the day, had urged Americanization on him and the children, but in so doing had unwittingly denied her grandchildren their right to an inherited Norwegian culture.

Her dream of sending a son to college came true, twofold. The oldest son as well as the youngest of their nine children earned college degrees.

Eleazer Cary Stangeland became a doctor and served in the Civil War. Bela died in Indiana of tuberculosis at the age of 26, leaving a young family behind.

Rosetta became a robust woman who lived to the age of 90 after raising 13 children. Maria was a working girl and never married.

Andrew Jackson (Jack), although born in Indiana, raised his family of seven children close to the grandparent's home in New York. He was tragically killed by the kick of a mule.

Mary Elizabeth became the mother of four children, and in her adult years strongly resembled her mother, Susan.

Finally, there was Bejamin Franklin (Frank) who became an engineer and inventor and worked for Fairbank Scales in Chicago before moving back to New York. During the great Chicago fire, he wheeled important papers on a hand truck for five miles to get them away from the devastation of the fire.

However it was the second born son, Tollak, the author's grandfather, a farmer as predicted, who passed on the Andreas Stangeland Indiana farm to future generations, and who kept alive the tradition of the annual July Fourth Stangeland reunion.

But that's another story.

You will also enjoy
reading these other
Scandinavian-interest
books
published by

North American Heritage Press

These are available at
your local book store
or Scandinavian gift shop
or may be ordered from
North American Heritage Press

P.O. Box 1 • Minot, ND 58702

(Please add $2.00 per book for shipping.)

The Scandinavian Heritage

By Arland O. Fiske

This hard-to-put-down book of 100 interestingly-told stories is about the people, places, traditions and history of Denmark, Finland, Iceland, Norway and of course Sweden. Well-known Scandinavian-American syndicated newspaper columnist Arland O. Fiske offers well-written and researched vignettes on topics which vary from Viking burial customs to the Scandinavian Royal Families.

Here's some excerpts from the book's foreword by Dr. Sidney A. Rand, former president of St. Olaf College and United States Ambassador to Norway:

"Arland Fiske is a good story teller. In these vignettes he has taken events in Scandinavian history and made them live and breathe. Some of them deal with well-known historical figures; others tell us of persons and places that do not dominate the pages of history. But there is a human warmth and interest in each one.

One virtue of this collection of articles is its breadth. So often we read about the Norwegians or the Swedes or the Danes or the Finns, they are presented almost as competitors for places in history. Here is an author who is attracted to and

NOW... The Scandinavian Heritage Book. Based on the popular syndicated column by well-known Scandinavian-American author Arland O. Fiske.

100 interestingly told stories about the people, places, traditions and history of Denmark, Finland, Iceland, Norway and Sweden.

charmed by the exploits and accomplishments of all the Scandinavians. The reader may make comparisons or draw contrasts; the author does not.

Fiske's collection of "little stories" is easily read and can be taken a bit at a time if preferred. Each story has its own attraction."

A best seller, now in its fourth printing!

---

248 pages, 6"x9", softbound · No. HP-120 · $9.95

The Scandinavian World

By Arland O. Fiske

CONTENTS

Well-known Scandinavian-American author and syndicated columnist Arland O. Fiske delights us, in his unique story-telling way, with stories and tales of the Scandinavian World.

The Scandinavian World

100 interestingly told stories about the people, places, traditions and history of Sweden, Norway, Iceland, Finland and Denmark.

Arland O. Fiske

Foreword by Alvin N. Rogness

248 pages, 6"x9", softbound   No. HP-121 $9.95

The Scandinavian Spirit

By Arland O. Fiske

"The Scandinavian Spirit is a charming potpourri of anecdotes and observations about Scandinavians of every stripe — saints and scoundrels, kings and country folks, pirates and preachers. Fiske's subject is anything and everything that anyone with Danish, Swedish, Finnish, Norwegian or Icelandic blood has done or said that he thinks might be of interest to people today. He has an uncanny ability to ferret out interesting stories and little-known facts that most of us would never discover for ourselves, and his folksy, down-home style makes you feel as if you are listening to the tales grandpa used to tell. So fix yourself a cup of rich Scandinavian coffee, settle down in your favorite chair, and prepare to enjoy a smorgasbord of stories that will brighten your day and warm your heart."

Dr. William H. Halverson
Professor at Ohio State University (retired)

Well-known Scandinavian-American author and syndicated columnist Arland O. Fiske delights us, in his unique story-telling way, with stories and tales of Scandinavian people, places, history and traditions.

"For Scandophiles — and there are acres of this growing specie — good things come in groups of three and Arland Fiske's third book on our Scandinavian heritage is full of interest. In pleasant, painless prose, the info is nicely sectioned off, the amount of each being not too much, not too little, just right. 'Know ye the rock from which thou wert hewn,' exhorts the prophet Isaiah. The Fiske trilogy fulfills that obligation."

Dr. Art Lee
Author of *The Lutefisk Ghetto*
Professor of History, Bemidji State University

Well-known Scandinavian-American author and syndicated columnist Arland O. Fiske delights us, in his unique story-telling way, with stories and tales of Scandinavian people, places, history and traditions.

---

256 pages, 6"x9", softbound   No. HP-124 $9.95

Prairie Wind, Blow Me Back

By Evelyn Dale Iverson

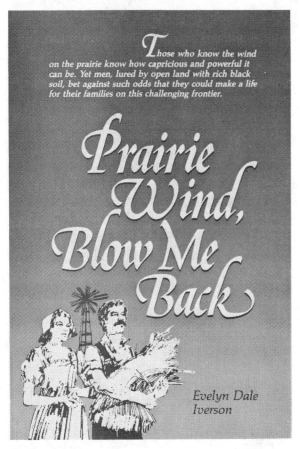

Those who know the wind on the prairie know how capricious and powerful it can be. Yet men, lured by open land with rich black soil, bet against such odds that they could make a life for their families on this challenging frontier.

Evelyn Dale Iverson

Rakel: *"How can Renhild be so devious? I think she is the most evil person I have ever met!"*

"Nils thought of the prairie wind as a sparring partner. How could he beat this fellow?"

PRAIRIE WIND, BLOW ME BACK.

But where? It depends who and where you are.

For Nils, when he was homesick and struggling, it was his childhood home. But later it was other things.

For most of us, it is a glimpse of a different world a hundred years ago, and what life was like "in those days."

And like Nils, before we leave it, a look at desires, priorities, and values.

—Evelyn Dale Iverson

About The Author...

Evelyn Dale Iverson is a granddaughter of Nils A. Dale in this story, and a daughter of Hans M. Dale, the infant who came in a covered wagon to Dakota Territory over a hundred years ago.

The author is a native of Canton, SD, where her father was a professor and later the president of Augustana Academy. She graduated from Concordia College, Moorhead, MN, when her father was treasurer of that college. He also owned a part of the homestead in Miner County, which he felt close to, and his family visited often.

Almost all the names in this book are real places and real people, with the exception of Arne and Renhild, who are composites of others who lived "in those days."

---

158 pages, 6"x9", softbound　　　　　　　No. HP-122　$7.95

Skis Against The Atom

By Lt. Colonel Knut Haukelid

The outcome of World War II could very possibly have been much different if Knut Haukelid and his small, but courageous band of Norwegian soldiers had not been successful in sabotaging the Nazi's supply of "heavy water." The "heavy water" produced at a facility in occupied Norway was vital to Hitler's race with the United States to develop the atomic bomb. Knut Haukelid's "Skis Against The Atom" gives the reader an intimate account of the valiant and self-sacrificing service that the not-to-be-subdued Norwegians performed for the whole free world.

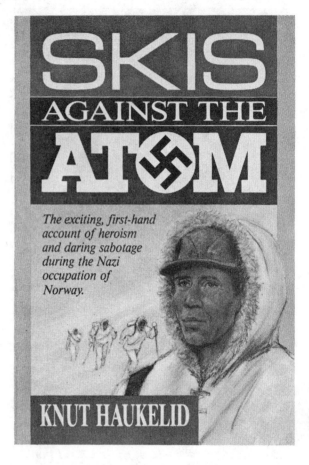

The exciting, first-hand account of heroism and daring sabotage during the Nazi occupation of Norway.

KNUT HAUKELID

Excerpted from the Introduction of Skis Against The Atom by General Major Sir Collin Gubbins, CO of Special Operation Executive

I am glad to write for my friend Knut Haukelid an introduction to this enthralling story of high adventure on military duty so as to give the background to the operations which this book so vividly describes, and to show how they fitted into the wider picture of "Resistance." I hope, too, it will enable the reader to have a fuller appreciation and understanding of the remarkable exploits of a small and devoted group of Norwegian soldiers.

---

252 pages, 6"x9", softbound   No. HP-123 $9.95